A GUY WALKS INTO A BAR

MICK WILLIAMS

Hydra
Publications

ISBN: 978-1-942212-75-1

Hydra Publications

Goshen, Kentucky 40026

www.hydrapublications.com

To my parents, who instilled in me a love for reading and music. To #1 Son and Grandson, who continue to remind me what life is about. And to Cathy.

PROLOGUE

I should listen to my gut more often.

Roses are red. Other than the dangerous thorns, roses are nice, right? A symbol of love men across the ages have given to lovers as a sign of affection. Blood is red too. It feeds the body, transporting valuable oxygen to keep us alive and invigorated. We'd die without it, something I'd soon find out first hand.

The vision, dressed in red, was at the other end of the bar. Her slender legs tipped with a pair of glossy red stilettos, were perched on the chrome footrest of the barstool. I think they stretched all the way from here to Canada. Maybe even to Heaven.

The first time she caught my eye, she did that hair thing girls do when they want something. She twirled her brown locks around her fingers as she maintained eye contact long enough for me to see that they matched her hair.

I always knew most predators had retractable claws. Hers were extended and painted a shade of red that looked as if she'd just ripped the bartender's throat out. In fact, he was missing, and my glass was empty. I hoped she hadn't killed him.

The devil is red too. And stop signs.

So why didn't I stop? Why didn't I just leave my empty glass and go back to my room?

Yeah, I should listen to my gut more often.

CHAPTER ONE

I help people. It's my calling. They have money, and I help them to get rid of it by selling them drugs. The large pharmaceutical company I work for rakes in billions of dollars every year by selling overpriced medicines to doctors. I don't get billions for my trouble, but they pay me well enough, which is why I'm in this bar, in this kind of hotel. It's nice enough that I can sit at the bar with no worries about the clientele, but not so nice that I can't afford to buy a drink or two.

There are four of us facing the large mirror mounted behind the bar, each separated by the barrier of an empty stool. Sitting between me and what I hope will become the focus of my attention for the foreseeable future are two people. One is a middle-aged woman who's just painted her claws, maybe to compete with the dream sitting next to her, and is fanning them as if she's waiting for an invisible Polaroid to develop. The other is a bulky man, dressed like me, but his clothes are twice the size of mine. I tend to keep fit, eat well, exercise. I do everything in moderation. This guy doesn't, evidenced by the extra stomach hanging over his belt. He's also looking for the bartender, but unlike my solitary wine glass, he has three empty beer glasses and a couple of shot glasses lined up to attention, awaiting new instructions like soldiers.

Because they banned smoking in hotel bars, without the overriding stench of tobacco, other smells have become prevalent. They didn't ban nail polish. I was about to tell nail lady they produce the stuff without the cloying aroma when the bartender reappeared. He was a young man, but he was sweating for some reason and looked as if he was trying to catch his breath after a heavy run.

"Sorry everyone," he said to his captive audience, "had to switch out a keg."

Bulky did the nod thing, and the bartender removed his dead soldiers and replaced them with a new recruit. Its frothy cap slid down the side of the glass onto the shiny bar top. A shot of Makers Mark followed it. Nail lady raised her painted hands in defeat when the bartender caught her eye. She spun her stool around, slid off it with the elegance of a rhino, and left the bar. It was just the three of us now. My stomach lurched as my dream leaned forward enough to catch my eye again and then leaned back. Her necklace swung out in front of her. It was the only jewelry she wore. No rings. Subtle, but I'm a man of the world. I know what to look for.

I pointed to my glass, and it vanished for a moment and reappeared full of merlot. One small sip for courage and I grabbed it by the narrow stem and walked casually to the other end of the bar. Bulky man watched me in the mirror. He was sizing up my chances of success and his smirk showed he had little faith in me.

As a single man I stay alert to opportunity, but picking up women in bars is not something I do on a regular basis. For one, it's tacky and can lead to all kinds of problems. The main reason is that it's a rare night when a woman as stunning as this one flashes the signs. One messy divorce scarred me enough to raise my standards. If I take a chance on someone, it had better be worth it. Therefore, the only thing I curl up with most of the time at night is a good book.

"Hi," I said, "I'm Paul." I offered my hand, and she wrapped those claws around it. Her handshake stroked against my skin.

"Hello, Paul. I'm Monica."

Monica? She looked like a Giselle or one of those names that promised all kinds of things, some of them legal. But she had a voice that would turn lions into kittens, and I couldn't look away from those eyes. They smoldered.

"Pleased to meet you, Monica," was the best sentence I came up with. "What brings you here?"

Damn it! What brings you here? Is this the first time I've ever spoken to a woman? Monica didn't flinch, though, just did the hair-twirling thing again and smiled. Something dormant stirred down below.

"Just passing through," she said. "What about you? What do you do?"

"I sell drugs," I said. I always say it like that. It makes me sound like a dealer, which promotes excellent conversation. "And you?"

"Ah," she replied, "I kill people."

She kept a perfectly straight face and, for a moment, I forgot the entire English language. I think my mouth dropped open and there may have been drool. She smiled again, and her eyes smoldered even more. "Just kidding. I travel a lot."

Bulky laughed to himself behind me. Bastard. It seems that smirk was justified after all. Her glass had a lone olive nestled at its base, skewered with a pink plastic sword. It looked lonely.

"Can I rescue that olive with a drink?" I asked. I can be smooth sometimes.

"Sure," she said. She lifted the glass as if it was a trophy awarded for finishing her drink, and slid the olive between her pouting lips. "Dry martini, with a fresh olive."

"Shaken not stirred?" I said with a raised Roger Moore eyebrow, trying to remain calm.

"I'm sorry?"

"Never mind," I said, deflated. I can fall flat on my face too.

Bulky was still chuckling to himself. I signaled the bartender to get her a new glass. He did and slid it across the bar toward us. I reached out to intercept it in a cool but casual fashion. The stem of the glass slapped the side of my hand, spilling some of the contents over my arm. I felt like a fumbling teenager who'd just discovered second base. Before things got any worse, I excused myself and headed to the restroom to regroup and clean up. My shoes made a good focal point as I shuffled past Bulky to the bathrooms. I prayed he didn't see my face in the mirror.

The men's restroom was cleaner than my kitchen; with white tiled walls that were so shiny you could comb your hair in them while you took a leak. The urinals had mountains of those weird-smelling cubes that drunks sometimes mistook for pineapple chunks. I ignored them with no call of nature to answer, placed one hand against the cold tiled wall and took deep breaths. My heart was slamming like a jackhammer and the clammy beginnings of a cold sweat were forming. I'm not saying it's been a while since I was with a woman of this stature but, well, it's been a while. Still, I couldn't stay in here all night. If this window closed, I'd never forgive myself. Hell, mankind would never forgive me!

I splashed lukewarm water on my face and wiped it off with a hand towel, slam dunked the towel in the trash can and made my way back to the bar. She was still there. Bulky had left, so now it was just the two of us and a bartender barely out of college.

"You're still here," I said with a smile as I slid onto the stool next to hers.

"Of course I am," she purred. "Where else is a girl going to go on a cool night in Kentucky?"

I started to give her the myriad of options and then reigned it in. "So, no concrete plans for the evening?"

"Only you," she replied.

I swear, she didn't bat an eyelid, just looked me right in the eyes. I don't think I cried aloud, but there was a strange mewling sound followed by that stirring down below.

"Me? You have my undivided attention, but what exactly do you mean?" I asked and rested my arm against the bar to prevent me from falling off the stool.

"Well. We're both here, both alone, and I assume both single. Do you have somewhere else you need to be tonight?"

"Me? No," I said, a little too quickly. Damn, I need to practice that. "I have all night."

"Then you only have one decision to make," she said. She leaned toward me, pulled the latest olive off the plastic sword with her teeth and took it between those red lips.

I think the next sentence came out in English, but I'd have to check the hotel's security cameras to be sure. "And what might that be?"

"Is this going to happen in your room or mine?"

After a second's hesitation, she passed me her glass to drain and we headed to the elevators. I pressed every polished button in that thing to make sure the ride to her room on the fifth floor took as long as possible to milk this moment. It was a miracle I managed it. I felt dizzy from lack of coordination. I was grateful to get in there without getting the bulge in my pants jammed in the closing door. If the hotel manager monitored the discreet camera in the corner, he wouldn't be turning the channel any time soon. The mirrored walls gave me a great three-sided view as she slammed me up against them and put those lips to good use. They were inches away from my ear, but I heard no breathing from her, just my frantic panting. I felt like a three-hundred-pound man who just finished a one-hundred-yard dash. Then she did that thing where, without me realizing it, she pinned my hands to the wall above my head, and my entire body was exposed and vulnerable. Fine by me, I thought. Have at it.

I think a random body part of mine bumped into every wall and door in the hallway as we did an epileptic dance to her room. By the time we got inside, my tie had almost garroted me and she was already barefoot. I pushed her onto the bed to try to gain a semblance of control and sent her purse flying across the floor. Its contents spread out and sought the underside of every piece of furniture in range. We ignored it and, for the next few hours, I found heaven.

CHAPTER TWO

A white streetlight shone across one side of the Capitol Bank building on Hillbourne and Main, casting dark, shadowy fingers up the tall wall that ran parallel to it. Traffic was light at this time of night, and hidden on the fifth story parking lot across the road was the only occupied vehicle.

Its two occupants watched as a lone figure climbed the wall and sat like a statue while a security guard made a routine sweep beneath it. Once the guard moved around the corner and out of sight, the figure dropped, landed cat-like beside the building and moved around the perimeter.

This was the fifth stakeout that Blaine Bell and Vince Molito had carried out together on American soil. Five out of five times they were successful and their reputation was growing as a competent and efficient team.

"You think that's her?" said Bell. He leaned over the steering wheel as if it would give him a better view.

Molito pointed at the bank. "Has to be. She's just like they said; stealthy, cool, efficient." He nodded as if to confirm it to himself. "Has to be."

The dark silhouette checked the doors and windows, then leaped onto a dumpster and used the extra height to reach the top of the building. The jet black clothing contrasted with the painted white of the roof and made her look like an ant crawling across a Formica tabletop. A large shoulder bag swung from side to side with every step.

"This I have to see," said Bell as he grabbed binoculars and slipped out of the car. He knelt below the lot's side wall and peered over the top. The figure reached into the bag, removed a tool and dismantled the steel mesh cover that protected a rectangular skylight. Once removed, another tool peeled back metal flashing from the edges and yet another removed the retaining bolts. The skylight slid to one side.

Molito joined the driver by the side wall. "Don't you think at least one of us should go in and watch her, see what she finds?"

"Yeah. You get down there, and I'll be ready with the car. Radios on."

They both flicked a switch behind their ears that opened channels on a top of the line wireless set.

As his partner began the descent to ground level, Bell raised the binoculars in time to watch the figure drop a small device through the hole in the opened roof. Seconds later, the streetlight and all other lights within a small radius blinked out, leaving the building in darkness. All shadows disappeared, and an eerie calm settled over the area. He strained his eyes enough to see the target rappel into the building. Torchlight danced across the window blinds before being quickly extinguished.

"What the hell?" he said into the mouthpiece.

"No idea," came a whispered reply. "That was so sudden I couldn't see a thing. Keep your eyes open."

Five minutes later, another light bounced in his peripheral vision as the security guard jogged back up the street to investigate. Nothing moved inside the building, but Molito had moved into position by the dumpster.

"Hey, you've got the guard coming your way," said Bell. "Get around the back but be careful. If he moves on the target, take him out."

"Got it. I hear movement on the roof. Get ready."

Bell strained his eyes again. The shadow moved along the parapet and back toward the dumpster. He crept back to the car, climbed in and turned the key in the ignition. The engine produced nothing but a click. He frowned. "What the fuck?"

He tried again, with the same result.

"Dammit," he said into the radio. "She must have dropped an EMP in there to disable the alarm. The radios are shrouded but the car's dead." A voice shouted from across the street. He looked again but saw nothing. "Molito! What's going on over there?"

"The guard appeared just as the target dropped onto the dumpster. As he reached the corner, she jumped him and chloroformed him. He didn't even have the chance to reach for his piece. Shit, she's seen me."

"I'm on my way," said Bell and ran down the stairs to the road.

He reached the bank and found his partner laid out next to the guard like two sardines in a can. He shook his head, pulled a knife from his jacket, and slid the blade into the side of the guard's neck before hoisting his partner over a shoulder.

When I woke the next morning, she was gone. No note on the pillow, no smell of coffee brewing, just my open half empty bottle of water standing by the lamp on the nightstand. Her bottle balanced on the drawers by the door, the plastic lid on the floor beside it. She must have left in a hurry.

I rolled onto my back, stretched my arms and laughed. I'd never had a night like that in my life, and I still had that glow of pride you get after a job well done. In fact, after that performance, I figured I should promote the Captain to General.

My mouth felt as if it held more gravel than the bottom of a bird cage and I'm sure I had a purple tongue from the wine. The bottled water was lukewarm, but it was wet. I rinsed my mouth with a small sip and placed the bottle back on the nightstand but didn't slide it far enough. It dived off the edge, tumbled to the floor and cartwheeled across the carpet. Water sprayed up the drawer fronts before the empty container landed upright on my untidy pile of clothes.

My bones creaked just as loud as the mattress as I slid out of bed and leaned forward to grab my pants. Something caught my eye under the nightstand, so I knelt by the bedside and reached underneath into the shadow. I pulled out a business card. The corners had curled with wear and there were lines of random numbers written on the back in black ink. I put it on the nightstand while I pulled on my crinkled clothes, then sat on the edge of the bed and looked at it. She must have missed it when she picked up the contents of her purse this morning, assuming she'd stayed until the morning. The front side had a line of professional looking font that said Monica Bridges. So her real name was Monica. That was disappointing. She worked for a company called SonicAmerica, but there was no job description, no branch address, just a cool logo and a cell phone number. I slid the card into my pocket. We could still try for a repeat performance in my room.

I was in the bathroom, zipping up after taking care of business, when I heard a knock at the door. My first thought was that I'd found the perfect woman and she'd just slipped out to get us breakfast. By the time I realized she'd have the key, the door burst open and a crowd of shouting, gun toting Feds filed into the room.

They fanned out like a synchronized dancing team and covered the room. Someone said 'clear' without too much conviction, maybe because they do it on TV. The lead agent peeled back one side of his standard issue black suit and flashed his badge at me.

"Sir, are you alone?"

Now, this wasn't the Penthouse. It was two rooms; one decent sized bedroom with a bed, a few pieces of furniture and a mini fridge, and the bathroom. The shower curtain made a staccato machine gun noise as he slid it to one side and stared at the empty tub.

"Ah, let me check." I paused for effect and stared with him. "Yes, it would appear so. What the hell is going on here? What are you doing in my room?"

"Unless you're Jane Bennett, which I doubt, then this is not your room. That's the name on the credit card that paid for it."

Touché, karma Gods, revenge is yours. Hang on, Jane Bennett? I followed him into the main room. His goons were doing a cursory search of the place while the hotel manager stood by the door. He waved his card key around as if he was trying to join the team.

The lead agent had one of those voices that commanded attention. He should work in radio. "So," he continued, "what are *you* doing in this room?"

"Okay," I said, "before we go any further, who exactly do you work for? Let's see some ID."

He flashed the badge again. I have to admit; it was pretty cool. Then he flipped open a wallet.

"Special Agent Lennon, F.B.I."

"Lennon?" I said. "As in 'John'?"

"Yeah, yeah, I've never heard that before, smart ass. Your turn. ID."

My fingers brushed against the business card as I reached into my pocket to grab my wallet. I left the card in place for now and handed over my license. Before I gave too much information, I wanted to see what this was about.

"So, Mr. Howard," he continued, "what's your relationship with Ms. Bennett?" He passed my license to a colleague who wrote my details down in his little notebook.

Who the hell was Jane Bennett? So was Monica Bridges really Jane Bennett? Was that even her business card? She didn't look like a Jane either. I'm still going with Giselle or Chantelle. Her name had to end in –elle!

"Well, relationship might be too strong a word," I started. I didn't need to finish. Lennon looked at me like I was one of his kids and I'd just spilled milk all over his new car seats. "And how long have you known Ms. Bennett?"

"You mean in the biblical sense, or…"

I got that look again.

"Okay. I met her at the bar last night. I'd never even seen her before then. What's this about, Agent Lennon?"

"And you were with her all night?"

"Yes. No. You know what, I'm not sure."

Lennon tilted his head like an attentive dog and smirked. "You have a lot to drink last night, Mr. Howard? Which was it?"

The weird thing is, I had no idea. My stomach felt fine, but my head was still all over the place. It seemed as if someone had crept into the room last night and drip fed me a bottle of bourbon.

"I know we fell asleep together, but when I woke up this morning, she'd already left."

"And you've no idea what time she left?"

"No. Not a clue. I must have crashed out. To be fair, it was a hell of a workout. And my head is a little fuzzy."

"Did she give you anything to eat or drink?"

"No. We came right here from the bar. I was drinking wine and she…hang on, I finished her drink. You reckon she spiked it?"

"Did you see it the whole time?"

I thought back to the sequence of events and couldn't be certain she'd drunk from her glass before she handed it over. I'd been in the restroom. Lennon was at least one step ahead of me.

"No wiseass answers this time?"

"I do that when I'm nervous. It's a defense mechanism. So you think she drugged me?"

"You should know the answer to that, Mr. Howard, but I can tell you one thing. She definitely used you."

"No kidding," I smirked, "and I enjoyed every second."

"As an alibi. We need to talk to her about her connection with multiple murders. We've got a new one here in Louisville. Last night. When she was with you."

A tornado blew through my head and cleared it out in an instant, but the room spun with it too.

"Multiple?"

"Multiple. She didn't by any chance leave you with any contact information, did she? I doubt she'd be that stupid, but you can never be sure. You know how it is, in the heat of passion."

"Yeah, okay, you can quit the sarcasm. You've got my attention."

I thought about the card, but my curiosity was piqued. Since it belonged to Monica Bridges and not Jane Bennett, I had no idea where this would go. And I didn't see her as a murderer, so I figured I'd keep hold of it for now. "No, she left nothing. Other than giving directions there wasn't much conversation. We had more of a physical evening."

"No comments on where she was going, or where she'd been?"

"Nothing."

"And you made no plans to see her again?"

I wish. "No. Like I said, she left before I woke. I expected that kind of night, though."

"Did you take any pictures?"

The question surprised me. "I beg your pardon? I'm not sure that's any of your business, and anyway, I might not be that kind of guy."

Lennon shook his head. I think I disappointed him. "We have no idea what she looks like. She's hidden her face from every camera we've found. Even the one in the elevator. The card she used to pay for this room originated in Virginia. We've been following a paper trail to get here."

I'm sure my face blushed at the mention of the elevator, and then I tried to describe her. I'm positive I overused 'smoking', but I did my best. The phrase 'She was my dream woman' is not a description the Feds can put on America's Most Wanted.

"If you put Cindy Crawford, Princess Diana and Famke Janssen in a blender...well, it would be messy, but you'd end up with Jane Bennett. She looked like a Bond girl and moved like a princess. And she had these smoking eyes." Damn it. There it went again.

The room search turned up nothing, which didn't surprise me. I'd already picked up the only thing on the floor that didn't come in with me last night. Lennon gave me the "we'll be in touch" speech and they all filtered out of the room like a bunch of penguins heading for mating season. I think my description got them stirred up.

CHAPTER THREE

"What do you mean, you lost her?"

Every word was clipped and precise, but the angry English accent still bounced off the sound-proofed walls like an errant basketball. A half dozen people looked up with concern and then diverted their attention back to high-tech computer screens that covered their desks.

"Bloody hell," he continued, "she's not your fucking car keys. You lost her? Wait there!"

Kyle Beck put the call on hold, slammed the receiver into its cradle and stormed over to his office. A hiss of air escaped the room as he pulled the door shut with a dull thud, and then he leaned against the desk and took a deep breath, forcing himself to calm down. The heat from his volatile temper rose in his cheeks, and his plush office chair whistled as he sank in to it. He pushed it away from the desk, swung his feet up on to the desktop, linked his ankles and picked up the phone. "Okay," he said, reconnecting the call, "tell me what happened."

His eyes narrowed and widened as Molito recalled the mission from the night before. The images of the woman in black prowling through the bank and eluding the guard flashed through his mind. Followed immediately by the image of her efficiently taking down Molito.

"So, what you're saying is that you got your arse kicked by a woman?" His harsh tone cut with a hint of ridicule.

Beck had met Bell and Molito on his final tour of Afghanistan. The three men completed three tours each in the region, Beck with the British SAS and the other two with the 82nd Airborne Division. They first met in Kabul and had bonded over whiskey and a mutual hatred of the Middle East and its residents. The rest of the team in the other room was handpicked from various agencies and units, recruited for their technical expertise. None of them had looked into the eyes of another before pulling a trigger or thrusting a knife through muscle. In that room Beck was untouchable. He was a God. Every word was a command to be followed, and followed without question. The banter shared with Bell and Molito didn't happen in that room, the bond between the men never exposed. Anyone speaking to Beck with the same tone of his tour comrades would be taken outside and shot, but the three men spoke alone as if they were propping up a bar in a dark corner of Kandahar.

"Fuck you," said Molito, trying to claim back some pride. "You know as well as I do that she's not the average woman. Hell, she'd be great on our team, if we could all keep our hands off her."

"Yeah," replied Beck, "but she's not on our team, and anyway, it sounds like she'd break your hands before you got past her bra strap. What about the guard? Did he see her?"

"Bell took care of the guard. No witnesses."

"Okay. Good. Well, we can put this one down to experience, mate. We've still got a few days, and I'm sure we'll soon pick up her trail, and we can get back on it, but now you know. You cannot underestimate this woman. We need that flash drive, Vince. It's worth billions. The fucking rag-heads might be stuck in the middle ages, but there's enough money over there to set us all up for life. Once we can prove what they're facing, they'll pay anything to stop it. Just keep behind her, keep your nose clean, and get ready to strike when I give the say so."

"No problem boss. Get in touch when you get a fix on her, and we'll be all over it," said Molito.

"I know you will," said Beck. "I know you will."

CHAPTER FOUR

I sat on the edge of the bed and turned the card over in my fingers. It didn't vanish or change into the queen of hearts; it remained silent and taunted me. Monica Bridges. Jane Bennett. Before I knew it, my fingers had dialed the cell phone number. The call connected and the electronic purring put me in a daze. I didn't get to sleep until late last night. A voice answered, cheery and pleasant, but not one I recognized. It jarred me back into the present. "Hi, you've reached Monica's phone. If you're hearing this…" I listened to the whole message and then disconnected the call without leaving a voice-mail. My Bond girl wasn't Monica Bridges. So who was Jane Bennett?

I went out to the parking garage to retrieve my laptop from the car, then got back to my room and connected to the hotel's Wi-Fi. I'm pretty switched on when it comes to technology. I can distinguish my gigs from my bytes. However, no amount of typing wizardry, phone number searches, or image recognition websites helped me narrow down the forty-seven million Jane Bennett's into the one I wanted to see again. Fewer than ten million Monica Bridges appeared online, but it didn't take a second to realize that, like Lennon, I had no idea what the real Monica looked like.

A shower washed last night's evidence away while I did a lot of thinking. Had I spent the night with a serial killer? Her hands were way too smooth. Killer's hands had to have calluses from digging holes in the desert or operating a wood chipper, not the velvety skin that stroked me into clawing the bed sheets like a cardiac victim. She did move like a lioness, and she was assured and lithe, but still...a killer?

The name SonicAmerica meant nothing to me either and I couldn't remember ever seeing it, and I drove miles for my job. The numbers on the back of the card looked like some kind of code. I remembered the first set began with KY-CB, which is probably what brought her here. Next to that were four numbers that slipped my mind, but they weren't familiar to me when I'd looked at them. Maybe they were the number to a safe deposit box. Isn't that what these things always boiled down to? The others had the same format as GPS coordinates. What can I say; I watch too much Discovery Channel.

I toweled myself dry and then flipped the laptop open again and searched for SonicAmerica. What did we do before the Internet? I would've had to flip through a phone book. I wasn't sure if they even made those anymore.

It looked like it was headquartered in West Virginia and had two big facilities. A glance at their homepage told me they were researching ways to use sonic waves and vibration in construction. It meant nothing to me. I could reach the first location with a four-hour drive and I could peddle my wares in West Virginia as well as I did anywhere else. Also, I've driven further for work without the added incentive of the Feds barging into my room. I searched for Google Maps and keyed the GPS coordinates from the card into the search engine. The screen turned blue. A few clicks on the Maps menu button and the image zoomed out until I was looking at the east coast. The coordinates placed a small red dot a couple of hundred miles into the Atlantic.

Chances are they weren't coordinates then.

I carried out my routine checks to make sure I left nothing behind and had zipped my laptop into its little case when I heard a knock at the door. The only people who knew my room number were Lennon and reception. I stormed over to the door and threw it open.

CHAPTER FIVE

A while after Jane Bennett charged her credit card, a notification appeared stating that she'd booked a room at a hotel in downtown Kentucky. Two cars made the seven-hour drive from northern Chicago and pulled into the parking garage beneath the large building. By the time they had convinced the front desk to give them her room number and made it up to the fifth floor, the target had already vanished, leaving behind a clueless idiot who knew even less than they did.

Cal Lennon was frustrated and drove aggressively around the maze of four-lane roads and one-way streets. His colleague, Eric Weston, sat in the passenger seat and checked card records and road traffic cameras on a laptop, hoping for another break. Lennon reached into the dual cup holder, took a mouthful of tepid coke and placed the can back in its holster next to a small cell phone.

They found the phone on the floor of a room in a mansion in Chicago. They'd emptied the house by setting off the fire alarms, knowing that their target was working inside there. Monica Bridges' room was easy to find but, other than the phone lying on the floor under a chair, it was empty. The gadget, their solitary lead, nestled in the SUV's cup holder. It was wrapped in a protective paper napkin like an egg to stop it from rattling against the plastic. Lennon jumped when it started ringing. By the time it chirped out its second dial tone, he'd released the steering wheel long enough to point to the laptop.

"Trace that call."

As if expecting the call, his fingers already flashed over the keyboard. With the advances in mobile technology, a laptop with the correct software and enough processing power could trace an active cell phone in the time it took to order a pizza. Lines zipped around the small screen as the program closed in on the signal's source, pinging from tower to tower until it settled on a building in downtown Louisville.

Lennon glanced at the screen and then across to his colleague, his eyebrows knotted in confusion. "Is that what I think it is?" He scanned the road ahead to find a suitable place to turn.

"It's The Malt House Hotel," said Weston. "Weren't we just there?"

"We were. Cross your fingers and hope the call's connected long enough to give us a name."

The address of the hotel appeared at the bottom of the screen even though both men already knew its location. Seconds later a cell phone number scrolled by beneath it, followed by a name.

Paul Howard.

"Well I'll be damned," said Lennon. "Maybe he wasn't an idiot after all. Call the other car and tell them to meet us there" He executed a U-turn across the median, causing commuters to brake and swerve. The horns and shouting voices faded into the distance as he floored the accelerator and drove back toward the hotel.

They merged behind the second car as they sped down the main street and then pulled in front of the hotel's entrance in unison. The guys in the front car entered the building as Lennon waited for his tech guy to latch onto Howard's cell phone signal. It didn't take long.

CHAPTER SIX

"Hello again, Paul," she said in that sultry voice.

I know my legs were still down there, but if the signal from my brain was getting through, they weren't listening.

"Would you mind if I came inside?" she said, standing across the threshold like a barred vampire.

"Are you going to kill me?"

"Not today," she said. My frozen legs and gaping mouth must have painted me fearful because she reached forward and placed a reassuring hand on my arm. "And, once again, I'm joking. Honestly Paul, once you get to know me I'm not that bad. Now can I come in?"

I stepped to one side, and she breezed past me. Her perfume washed over me, and that familiar stirring started again. The red dress and stilettos were gone, replaced by a black tee shirt, pants, and tennis shoes. She still looked amazing. "You look like a ninja," I said.

"I have a strong need to be stealthy," she replied. "I saw you met Agent Lennon."

"Are you following me?"

"No. They were following me. I side stepped them and watched them enter the hotel. Once they left, it didn't take me long to find your room number. I need to ask a favor of you."

"Will you still be here when I've done it?" Petulance is not a good character trait, but it came naturally to me.

"I'm sorry about that," she said with a pout. "I had to be somewhere early and I didn't want to wake you."

"You drugged me! I would've slept through an earthquake! What did you put in that gin?"

"I put nothing in the gin. I was drinking that."

"But I thought…"

"I did put a mild tranquilizer in your water bottle."

"Damn it! Why? What are you involved in? Hell, let's start at the beginning. You used me."

"Whoa, slow down. Too many questions…and it's fair to say we used each other."

"I don't remember drugging you."

She lifted her hands in mock surrender. "Fair enough, you win that one. I needed to be sure you'd be there all night."

"I could barely walk by the time we were done. Believe me, I wasn't going anywhere."

"Maybe, but I had to be sure," she said. "I needed an alibi. I'm sorry."

"An alibi for what? What's going on? Apology not accepted, by the way. And first things first, I don't even know your name."

"It's better if you don't get involved," she said. "And my name is Sabrina. Sabrina White."

I should mention that I'm dealing with trust issues since my ex-wife shared a drink and herself with an ex-friend of mine. My young daughter Kacie says I need to move on and get over it. When did kids become therapists? Still, I do my best to give people the benefit of the doubt; even when they drug me.

"Are you sure?" I said. Okay, sarcasm is not a good trait either. "Did you check today? You're not Monica Bridges or Jane Bennett?"

She didn't hide her surprise; the expression on her face spoke volumes. I just stared and waited for a response. The edge of the bed dipped into a pleasant smile as she sat on it and clamped her hands between her thighs. When she looked up at me, it was with eyes that looked as if her puppy had just died.

"How did you get those names?"

"Lennon told me about Jane Bennett, but Monica Bridges involves me finding a business card you dropped."

"So you found it?"

"I've got it. It intrigued me, so I've been playing Sherlock Holmes. I thought the large numbers might be map coordinates, but that didn't pan out. And the smaller number, the one that starts with KY-CB? Is that a safe deposit box number?"

"No. I checked. That's why I needed an alibi. I was with you all night until early morning. Don't be offended. By the way, I had a good time. Still, I figured the CB referred to Capitol Bank, so I sneaked out and paid them a visit. There were nowhere near enough deposit boxes to warrant that high a number."

"Compliment accepted, although it's a little late for your alibi. Lennon knows you weren't here until morning. Oh, and I called the cell phone number," I said.

A look of sheer panic crossed her face, and she shot to her feet. Her sudden urgency scared the crap out of me. "Tell me it didn't connect."

"I could, but I'd be lying. It went to voicemail."

"What? Shit! Get your things together. We've got to go. Now!"

"Go where? And why?"

"Anywhere. Because they're monitoring that number. I'm sure the guys chasing me have her phone. I couldn't find it in her bag so I called the number on the card and they were on to me again in no time. If your call connected, then they're coming for you too. They've got your number, and they'll trace you. You're involved now, whether you like it or not. They've been chasing me for the same reason, and I've not been able to work out why. Where are you parked?"

"What makes you think I have a car? And I still have no idea what's going on. I'm not ready to go racing off with you." I felt like I'd arrived late for a meeting and they were just wrapping up.

"I've been followed across states because of a phone call. Something big is going on. If you want to sit here and wait for the bad guys to turn up, be my guest. But you're a sales rep," she said, "of course you've got a car. And Jane Bennett will have reported hers stolen by now, so mine's useless. So come on. Move!"

"It's in the adjacent garage," I said defeated. "Follow me."

We got out into the parking garage without the front desk seeing us. This garage wasn't covered with the standard camera package and the ones they did have didn't seem to be in good shape. My sedan was parked in the corner next to a wall. Half the chance of someone dinging it. She threw her stuff behind the seat; I dropped my small suitcase in the trunk.

She made her way around to the driver's side. "Hold up," I said. "I'm driving." After a small argument, she relented and walked around to the other side of the car and climbed in. "Okay, where to?"

"Head east to the highway," she said. "I'll direct you from there."

As I drove out past the hotel entrance, a couple of familiar looking black SUV's pulled up in a tidy line. A steady stream of Feds jumped out and went inside. I didn't see Lennon.

"Seems we were just in time."

Sabrina, if that was her name, didn't even glance at them. "Get onto I-64 and keep going east. We're going to visit Monica Bridges."

"First things first," she said, "I might be a thief, but I'm not a killer. And I'm not a common thief either. If anything, I'm more like an executive thief. More professional."

Sabrina looked so intense I had no choice but to give her the benefit of the doubt. Her hands were clamped together like a vice, and she sat back as if glued to the passenger seat.

"And I don't know where Lennon is getting his information, but I haven't killed anyone. You have to believe me. I may have knocked out a couple of guys here and there, but I'm no killer. And don't trust Lennon either. His credentials haven't checked out yet."

I did one of those double takes and caught her eye. "Even if I believe you about the killer thing, what the hell is an executive thief? Are you really trying to make stealing things sound cool?"

The black ribbon of I64 unraveled behind us at a good speed. Her voice still sounded like cotton candy floating on clouds, but without the benefit of alcohol and dim bar lighting, the hypnotic effect that had lured me the night before was missing. We'd played the silence game for a while as she wrung her hands again. I was waiting for her to open up and confess everything. I think she was just waiting for me to say something that justified us being in the car together. There's a limit to how much country radio you can listen to until someone caves. It was her. I'm not proud.

"It's not like I steal bras and panties from Walmart," she continued. "People pay me large amounts of money to get things for them; paintings, sculptures, jewelry. You name it. If it's out there and someone knows about it, there's always someone who wants it. I fulfill that demand. Monica Bridges was just another mark. They wanted me to go to Chicago and get a flash drive from her room. She was attending a conference in this big fancy house. I found her room and looked around but, no sooner had I picked up her purse, alarms sounded. Once I got out to the car, I emptied the purse and then ditched it in a trash can. The damned thing's fluorescent. I didn't find a flash drive, just regular stuff, so I kept the cash and her credit card. I hadn't driven a few miles when Lennon and his goons were chasing me with guns. There was no reason I could think of. The only thing I took was that purse. When I lost them, I circled back to the trash can and picked it up, but I still couldn't find anything in it. When curiosity got the better of me, I called that number. Since then they've been chasing me and I have no idea why. I can't do my job with people following me. I have to find out what's going on and I'm hoping Monica Bridges can help."

"Well, in your line of work, it's not like you can just turn yourself in and ask them. How did they know to look for you in the first place? Did someone see you at the house? And who is the 'they' that used your executive services?"

"I'm certain no one saw me. The house was full of people so the alarms shouldn't have been set, but I did disable the surveillance system before I went inside. I had to search a couple of rooms before I found hers and the first one was a kid's bedroom. Maybe there was one of those monitored nanny-cams hidden in there. I'm sure they traced her credit card and found the rental car, though, so I ditched it and borrowed Jane Bennett's."

It was like when you hear one of those inappropriate jokes that take you by surprise. You know you shouldn't laugh, but I had to. "Borrow?" I said. "Don't you mean take?"

"Hey, it was her fault. If you want to step out to smoke a cigarette, then don't leave your keys in the ignition. Smoking is no good for you. I hope she learned a lesson."

I had all kinds of comments about moral compasses spinning out of control, but I wanted to concentrate on driving, and I was still only about eighty percent sure she wasn't a killer. "And who employed you?"

"I have no idea. Everything is done by email. In my line of work, names are never used. I was to email them back once I had the drive, and they would send drop instructions."

"Okay, well how do you know how to find Monica Bridges?" I asked.

She relaxed enough to reach behind me and pull a purse onto her lap. It was one of those Vera Bradley things that looked like an explosion in a paint factory. The main body of it was a swatch of fluorescent material with a strap that had a bulky pad in the middle for shoulder comfort. It amazed me that anyone could carry one of them around without getting a migraine. She rummaged inside and pulled out a handful of papers and a notebook.

"Rule number one," she said, waving the paper at me. "Don't keep your diary in your purse."

"I'd say rule number one should be 'don't keep a diary'. Why would you want to put all of your intimate details in writing? It's just asking for trouble."

"Well, you'd have to be crazy or naïve to write your full details at the front. Her full name is Monica Jane Bridges. She's forty-eight, has a high-powered position with SonicAmerica, and lives at the address we're heading to. She's also been doing a lot of research about DARPA."

"Never heard of them," I said. "What are they? Some kind of banking organization?"

"Nowhere near," she said. "I did a load of research of my own." She shuffled through the papers and moved one to the front of the pile. "Defense Advanced Research Projects Agency. It's a government agency, run by the Department of Defense."

"Are you going to get all X-Files on me?" I asked.

"Not quite. You know how we worry that other countries have cooler stuff than we do? DARPA does the research to make sure we stay ahead of the others. At least as far as they know. Apparently, it freaked the government out, back when the Russians got a rocket into space ahead of us. They never wanted to be behind again, so DARPA has a full time job to push technology forward, with a three-billion-dollar budget, no less. They're based in Virginia."

I whistled. "That's a fair chunk of change. I'm sure there's a lot of political intrigue and maneuvering involved. But why would Monica be involved?"

"No idea. I've been through every page in her purse, and I can't find any connection."

"How dangerous is this?" I asked. "I mean, really? What if I go to the police and just tell them about the drive and put everything out in the open? Am I in real danger, like the life-threatening violent kind?"

"They shot at me when I was running away in Chicago. Does that count?"

"Did you give them a reason to?"

"No. All they knew was that I tripped some alarm at the house."

I stared at the road in silence. I might be allergic to life-threatening violence. What if it brings me out in a rash of bullet holes? I hoped Monica Bridges knew something.

CHAPTER SEVEN

M onica Bridges stared at the rows of wine bottles seated in the oak rack on the wall facing her. It had taken her years to build up the collection while her husband worked overseas, sometimes for months at a time, but it now sat gathering dust. Faint light bounced off the curve of the glass as the bottles pointed at her, almost accusing her of neglecting them. In the top left corner, a small cobweb hung like a silk curtain. Its resident sat back in the shadow on guard, watching her, as if it knew she was no threat.

While he'd been away for months, her work kept her busy enough to be away from home for weeks, her research eating into her days like a cancer, stealing away the hours. The projects she and her team worked on had high-level clearance but, unlike her husband, she shared her successes and failures with him when he returned, even showing him diagrams of the painstaking advances they'd made.

His job was a mystery. She suspected that he worked for either the government or the military but, other than that, nothing. She didn't even know his title. "You know how it is, baby," he often said in his deep, soothing voice, his accent so familiar to her now she never noticed it. "I told you about all of this before you married me. You have to just let it go and trust that I'm doing important work for the good of the country."

She didn't argue. Born into an average life, Monica went through high school and college with top grades but without a single date. She wasn't unattractive, but she wasn't what she would call model material either. When God gave out brains, her mother said, Monica was at the front of the line. Mom never mentioned where she was in the line when God gave out looks.

When her husband first approached her, she was at a gala dinner. SonicAmerica had produced a machine that would revolutionize deep-sea research. Government and independent contracts rolled in. As the lead on the research team, she was instructed to 'dress to kill' and told that the night was all about her.

Kyle approached her early into the evening as if he sought her out. She thought nothing of it. Her research had resulted in the break-through they needed to complete the project and almost everyone in attendance had spoken to her. Kyle was different, though. He touched her arm when he spoke, and laughed at her attempt at jokes. He wasn't standoffish like the other military and government types. When he smiled at her, his eyes had sparkled and reminded her of Steve McQueen from her mother's favorite movies. He was so far out of her league they weren't even playing the same sport, so when he proposed she didn't hesitate to say yes. For five years she gave him everything she had.

Fresh tears welled up and rolled down her cheeks as she shifted in her seat. She should have been cried out after five days. Her stomach grumbled a protest, demanding to be fed. A cheese tray from the fridge under the wine bar lay empty on a side table, next to the zip ties she'd severed with a corkscrew. One bottle of water and a small bunch of grapes remained in the fridge. They had to be rationed as best as possible. Rows of wine bottles were stacked to her side, but she didn't dare drink any them. The alcohol would dehydrate her. She couldn't afford for that to happen

Despite having the run of the basement, she could go no further than the top of the stairs. A thick iron bolt held the sturdy door shut. She was stuck in this house. Alone.

CHAPTER EIGHT

Welcome to West Virginia. Wild and wonderful.

That's what the sign said as we crossed the state line. I'd had wild and wonderful once this week and, while I was game for more wonderful, I figured wild could sit this one out. We pulled into a Burger King for something to eat and Sabrina typed Bridges' address into her phone's GPS. The screen zoomed out and showed a little dot in the middle of nowhere.

"You know that area?" I asked.

"No. Looks like she lives off the grid."

"The benefits of a high powered job. It must be nice."

"I don't know, my job pays well," she said. She tucked a stray lock of hair behind her ear and smiled. Faint crow's feet perched at the side of her eyes. I wondered if they came from a lot of smiling or a lot of stress.

"Yeah but the benefits suck, right?"

"Depends on how you look at it. I get a lot of paid vacation, and I get to travel, and I can get whatever company car I want, whenever I want one. I'm in an incredibly low tax bracket too. The health insurance isn't so great, though. And they definitely don't cover gunshots."

If I've had a weirder conversation, I don't remember it, but I was pleased that she seemed to have relaxed a little. We dumped our trash and walked back to the car.

I glanced across to her as she fastened her seat belt and shuffled to the back of the seat.

"I noticed you're a tense passenger. You don't like sitting in that seat, do you? What's that about? Don't you trust my driving?"

She stared at the space between her feet, and was silent for a while. It was as if a dark cloud entered the car. When she spoke, her voice trembled and sounded nervous.

"It's not that. To be honest, I'm a control freak when it comes to driving. Both my parents died in a wreck. I was buckled into the back seat while my mom went headfirst through the windshield. She didn't wear a seatbelt. My dad did, but his chest crushed against the steering wheel. I watched him die in hospital." She looked back at me, her eyes misty. "Morbid, huh?"

"Shit Sabrina," I said and wished that the driver's seat would open up into a chasm and swallow me. "I'm so sorry. Me and my stupid mouth. Were you okay?"

"The strap dislocated my collarbone, but it saved my life. Don't worry. It was a long time ago, but I'm still wary in a car. You should be honored, though. I don't think I've mentioned that to anyone in years."

I reached for the door handle. "Hey, if you want to drive, I understand."

"That's not necessary. Face your fears, right? Anyway, you seem to be a decent driver. Must be all the miles you put in doing your job."

We got back on the road, and I drove with the hesitancy of a pensioner until she told me to get over it and drive properly. Soon the frequency of the buildings dwindled, and a green patchwork of farms spread out before us. The hum of the smooth asphalt transitioned into the crunch and pop of gravel as we trundled down smaller roads. The GPS dot grew larger. After a couple of miles, Sabrina pointed to a small side road that snaked away to the right and disappeared into a wooded area.

"It should be down there," she said glancing at the phone, "about

200 yards. See if you can find somewhere discreet to hide the car. We should walk the rest of the way and try to stay out of sight."

I found a small gap in the tree line, and reversed the car in as far as I dared. If we needed to get away in a hurry, I didn't want to do too much off-roading. Sabrina grabbed a large over the shoulder bag and threw the strap over her head. I looked at it with a frown. It looked pretty heavy.

"Tools of the trade," she said.

"Damn. Which trade? Mining?"

"At some point, you'll thank me for the contents of this bag," she said and strode off ahead of me.

We kept to the side of the road in case anyone else visited and crept beneath the overhanging canopy. The further along the road we walked, the thicker the canopy grew until it felt as if we were traveling through a leafy tunnel. It took about ten minutes for us to reach the house. The tree line angled back, and the lush grass ended at two rows of strategically placed stones that directed us up to the front porch. The gravel road widened and swept around one side of the house and reappeared on the other. I was sure I could hear running water somewhere in the distance.

Sabrina beckoned me to one side. "Let's stay in the trees and check around the perimeter. It doesn't look as if there's anyone home, but I've been surprised before. Best to be sure."

It was easy to tell if anyone was home. The house was beautiful, built from stained wood with huge windows that reached up from a few feet off the floor to just under the gutters. It had more glass than an Irish pub crawl and was pretty much see through. The only way anyone was home was if they were asleep in bed or dead on the floor.

I followed Sabrina through the brush, and we crept around to the back of the house. She glided forward in silence while I alerted every bird within a hundred miles with my clumsy movement. My dress shoes didn't help. I made a mental note to pick up some casual wear.

A garage that sat on a raised platform broke the smooth curve of the circular driveway. A stream flowed beneath it and trickled into a winding creek. I could live here if I had five jobs and a small inheritance. The garage was empty.

"Okay. Seems to be clear," she said. "Let's check out the alarm system. There's bound to be one."

We walked up to the back door, and she leaned forward and cupped her hand against the glass. "Tut, tut. There's the panel, right by the front door. It looks pretty old. I don't see any cameras, which surprises me. This must be one of those low crime areas where people think it will never happen to them. Still, you'd think someone in a position of responsibility would be more security conscious."

I trailed behind her again as we moved around to the front door. She placed her bag on the porch and reached inside it.

"You see the small cable at the bottom of the panel? That's a good, old-fashioned phone line. As soon as this thing trips, it'll transmit a signal to a monitoring station. It might even go directly to local law enforcement with this place being so remote. Once I open the door, I'll have maybe twenty or thirty seconds to disable the alarm. I'll cut the cable first to kill the signal and then I'll take care of the panel."

"Thanks for the walk through," I said, "it's always nice to watch a professional at work."

She rolled out a small black pouch that looked like the kind of thing torturers carried around and took out two small picks. Not a minute later the door swung open, and the alarm began to beep. A stern lady said, 'Disarm' over and over through a small speaker. Sabrina strolled over to the panel, took wire snips from the bag, and cut the phone cable.

"I assume you have the skills to disable the alarm panel itself?" I asked. Maybe I should have asked that before we entered the premises.

"Of course," she said, and proceeded to smash the crap out of the panel with a hammer. Six good swings and it was a tangled mess of plastic, wires, and circuit boards. "They're not as complicated as you think. The main thing is to prevent the signal from transmitting but still, the siren can be distracting when you're trying to work."

CHAPTER NINE

Kyle Beck stood with his hands rested on his hips and looked over the shoulder of an operative. The young assistant controlled a miniature joystick with one hand while the other tapped away at a wireless keyboard. Each movement adjusted the picture on the large screen in front of them.

"We picked them up again just as they entered West Virginia. They're eating Burger King at the moment, but they've been in there a while."

Despite its size, the screen resembled a photograph, the image crisp and crystal clear. Beck could even make out the license plates of the vehicles parked outside the restaurant and see people eating lunch through the foggy windows.

He was familiar with drones and their capabilities, although military models were much more advanced that the small thing he opted to use for this job. This thing flew at less than a hundred feet. Military drones reached 60,000 feet and still projected perfect images. This smaller model wasn't as reliable or as stable as its larger brothers, but its size made it much less visible for close up work.

The military had embraced drone technology and used them for many things. During Beck's time in uniform, they checked the road ahead for the black ops missions he'd ran. Better to avoid confrontation than to have to shoot your way through it. Even a stray herd of goats could be enough to jeopardize a mission that's months into the planning and might cost well-trained men their lives.

"Are Bell and Molito in position yet?" he asked.

"No sir, they're still a few miles out. Last I heard, fifteen minutes away."

"Okay, follow the vehicle and update their cell phones' GPS. Once she gets what we need, we'll move in and take it."

"Yes sir, I'll keep them up to date."

They watched as the two targets left the restaurant and, after a short discussion, climbed into their vehicle and headed away from town. As the car rejoined minimal traffic, the operator adjusted the small joystick to keep the sedan in the center of the screen and tracked it through the town and out into open countryside. The dark lines of highway turned into chalk lines as the roads grew smaller, and the target wound its way around the landscape.

Just as the vehicle turned off onto an even smaller side road, the image rocked as black shapes flew across the screen. Then it jarred and spun. Blue sky and clouds filled the screen with fleeting glimpses of trees and grass as the drone began a free-fall. The operator fought with the joystick and punched keys, but the image continued to spin.

"What the hell is going on?" said Beck, his eyes flitting back and forth from the screen to the operator's frantic fingers.

"I think it was a flock of birds, sir. They must have flown into the drone. I can't stabilize it. I'll have to reset and restart it so it's not fighting against its propellers."

"Do whatever you have to do. Just get me that fucking image back. Now!"

The young man ran both hands across the keyboard, his fingers a blur of motion as he attempted to correct the drone. Five minutes later, a still image reappeared. The drone lifted out of grass and into the air again, and the search began for the target. It was nowhere to be seen.

Beck pointed to the keyboard. "Zoom out. Show me the lay of the land."

Roads and buildings shrank as more of the countryside filled the screen. He leaned forward and pointed to a dense patch of greenery.

"I'll bet they're under that canopy somewhere. Don't worry; we still have the tracker. We'll find them again."

CHAPTER TEN

I felt like a goldfish.

One whole side of the Bridges' residence was a one level open plan room with minimal furniture and a seating arrangement smack in the middle. Don't get me wrong; it was still an amazing room with glossy hardwood flooring and cedar posts between the gaping windows, but that's pretty much what it was. A room full of gaping windows.

I checked upstairs to make sure no one was sleeping and then came back to the main downstairs room, sat on the center stool, and spun around like a kid in a playground. Sabrina tossed me a pair of latex gloves.

"Don't touch a thing without putting these on first. You take upstairs and I'll check down here. We're looking for a small flash drive. Look under drawers, bedding, behind pictures. I'm sure you know the drill. If you find anything locked, call me. And don't rush but don't dawdle either, we don't know how long we have."

"Got it," I said and snapped the gloves against my wrists for effect.

The stairs didn't make a sound as I climbed them. The solid boards took my weight with ease. Upstairs felt more enclosed, with a single hallway dissecting the space into two equal sized halves. The side on the right was to the back of the house and was one long bedroom with an en suite at the far end. It had the same hardwood floor as the lower level, but had thick wool rugs cast around at random angles like magnets on a fridge door. None of the bedroom furniture matched as if each piece was handed down as a family heirloom. The dresser had a photo on either side of the mirror. There were no brushes or perfume, no trinkets or jewelry boxes, just two pictures and a thin layer of dust. Both pictures showed an average looking woman. The first showed her sandwiched between two smiling pensioners. The other showed her standing on a stage, suited and booted, receiving an important looking award. It looked as if Monica Bridges was married to her work and loved her folks.

A search in and under each drawer revealed nothing other than a collection of dangerous looking women's accessories hidden beneath her underwear. Nothing was hidden in the bed either, and it took longer to replace the scatter cushions than to search it. All the other pictures hung flush to the walls and concealed nothing more than fresher looking paint when I pulled them back. I was about to move into the bathroom when I had a moment of genius. I remembered a movie from years ago, where the room in question had a small hatch built into the floor, hidden under a rug. After a considerable amount of lifting and back straining, I still came up empty. I was in a room on the other half of the house, which was kitted out as a home gym when Sabrina shouted from downstairs.

"I found something here. You have any luck up there?"

"Not yet," I shouted, "I'm almost done, though." Curiosity got the better of me, so I breezed through the rest of the search and then made my way back downstairs.

I found her in a home office, kneeling in the far corner in front of a safe the size of a small storage shed. She had the cup of a stethoscope positioned just below the dial and was turning the wheel click by click, listening to the box's heartbeat.

"You really use those things? I thought they were just for effect on television."

She stopped turning the wheel and turned to face me. She didn't look impressed. "Yes, they're invaluable to hear the tumblers. Now be quiet while I do this, we've already been in here too long."

"Sorry," I whispered, and stood in silence to watch her work. Her hands moved with a surgeon's precision as she manipulated the wheel. A few minutes later the safe door swung open in slow motion as if it was moving through water. She helped it along and pushed the metal slab back on its huge hinges.

The contents took my breath away. The top half must have doubled as a filing cabinet with tidy piles of manila folders on each side and a small metal box in the middle. Nothing too important up top, but underneath were stacks of money blocks. Row after row of presidents stared back at us through shrink wrap as if they knew we shouldn't be there. There was enough cash there to buy a small island, or at least I thought so. Sabrina ignored it and went straight for the box.

As a kid, my sister had one of those boxes where you opened the lid and a plastic ballerina pirouetted to chiming music. This box looked just like it. Sabrina placed it on the floor and pulled a key from her back pocket. "Found this taped to the underside of the desk drawer," she said, waving it at me. "If it's hidden, it's important, right? Let's see what's in here."

The key fit the lock, and at a half turn, the lid popped open. There was no ballerina. After a quick glance inside, she snapped it shut. "Okay, I found it. Grab the files off the top shelf and let's get out of here. The clock's ticking. I can check this in the car."

I slid the folders onto my arms. They weighed more than I expected and I had to fight with them for a moment to stop them sliding onto the floor. I should get back upstairs to that gym. "What are we going to do with all of this cash?" I said.

"We're going to do nothing. It doesn't belong to us."

I looked at her as if she had two heads. "But…"

"But nothing. I told you, I'm not that kind of thief. I have a strict code I adhere to, and I do what I'm hired to do and nothing more. That's why they pay me what they pay me. We came for the flash drive. We have it. Let's go."

She'd left the room before I got up from the floor. I love a woman in charge.

CHAPTER ELEVEN

The two SUVs buzzed along Interstate 64 like a pair of carpenter bees; jet black, single minded and relentless. The drivers stuck to the speed limits in the town center, but once they reached the outskirts, they put their collective feet down and moved at a faster rate. They remained alert, however. The tin FBI badges they wore might fool the unsuspecting public with some aggressive acting. The average person never saw a real federal I.D. other than on television, but the average law enforcement officer could tell the difference. They didn't need the added complication of being pulled over by an overzealous cop.

Using his cover, Lennon interviewed the girl behind the main desk. They'd missed Howard and the woman at the hotel by half an hour, but a busboy had spotted the two of them sneaking out into the parking lot through a rear entrance. They were still together.

He took his eyes off the road long enough to glance at the laptop screen. Miles still separated them from their quarry but the gap was closing. The inside of the SUV sounded like a critical care unit with the signal from Howard's cell phone pinging with the rhythm of a heart monitor.

"Dammit Weston, can you turn that down?" he said. His patience had finally snapped as they left Kentucky and narrowly avoided being side swiped by a local driver making a turn with no signal. The FBI did not drive around in SUVs with huge dings and scratches down the side of them and it would have weakened their cover. Good evasive driving ensured the vehicle remained pristine.

His team was considered a 'second tier' team, a unit designed to mop up loose ends. No one in the team had any family. No wives or lovers. No ties to any particular state. They existed on the understanding they didn't just have a job; they were the job. Every one of them was a top-notch marksman. And they were all expendable.

The Consortium knew that only one threat remained that could jeopardize the plan, and even then, the threat was considered small. That being said, too much could be lost to take any chances, however small. With all other resources 'otherwise engaged' as zero hour fast approached, Lennon's team was tasked to take out the thief. It would have been much easier if they had known her identity or even what she looked like. They'd overheard the only concrete information they'd obtained on intercepted chatter. It was a request from the splinter group to acquire the flash drive at a conference in Chicago. After crashing that party, they just missed her and, now in Kentucky, the same thing had happened again.

Lennon knew that she was smart, but no one was infallible. Everyone made mistakes eventually. Everyone.

"Shit!"

I'd driven us back toward town and parked in a small clearing so that Sabrina could check the contents of the drive before we made our next move. She slapped the laptop lid closed, climbed out of the car and slammed the door. The vehicle rocked with the force. Once it settled, I walked around to her.

"What's wrong?" I asked.

"That's not it," she said.

"The drive? What, it's not the right one?"

"No. This must mean something. Otherwise, it wouldn't be locked in a safe. To me it looks like a photo album of her and a boyfriend."

"I don't remember any pictures of a boyfriend at her place," I said, "just the usual family shot and a random ceremony. No significant others on display. You're sure it's a boyfriend?"

"I'm not sure. We need to go through those files and see if we can find anything in them. We have to find her."

I got the files from the car and spread them across the hood. Over the wooded area we'd just vacated, a hawk swooped into hunting position and hovered. Could that mean things were moving by the house?

The folders were labeled with every cool name in the book: Vector, Equinox, Ghost Swimmer. Each of them contained detailed blueprints of complicated looking machines. One looked like a plane, one like a shark, all of them too complex for me. A file marked DARPA contained a layout of a facility that might have been a research building or laboratory. It was the thickest file of them all.

Sabrina waved a page in the air. "Here, I found something, an address for SonicAmerica. It's in Virginia. She must commute from home to Virginia and have another house that she uses during the week. Are you up for a road trip?" She looked up and then over my shoulder and pointed into the sky. "You see that?"

I followed her finger. The hawk was still hovering over the area near Monica's house. "Yeah, that was there when we parked the car - looks like a hawk."

"In the same spot?" said Sabrina. "Hawks don't hover like that for too long, they move around to hunt. That's not a hawk, that's a drone. They're onto us."

As we watched, the shape shifted, moving above the trees and tracked forward in our direction. It was still a distance away and, to me, still looked like a black dot in the sky.

As if someone flicked a switch, Sabrina went into professional mode and gathered up the files. She seemed to weigh up her options and then climbed into the rear seat. As she fastened her seatbelt, I fired up the engine and pulled the car forward.

"Where to?"

"Just drive," she said. "I need to think. Go!"

She didn't need to tell me twice. The tires screamed like a scalded cat and sprayed gravel up the side of a parked car. I'm sure I gave someone a dozen stone chips.

"Is there an airport near here?" she asked.

My turn to think. "Yes, about ten miles away, but it's back the way we came. You know we'll have to drive under that drone."

"Do it, as fast as you can. Head for the long term parking garage."

I looked over at her and she gave me that 'trust me' look that beautiful women do so well. The car spun around in the road as I yanked on the parking brake, wrenched the wheel around and floored the accelerator. We lurched forward again. The black shape dipped and scythed through the air and a glint of light flashed off its underbelly as we roared beneath it. Sunlight off glass. She was right, they were following us. And watching us.

Every time I turned a corner she craned her head in the rear window and followed the drone as it followed us. I don't know how she stayed in the seat. From time to time, I caught a fleeting glimpse of it through the open side windows. It had a huge advantage over my driving; I had to make every turn whereas it just flew over them. This was the first time I'd been followed and my hands were sweating like a con man in a line up.

Before long, the airport's control tower and its radars waved to me in the distance. "So the plan is to lose them in the parking garage?"

"I hope it's better than that," she replied. "Airports don't like to share their airspace. A lot of drones have programming called a GPS geofence built into their firmware. If they fly too close, the program forces them to land themselves a distance away from it. I'm hoping this has one of those. And anyway, we need a new car. They've tagged yours. Keep driving and I'll direct you."

"For the second time this week," I said with a smile. She laughed and shook her head. "How do you know all of this stuff?" I asked. "Did you go to spy school or something?"

"I have a mentor of sorts," she said, "but I read about the drones when I was researching Monica."

I was glad she could laugh, because I was getting scared. I've never even gotten a parking ticket and now I might be fixed in the Feds' glassy gaze. My skin crawled and, with every heartbeat, blood rushed like a loud whisper through my ears while the drone above us didn't make a sound. Ahead of us, the road dipped as a bridge spanned the road. I braked beneath it and hid for a moment before poking the nose of the car forward. The drone was above us, hovering silent and ominous, waiting for us to move. Tires squealed as I floored the accelerator again and raced for the airport entrance. In my peripheral vision it flitted after us. As we grew closer, I had to slow down and merge with traffic. My panic grew. I half expected the thing to land on the roof, but moments before we entered the garage, Sabrina shouted "Yes!" and clapped me on the shoulder.

"Thank God," she said, "it's descending. Pull over so I can see where it lands."

"What?" My head spun so quickly I'm surprised I didn't get whiplash. "I drive like a maniac to outrun the thing and now you want to watch it? I feel like the jury just cleared us and you want a retrial!"

She laughed again and let out a whoop of victory. "Paul, can you imagine what information might be on it? Or how useful it could be? You look around and find us a new car. I'm commandeering it."

Kyle Beck squeezed the hard foam headrest of the empty chair in front of him like a tension ball, his tanned forearms rippling with the effort.

When the drone had begun its smooth descent, the operator had excused himself from the room. He was sure he'd live to see another day, but this wasn't the first time he'd seen Beck's temper. The man's face changed like a mood ring on a bad day, alternating in shades of red and purple. He also knew he'd feel the full force of it.

As the drone made its steady descent to the ground, the final things they'd seen were the control tower of the Tri-State Airport in the distance, then the exterior fencing of the airport itself and, finally, lush green grass. Once landed, the drone's power shut off and the screen went black.

The operator reentered the room through a small side door and walked back to his desk. Beck continued to massage the back of the chair as the younger man eased himself back into it. The tension in the room crackled as Beck spoke, his voice simmering as his trained anger reigned itself in.

"What happened?"

The operator took a deep breath, aware of his exposed back. "Sir, you wanted a small drone that could do close up work if needed. It was just a modified Phantom, sir. It has a built in program that they must have known about, a failsafe that causes it to land itself if it flies into restricted airspace. I had no idea they'd know about that."

"No fucking kidding," said Beck, each word spat out like a bullet. He walked forward and addressed the room. "Where are Bell and Molito?"

A brief barrage of keyboard taps came from the far desk. "About thirty minutes away, Sir."

"Can you pinpoint where that drone landed?"

"Yes, sir."

"Text them the co-ordinates and get them to pick it up and then track the woman again. Do we have better units we can use, something that won't decide to fucking land itself? This is getting to be embarrassing."

"Yes Sir," said the operative. "It won't be as discreet, but it has no overrides and is much more stable."

Through the glass partition to his office, Beck saw the light on his secure phone flash.

"Find them and launch it. Don't mess up again."

He walked back to his office, the chatter of key presses fading to silence as he pulled the door closed.

"Yes?" he said into the mouthpiece.

"How are we progressing?"

No introduction, no formalities. The Middle Eastern accent was unmistakable, and Beck's heart rate increased.

"We're moving forward. The target was located and we'll have the drive within the day. Everything is as we agreed."

"Good. My source tells me that the launch date was set. You've got three days to neutralize the threat. After that, our countries will be at war, and we will spend our money elsewhere."

Beck bristled at the threat. "I told you, we have everything under control."

"You'd better. You will be held accountable."

The line went dead. Beck sat back in his chair, took a deep breath, and used the back of his hand to wipe away a bead of sweat.

CHAPTER TWELVE

I t's amazing how many people don't lock their cars in long term parking, as if they expect them to be stolen, and would rather avoid damage to the locks. It might be days before they even realize they're missing.

Sabrina told me what to look for and how to get it started. I found a suitable model on the second level. I waved someone's parking permit in front of the barrier and drove the Lexus under the saluting arm out into daylight. By the time I reached the end of the exit ramp, she was walking up the grass verge with the drone under her arm. I pulled over to the side of the road, popped the trunk, and joined her.

The drone wasn't what I expected. Parents could fly this one with their kids in the park. The only difference was the technology strapped to its undercarriage. I'd never seen a camera like this. The shiny glass lens was mounted on a swivel mechanism. It looked as if it could double back and check out its stomach, and the aperture had more eyes than a spider. The whole thing was colored stealth gray. Had it not been silhouetted against the bright sky at that moment, we could have been followed for days without noticing it.

"I expected something classier, like a miniature plane with little rockets on the wings or something," I said, and pointed at Sabrina's electronic hostage. "I'm sure you can get one of those from Toys R Us."

She turned the machine over in her hands. "Depends on what you want to achieve. If you flew a miniature plane with rockets on the wings through the park, you'd freak a few people out. In fact, you can bet that someone somewhere would take pot shots at it. If you flew one of these through the park, most people would probably just wave and smile for the camera. It's very discreet., And, I doubt you'd get this at Toys R Us. That camera's worth more than your car."

"You reckon it's the Feds again?"

"I'm not sure, but I wouldn't be surprised. They've been my shadow for a while."

She laid the drone flat in the trunk, rummaged in her bag of tricks, and resurfaced with a small tool kit.

"Is there anything you don't have in that bag?" I asked. "You know, like a helicopter or a Humvee?"

"I don't have any wine," she said with a pout and a slight smirk.

"We can sort that out easily enough. To be honest, after today I wouldn't mind a bottle or two myself. We should think about finding somewhere to spend the night too. We won't reach SonicAmerica before nightfall. I'm going to assume that, even if Monica Bridges doesn't work regular office hours, she'll be much easier to find during the day."

She propped the drone up on her bag and removed a small panel on its side. "Do you have any cash? They'll be tracking the credit cards I've been using by now and I'm sure they'll be watching yours as well. I've got my cards but I don't want to use them unless I have to. They have no idea who I am and I like that anonymity."

I rummaged through my wallet. "Enough for one night," I said, "but probably only for one room."

"That's fine."

"With one bed."

"It's not like I don't know what you've got, Paul." Her eyes didn't flinch from her work, but those sexy crow's feet appeared again. "We can share a bed, but no touching, okay?"

"Sure," I said. I hate to admit to being disappointed. My self-control didn't need that kind of test either.

"Don't think I'm weird," she said, "but we shouldn't get involved. One night is fun; two nights is the start of something. I don't want to start something. That's not a good thing in my profession. What I do is dangerous. And, people get hurt."

"Hey, I understand.. And, for the record, I already think you're weird." This whole conversation was weird so I changed the subject. "So, what's behind the panel?"

"I'm hoping there's a power pack of some sort. I need to disable this thing until I can get help to reprogram the software. It will have its GPS, which means they can track it. I'd like to get a decent night's sleep before they start chasing us again.. And, it would be really nice if it had a hard drive I could take a look at. If it was recording images we may be able to see where it was launched. And, who launched it."

Six tiny screws later and surgery was complete. The small panel lay to one side and a spaghetti jumble of wiring faced us. The drone looked nowhere near as sinister lying there with its stomach contents exposed. Sabrina pried the wires apart and pulled out a small metal pack that looked like a hard drive to me.

"Well, there's no hard drive," she said, "just a battery pack, so the transmission went right to whoever sent it. Not now, though."

"Did you say you could reprogram this so you can control it?"

"No, but I know a man who can talk me through how to do it," she said. "Come on, I'm starving. Let's get something to eat and then find somewhere to spend the night."

Speed Dial One.

No name. No designation. Just Speed Dial One. That was Cal Lennon's name for his superior, the man who called to give directions and check on progress. They'd never met so Lennon had no idea what the man looked like. When his cell phone screen flashed 'SD1', he wasn't even sure if that was his real voice on the phone.

What he did know was that SD1 on his phone probably appeared as Speed Dial Five on someone else's. The Consortium was comprised of elected officials, of prominent politicians, and of the country's movers and shakers. The people behind the scenes that made things happen, the one percent that controlled economies. Layers existed between Lennon's superior and the people in control to protect them and ensure a compartmentalization. The only thing Lennon got from them was his orders.

He accepted that he was nothing more than a blunt instrument, a tool for higher powers to use to clean up messes and carry out the dirty work. They never got their hands dirty. For what they paid him, he had no problem with that. Ignorance was bliss and, whatever the Consortium had planned, he was blissfully ignorant. And very well paid.

The sun grew tired and sank behind the horizon behind them when the flashing icon on the laptop screen blinked out. As that light died, the light on Lennon's phone flashed. He pointed to the screen with a frown, indicating to his colleague to investigate the signal loss, as he answered the call.

"Yes, sir?"

"How is the target?"

As always, the voice sounded natural. Lennon always listened to see if he could pick up any inflections or accent that might give him a clue who he reported to. He heard nothing but a neutral, monotone American accent.

"We are en route to intercept, Sir. Expect completion by sunrise." He looked again at the screen and hoped his voice had remained steady and had not betrayed his concern. There was still no signal, despite Weston's frantic efforts.

"Good. You need to ensure the job is done by Monday. Don't disappoint me. Kill the woman and destroy the drive."

"What? Why the sudden rush? We had a while to get this done quietly?"

There was no waiting for confirmation or a goodbye, just silence. The call disconnected.

Lennon placed his phone in the cup holder next to the tissue wrapped phone and looked at his colleague.

"Well? Any luck? What happened?"

Weston shrugged his shoulders. "No idea. Either he switched off the phone or he's somewhere dense enough to block the signal."

"Where was the last location before the signal died?"

Weston punched coordinates into the SUVs dashboard GPS and pointed to the image. "They entered West Virginia here, headed toward this town."

Lennon ran a hand over his close-cropped hair. "Okay. I'll get us as close as I can to where they vanished. Pray that the signal comes back or we spot them on the road. They want the job done by Monday."

Weston stared, wide eyed. "I thought we were under no time restraints?"

"So did I," nodded Lennon. "That must have changed. You're aware of what happens if we fail, right?"

"Yeah," said Weston, "and I'm too young to die."

"Me, too. I'd like to see what's on that drive that's so important. You're still monitoring his family?"

"Yep." Weston opened another window on the laptop. "I made a comprehensive list of all of his known relatives as soon as we had his driver's license details. He doesn't talk to them much. No communication so far. I'll keep an eye on all the usual channels. Something will crop up. It always does."

"It had better," said Lennon. "I get the feeling this job is much bigger than we think."

CHAPTER THIRTEEN

I forced my eyes open and focused on curtains I didn't recognize; from a bed I didn't know. The glow through the fabric looked as if a huge grass fire burned in the distance as the rising sun peered out over the black line of the horizon. My back popped and cracked in all the wrong places as I levered myself upright. I could hear Sabrina moving around in the bathroom. The motel's hairdryer sounded like a plane coming in on a final approach and one of its engines had died.

The room had one of those two cup coffee machines that spurted radioactive sludge into a chipped mug. Our empty wine bottle from last night sat beside it. I poured the dry grounds into the strainer, topped off the water, and picked up my phone to check the time. With everything that had happened, I hadn't even glanced at it for hours. The battery was drained. I plugged the charger cable into an outlet and after a few seconds the blank screen lit up and the time appeared.

Sleep was elusive last night. There's nothing quite like having government agencies chasing you with advanced technology to make you paranoid. The thing is, I had this nagging feeling in my gut that said I was only involved in this mess because I was with Sabrina. What if they were only after her and she was dragging me around like a portable Kevlar vest?

My dusty shoes lay by the side of the door where I'd toed them off last night. She was still in the bathroom making all kinds of noise. It would be easy to slip out of the room and get a bus back home. No harm, no foul. Except the stolen car I drove yesterday had what we thought was a dismantled government drone in the trunk. That was probably a slight foul. Definitely some harm. Then I remembered the minor breaking and entering I'd committed. She'd mentioned shooting too. Had I not met Agent Lennon, I would have dismissed this as a wild story and moved on. He seemed pretty desperate to get her, though, and she seemed desperate to avoid him. There was no faking there.

My daughter's voice banged around inside my head, her irrational argument that I should trust a little easier conflicting with my well earned and rational distrust of women, especially women that drugged me. Somehow, though, bit by bit, Kacie's voice seemed to be winning, and at least for the time being, I curtailed my natural instinct to run in the opposite direction.

The bathroom door screeched across its dry hinges as Sabrina sashayed into the room and my mind was made up for me. She appeared wearing a black dress suit with heels like one of those sexy headmistresses they show on late night TV. All she needed to complete the outfit were the wide framed glasses and a wooden ruler. Her hair rappelled down her shoulders in ringlets and her face looked exactly like it did when we first met. Damn, she was gorgeous. My mouth obviously fell open because she pointed at it.

"What?" she said.

I shrugged my shoulders and closed my mouth. I had no words.

"If we're going to visit Monica Bridges at work, we have to look like we belong there," she said. "Come on, shower and tidy up. I pressed your clothes while you slept. You just need to shave and clean your shoes. We're going to pretend to sell something to Monica."

Like I said, all she needed were the glasses and a ruler.

I felt guilty about the Lexus we'd borrowed. Years ago, as a young boy, I stole a pack of baseball cards from the small grocery store down the road from our house. I smuggled them out in my jacket pocket and hadn't dared look at them until I got home and into the safety of my bedroom. That night I didn't sleep, paranoid I'd be caught but, instead of returning them, I buried them in our garden and hoped that no one saw me. The Lexus was too big to bury. I determined to treat it with respect and hope its owner retrieved it in one piece once we reached safety. That was the only thing that forced me to climb back into it.

The Lexus had one of those top of the range GPS systems built into the dash. It also had cameras, parking assists and a music system Jay-Z would be proud of. It would probably pick up the Playboy channel after midnight too. Sabrina's nimble fingers entered SonicAmerica's address into the GPS and MapBitch told us it would be a five-hour road trip.

Sabrina let me drive. We moved non-stop at a steady rate, other than stopping at a McDonald's for a cheap breakfast. Halfway through the trip we reached the Monongahela National Forest. I'd never seen scenery as stunning as this before, especially when we came upon the Appalachian mountain range. Its jumble of colors, a mishmash of reds, browns, greens and steely grays, topped off in places with an icy cap, cut a swath through the green carpet that it ran through. Despite all the natural beauty on display, relaxation eluded me. The nagging suspicion that we were still being watched kept picking at me. As Kurt Cobain sang, "Just because you're paranoid don't mean they're not after you." In our case, it seemed they were. Every time the road straightened out I craned my neck under the windshield and checked out the skies.

My stomach lurched at one point when a black dot flitted over the trees to our right, but Sabrina assured me it was just an eagle. I pointed out to her that, since we stole the first drone, whoever was trailing us would be a little more cautious if they sent another.

We'd driven quite a distance with little conversation. She still seemed tense, but as we spent more time together, she seemed to relax a little and was looking past me at the landscape when her eyes turned to focus on me.

"So, what's your story, Paul Howard? I could tell a mile away you were single. Does the job scare the ladies away, or are you a player?"

I did one of those exaggerated laughs people do when they want to mask discomfort, but she saw right through it.

"Yeah, yeah, whatever," she said. "You're no shy boy. I can read people."

"Well," I said, "you want my whole story in one minute? I married young to my high school sweetheart. Got pregnant way too soon. Her, not me. We raised a beautiful daughter named Kacie. I got this decent job, which sent me on the road a lot. Then I got home one night and found my best friend with my wife. We went through a messy divorce, which wiped out most of my hard earned cash. I've had a huge distrust of women and best friends ever since. There've been a couple of short-term relationships, but then I'm back on the road. It seems I can either have enough money to be comfortable, or love. Not both."

"Wow. Check out Mr. Cynical."

"I'm working on it," I said, "but it does seem to be taking a while." I changed the subject. "So, what exactly are we going to sell to Monica?"

"It doesn't matter what we're selling," she replied. "The sales angle is just a means to an end, a way to gain access. Once we're in the door, I'm sure she'll want to hear what I have to say. I can be quite persuasive."

"Oh, I know that," I said.

She laughed. It was one of those infectious laughs they build into children's toys. "I don't remember there being much persuasion required, mister. If I'm honest, I do feel a little guilty now, though. I'm sorry I got you into this. And for the record, don't be so hard on yourself."

"Hey, saying 'no' was always an option," I said. "And thanks."

"It was never an option. Not a chance."

As my laughter subsided, my paranoia was rewarded. I made a tight turn around a sharp corner and, as the road straightened out, I glanced in the rear view mirror and the smallest of movements caught my eye. At first, I thought it was an insect in the back window but it didn't buzz and fly around. It was distant, but constant.

My stomach churned. We had company. Another drone. They were back.

CHAPTER FOURTEEN

B eck pushed open the small side door of the control room and stepped out into a large tube. That's what the walkways in this place felt like to him. The round concrete corridors were like something out of a Star Trek movie. They ran in a circle around the perimeter of the complex, with other corridors on one side that branched off toward the center like the spokes of a wheel. The constant hum of generators was background noise to him now. Having spent a lot of time in here, the filtered air that pumped through the metal vents no longer felt artificial, but blew like a morning breeze that cooled the sweat on his face. Down lighters sunk into the top of the curve cast circles like spotlights onto the mesh floor beneath his feet to compensate for the lack of natural light.

There was no sound as he walked along the corridor, rapping his knuckles against the dense curved wall, each contact a dull thud. At the first corner he turned and moved toward the center of the complex. The corridor ahead ended thirty feet away in a stout steel door with no window or handle, just a panel to one side at chest height. Beck walked up to the door, took the plastic card that hung around his neck on a lanyard, and swiped it against the panel. The heavy door slid open with a whisper to reveal a dazzling circular room.

The whole space flashed and blinked with light. The circular wall was a roundabout of monitors, each showing a detailed map, with cities and roadways etched into the glass screens with more light. Saudi Arabia. Iraq. Afghanistan. Israel. Egypt. He knew them well. He'd eaten and slept in each one, killed in each one. Straight ahead of him was a screen with an exaggerated digital clock display that glowed with red numbers. It counted down in silence. Right now, it said 38:58:48. Less than two days until either the end of the world as it was now or untold riches.

For the first time, the slightest pang of guilt surfaced in him. None of the surrounding team had any idea about the existence of the flash drive, or of his agenda. Part of him hoped that the drive disappeared and the launch would go ahead. The whole Middle Eastern region would be decimated and plunged into war with numerous countries. Beck had said over and over that the people there would never advance into the twenty first century and that the best thing for the entire place would be to bomb it into a sheet of glass. They could build a huge tourist attraction on it. If they recovered the drive, however, he would sell it to the rich Saudi princes for more money than he'd ever spend. Then maybe he'd wage his private war.

This room was one of four that made up the large central hub of the facility. The other three rooms were of no interest to Beck. He had no use for laboratories or research stations. The room he stood in was the only one that mattered and the only man that interested him was the one posted here.

Dave Jones was a friend from the front who had partnered Beck on many missions. He was efficient, capable, and completely trustworthy. He was also a fool who followed every order to the letter. He had one job. To make sure no one touched anything in this room and that the countdown continued. The two workstations in here, positioned under the counting clock, could end the world. Jones had no idea.

Beck nodded to him. "Everything okay?"

"Yes, Sir, it's all good," said Jones.

"As you were then, soldier," said Beck. He smiled and offered a mock salute. "Payday is fast approaching."

Jones grinned, returned the salute, and turned his chair back to watch the screens.

Two days. In two days, he would have more money than some kings as long as he got that drive. With the drive he could avert the launch, get millions of dollars from the raghead fuckers, and buy himself a nice island to retire to. If not, the original plan would go ahead anyway. Oversee the launch, start the war, sit back and bank the money anyway. Not as much, but still. It was a win-win situation, but the first win outweighed the second by a huge fortune. Hate them as much as you like, but the turban-wearing bastards had money to burn.

Muscles cracked as Beck flexed his neck from side to side. A headache was forming at the back of his head, but he knew techniques to alleviate the pressure. Bell had called back to say that the drone had vanished, despite checking exactly where it had landed. Someone, he assumed the woman, had taken it.

The next drone was launched from a secure location on the east coast of Virginia and took just over two hours to get into position. The operator heaved a sigh of relief as the camera cleared a tall outcrop and the sedan appeared, exactly where the tracker said it would be. Beck re-entered the room just as he relaxed and took up position behind him.

"That's them?" said Beck.

"Yes, sir. We're back on track."

"Good. Forward the GPS details to Bell and Molito and keep their phones up to date. Let's end this once and for all."

I went into full panic mode.

"How the hell do they keep finding us?" My voice was so high pitched I half expected a pack of dogs to come bounding around the next corner. Sabrina looked as if she was about to slap the crap out of me.

"No idea," she said. "Calm down and think. I remember there was a single camera on a pole back at the motel parking lot, but I saw nothing else that could have given us away." She turned in her seat to face me. "You reckon Lennon planted something on you?"

"No. No way. I went nowhere near him or his goons and my stuff was in my room, not yours, so they couldn't tag that either. This is starting to piss me off."

"It's only just starting to piss you off? One octave higher and you'll crack the glass. Keep driving as you were and we'll wait for an opportunity to try to lose them again."

I gestured through the window. "Sabrina, we're in the middle of a National Forest in a stolen car and the Feds seem to have a damned satellite trained on us. How are we going to lose them?"

"Listen to you, O ye of little faith. Opportunities always present themselves. You just need to be looking for them."

Ten minutes later, an opportunity presented itself as we drove onward into the heart of the forest. The canopy above us thickened until only tiny stabs of light cut their way through to mirror ball the road ahead. A small brown sign at the side of the road directed us right to a Ranger's office or left to a rest area. Nothing more than a small parking lot, the rest area sat in the shadow of the canopy. A handful of vehicles dotted around the lot, their owners either walking dogs or walking themselves through the forest.

I parked next to a decent looking truck, a blue Ford F150 with a covered bed and tinted windows. The wheels were sparkling chrome and it had a bumper sticker that said 'Don't follow me just because you're jealous' on the tailgate.

"Looks good to me," I said.

Sabrina looked it up and down like a potential date. "Don't you think it stands out a little?"

"Hide in plain sight, right? Isn't that what they say? They won't expect us to be driving something like this. It might as well have flashing lights and bells on it. We should hang around here for a while and let them search for us. In fact, before we go any further I need to check in with work before I lose my job." I pulled my phone from my pocket. A small cross-hovered at the top of the screen. The thick canopy killed any signal I had.

"It's a good thing," said Sabrina, "you know they'll be monitoring your phone too. Maybe that's how they keep finding us. Take out the battery and kill the power."

I did as she said, placing different parts of my phone in different pockets for good measure. "What about yours?"

"A friend hacked my phone and took out the GPS. It's literally just a phone with a camera."

I nodded toward the truck. "Want to try it?"

"It's as good as anything else here."

"Okay," I said, "you get it open and I'll get our things together."

A few minutes later we exited the canopy and drove back into sunlight, the truck's engine making light work of the rise and fall of the mountainous road. I still didn't feel good about taking someone else's property, but until this was resolved I'd probably have to do a few things I didn't like.

If our spy was out there looking for us, I didn't see it.

Not for the first time, Monica Bridges wished that she'd pushed harder in her argument to get a sofa for the downstairs room. Kyle said that bars didn't have sofas in them. He should know, he said, England existed around a bar culture which consisted of high stools positioned around a bar top. To make socializing easier.

It didn't make sleeping easier. Her back twinged as she tried to straighten it, and her bones ached with a constant throb from spending nights asleep, curled up on the carpeted floor. Thank God she'd won that argument, otherwise she'd have been sleeping on ceramic tile. Pain shot up her arm as she tried to lift herself, a reminder of the cuts around her wrists, her reward for cutting through the zip ties.

It took her a moment to work out what had woken her. Her imprisonment was like solitary confinement, with no noise or contact with anyone. The stories of confinement seemed to be true. Deprived senses were affected. She could smell and taste the fruit and cheese she'd eaten, see their color and feel the change in temperature when she'd taken the tray from the fridge. Her ears had heard nothing for days, not since he'd locked her down here, but now there was a muffled ringing.

The phone upstairs.

She summoned energy from somewhere and ran as fast as she could up the stairs, taking them two at a time. Her heart thudded in her chest and her breath came in gasps as her aching body protested. How long had it been ringing? Was there someone at the front door trying to get her attention? Help was finally here.

She hammered her hands against the door, the shock of the impact jolting her shoulders, and she cried in pain as the pressure opened the cuts around her wrists. Small specks of blood spattered against the white painted door and smeared as she continued the barrage.

Then the ringing stopped.

In the silence, she beat at the door even harder and screamed until her sensitive ears vibrated. Her desperation ran in tears down her face. She continued her efforts until her strength drained and all the energy left her muscles and she sank, exhausted and sobbing, to the stairs. If anyone was out there, they hadn't heard her.

Her stomach took a leap and a sudden sense of fear startled her. Maybe it wasn't help. Maybe he'd come back to finish the job. She fought her fear, ran back to the bar, grabbed the corkscrew and stood at the bottom of the stairs with the weapon threaded through her fingers. Every muscle was tensed and she heard her breath rasping through her teeth. A mist of spittle sprayed over her chin, but she ignored it. She held her breath and listened. Nothing. No sound. No footsteps coming through the ceiling above her. No bolt being shifted on the door.

She wiped her chin, turned a stool to face the stairs, and sat. She placed the corkscrew on the bar in front of her. Then she cried.

Lennon sat bolt upright as a loud knock woke him. He swung his legs out of bed, stepped into his pants, and looked through the door's peephole. Weston saw his shadow and shouted through the door.

"We got another signal. They're on the move. The other guys are already in their vehicle and we're ready to go."

"Give me a few minutes," said Lennon. "I'll be right with you."

Ten minutes later they were winding through the scenery and had passed the sign announcing their arrival at Monongahela National Forest.

"We're about ten miles behind them," said Weston.

Lennon looked in the rear view mirror to make sure the other vehicle was keeping up with him. Its tinted windows reflected sunlight back to him as acknowledgment. He ran through his mental checklist, the one he relied on when he knew he was about to take a life. His unregistered pistol was behind him in a hidden pouch beneath the rear seats. The setting ahead was perfect; a dense forest with many concealed areas. The chance of witnesses was slim and there were many hiding places for the bodies. Everything was coming together. He pressed harder on the accelerator and the SUV lurched forward.

CHAPTER FIFTEEN

The operator continued to keep the sedan in the center of the screen. Beck perched behind him again like a pit boss and admired the way the vehicle hugged the turns and moved smoothly onwards.

"Zoom out, would you? I want to see the road ahead. We can't afford to lose that car again and we don't know how long we can rely on the tracker alone. Bell and Molito need to get closer, but not too close. We don't want to be seen."

With a quick nudge of the joystick, the landscape blurred away from them and then reformed. The natural beauty of the National Forest was obvious, even from thousands of feet in the air. Lush green was broken up with dashes of color, and roadways snaked through it like veins.

"Get the team closer before they vanish under that canopy," said Beck, pointing to the screen. "I'm sure there are plenty of different routes to take once you get under there. Pull up a road map of the forest just in case." His eyes flitted over the landscape and paused as he spotted two black dots trailing the car. "Wait a minute, what have we here? Zoom in on those marks back there."

Another nudge of the joystick.

He laughed as the two SUVs appeared on screen. "They're so fucking obvious aren't they? Look everyone, the Feds are on the scene. You'd think they'd have moved on from tinted black by now wouldn't you? All right, we can't afford to have any gatecrashers to the party." He paced across to the back of the room and pushed a button on a hands free unit sitting on a rear desk. "Molito?"

The reply was instantaneous. "Yes, Sir?"

"Where are you?"

"Just entering the National Forest. Making good time."

"Good. You have company."

"We do?" said Molito. Beck detected a hint of pleasant anticipation in the words. "In front or behind?"

"Two SUVs, about three miles behind you. Looks like Feds. How much do you want to bet they're after the same thing we are?"

"I wouldn't take that bet," said Molito. "I doubt I'd like the odds. I'm guessing that offing a few Feds won't ruffle too many feathers?"

"None whatsoever," said Beck. "They're just gnats in a swarm. Go ahead and do what you do best."

They contemplated setting up a kill zone just past a bend in the road, using a rifle aimed down from a rising embankment. Bell pointed out the issues of trying to take out two vehicles with one rifle with no distraction. As a rule, FBI teams hunted in packs of two. The chances of taking out four men in two moving vehicles with rifle-fire were small, so they came up with another plan.

Blaine Bell had carried out the 'hood up' plan before, when he and a Seal team had taken out a small Afghan convoy. His team of five had wiped out the four-vehicle convoy on a dusty road in Kabul with no friendly casualties.

He steered the car toward the center of the road as his heartbeat raced. The moments before an expected confrontation always energized him, his mind and muscles more alive than ever as if low voltage electricity flowed through his body. The land at the side of the road rose to about twelve feet, then leveled off and sloped back into the forest. Molito scrambled up the bank as Bell parked the vehicle across the two lanes, enough to stop traffic but not enough to seem obvious. He lifted the hood so that the SUV appeared helpless. Whether the arriving driver wanted to help or not was irrelevant, the road was blocked anyway.

Molito signaled from the top of the rise. "Just the two vehicles. Nothing else coming in either direction."

Bell gave the thumbs up as his colleague lay flat and disappeared from view. Seconds later, the barrel of the sniper rifle poked over the ridge. Bell leaned under the raised hood and rested his pistol, a 45 Sig P220, on the air filter.

A few minutes later, the bass rumble of tires approached the corner. Bell ran the back of his hands over the oil filter to make them look worked on and then waited. The SUVs rounded the last bend and slowed to a stop. Doors opened and closed. He counted two slams. One vehicle still held its occupants. Typical FBI protocol and exactly what they had expected. One team stayed back to monitor proceedings while the other investigated. One for him, one for Molito. Once he heard footsteps, he leaned out from behind the hood.

"Hi guys. I hope at least one of you is a mechanic."

Two guys in standard issue suits walked toward him with their hands close to their sides. They were armed. He also noted that the lead vehicle was the one investigating, which was unusual. The rear vehicle normally made the move so that the vehicle in front had a clear line of sight should anything go awry. Feds didn't break protocol often. Something wasn't right. As they got closer, the two men separated, one moving toward either side of the car. The guy on the left opened his mouth to ask a question, which was the signal Molito would be waiting for.

Two shots sounded, one quickly after the other. Red tinted glass crystals sprayed from the rear SUV as Molito's rounds found their targets. The two men approaching dived toward Bell's car and out of sight.

Bell moved to the side of the vehicle as soon as Molito opened fire.

He crouched and stepped around the hood, pistol raised. Two louder cracks echoed between the vehicles and he stopped, confused that he hadn't pulled his trigger yet. A stabbing pain began in his ankles and shot up his legs and he collapsed onto the hard asphalt and noticed that both his ankles were bleeding. Once his head reached ground level, he glanced under the car. The guy on the left was lying under the dip of the spare tire, looking back at him. He fired again.

From this range, Molito could see the hairs in the guy's ear in his crosshairs, and the line where his sideburn met the smooth shaved skin of his face. He aimed at the ear and squeezed the rifle's trigger. A round left the chamber with a suppressed hiss. Without waiting to see where the first shot went, he moved the sight to his left to focus on the passenger. Again, he squeezed the trigger and then took a moment to inspect his work. The passenger was leaned against the door column with most of his head gone through the smashed side window. The driver lay motionless in his lap. He scanned further left. The two men in the road had dived in front of the car Bell was 'working' on.

Two more shots broke the silence. Molito couldn't see his partner on the other side of their car, but he knew the difference in sound between a 9mm shot and a 45. Those shots came from a 9mm. That meant Bell hadn't been able to fire his Sig. The 9mm spat out one more round with no response and, as the percussion faded into the forest, Molito knew that Bell was dead. The first guy had vanished, and the other was out of sight below the front of the car, hidden behind the engine block.

He squeezed off another round, which ricocheted harmlessly away. The guy at the front returned fire, but the bullet impacted with a dull thump in the earth below him. Another gunshot sounded and the dirt in front of him kicked up into the air and sprayed against his forehead. They were on to him.

Outnumbered and outgunned, he stayed low and shuffled himself back from the edge of the embankment and ran in a crouch to the relative safety of the forest.

It took us another two hours to reach our destination. In that time, neither of us spotted our flying friend.

The SonicAmerica building was a work of art. It wasn't so tall that it dominated the skyline, but it stood out in a row of imaginative architecture. Tall red brick walls on either side swept back like opened curtains and were illuminated by down lighters that shot dancing rainbows of color down them in random patterns. The brick sandwiched a wall of windows, each row with its glass angled in a different direction, which bounced the sunlight all over the place. I could see where Monica got the inspiration for her property. Other than the brass parts of a huge revolving door in the center, the entire front was glass.

We wrapped up the packaging from the fast food lunch that Sabrina's remaining cash had bought us. The restaurant's free Wi-Fi enabled us to do more research on SonicAmerica too. They specialized in producing equipment that used sound waves and vibration. I had no idea this technology even existed. SonicAmerica products were used in all kinds of applications, from drilling on deep-sea oil rigs to land excavation in dense forest, just like the one we'd driven through to get here. They created sonar that was used on experimental submarines in the Atlantic Ocean, and by forensic anthropologists to scan for fossilized remains in Peru. It was an impressive résumé but, as detailed as the website was, it made no mention of its employees. We still had no idea what Monica Bridges did for a living.

"Let me do the talking," said Sabrina. "This isn't the first time I've weaseled my way into someone's office. The secret is to be confident and believe that you are who you say you are. You just stand back and believe that you're my assistant."

"Don't forget what I do for a living," I said, feeling a little short changed. "I do believe that I sell things, because I really do sell things. I walk into places like this every day."

She ignored me, so I followed her across the parking lot and through the revolving door. It completed its perfect circle in silence, the huge weight of the thing balanced like a spinning top on well-oiled bearings. The interior was just as impressive. Glossed marble covered the floor in an intricate design with a subliminal pathway worked into it that led to a steel and wood desk three times the size of my bed.

Sabrina did that hair thing again where she tucked a piece of it behind her ear, and then tilted her head. I'd seen this move a few times now. It was interesting to watch her work her magic on another unsuspecting soul.

"Hello," she said. Her smile would have caused a few wrecks outside if it was reflected through that crazy glass out front. "You have a beautiful building here."

"Well, thank you so much," said the receptionist who countered with a dazzling smile of her own. She was as polished as the floor and looked like the type of girl who only drank peppermint schnapps so her breath always smelled nice. "We are very proud of our company."

And the billions of government dollars too, I thought.

She leaned toward us with confidence. "How can I help you today?"

"Hello. Yes, we have an appointment with Monica Bridges," said Sabrina.

The receptionist frowned and looked at her as if she was about to erect a wall between them. Sabrina breezed through it like a pro. "Oh, I know, we're a little early. We can take a seat if you like, but Ms. Bridges is quite anxious to see us."

"She must be more than anxious," said the receptionist. "I'm afraid you may have made a mistake..."

"Well, we did make our appointment quite a while ago."

"It must have been a long time ago," she said, and eyed us suspiciously. "She called in about a week ago. I took the call. She quit and no one's heard from her since."

CHAPTER SIXTEEN

Lennon wriggled out from under the car, struggled to his knees, and knelt next to his colleague. Weston had moved around to the side of the vehicle and was using the wheel as cover.

"You okay?" asked Lennon. He took deep breaths to calm his adrenaline as he dusted off the front of his jacket.

Weston was pale, but nodded. "Yeah. You?"

"Yeah, I'm all right. What the fuck was that?"

"I'm going to go out on a limb," said Weston, "and say that that was an ambush."

"Okay smart ass, spare me the dark humor. Why us? There's no way a couple of robbers would try to hold up two Federal looking SUVs."

Lennon looked over Weston's shoulder and slid with his back against the door panel to the ground. The red mist inside the SUV and the shattered glass and bone fragments over the road told a grim but obvious story.

"Shit. Platt and Sullivan both bought it. I managed to get one of them but we still need to see what's going on. Cover me. I'm going to run to the bottom of the embankment. If the shooter is still up there, the incline will hide me."

"Got it," said Weston. He rose above the car's hood and aimed at the ridge. "Ready? Go!"

Lennon launched himself off the door, spun, and ran across the road as Weston fired a volley of shots into the soil above them. Small rivulets of dirt ran down to meet him as he scrambled up the bank and stopped just shy of the top. He looked back to Weston, who gave him first a shrug, and then a thumbs up. Pushing off the balls of his feet, he forced himself over the ridge and landed on his stomach. He swung his gun from side to side as his trigger finger tensed, millimeters away from completing the pull.

He was alone.

The shooter must have left along a sloping grass plain that blended into a busy tree line, so he ran in a zigzag pattern up to the forest's edge and knelt behind a tree. Nothing moved ahead of him but leaves, waving in a faint breeze. There was no sound but rustling and the flutter of spooked birds returning to the safety of high branches. Whoever was up here was now long gone, vanished into Mother Nature's excellent camouflage.

Satisfied that they were alone, Lennon made his way back to the top of the embankment and picked up three shell casings scattered in a patch of flat grass. More flat grass and broken blades behind him showed the route the shooter had taken as his retreat.

Weston was leaning against the rear SUV when he returned to the roadside. "I guess you'd better call SD1 and let him know what happened here," he said. "We're two men down."

"Not yet," said Lennon, "there's more going on here than he's telling us. They change the timing of our whole mission and, all of a sudden, we drive into an ambush? That can't be a coincidence. I want to have a look around first, see what I can find. You clean up these two, make sure you leave nothing behind. If anyone shows up, give them the usual FBI crap. And watch that ridge in case our man comes back."

He made his way back to the parked car and approached the dead man lying in the road. The guy was about thirty, a solid mass of muscle, with the no nonsense hairstyle of a military man. Lennon searched his pockets but found nothing but a cell phone and the car keys. He wasn't surprised. From the guy's dress and the tactics he'd used, he knew now a kill team had hit them. There would be no I.D. and nothing in the car to identify him either. He pocketed the phone, picked up the guy's gun, and opened the car door.

Fast food wrappers filled the rear foot wells and, other than a spare handgun slid into a holster under the steering column, the car was empty. He started the engine and moved the vehicle to the side of the road, then wiped down the steering wheel, took the gun and the keys, and walked back to the SUV. Weston was already inside.

"The other car clean?" said Lennon.

"Yeah. Anything over there?" said Weston, nodding to the carnage ahead of them.

"Just this," said Lennon. He retrieved the phone and pushed the power button on its side. One swipe of the glass and a map appeared, with a small flashing dot moving away from them to the east.

"Well, well, well," he said, "what have we here?"

"Looks as if we're following someone," said Weston. "Those boys must have been pretty confidant, not password protecting their phone. What do you reckon? Leave SD1 hanging a while longer and see if that someone is who I think it is?"

"Sounds like a plan," said Lennon. He started the engine and, with one glance at the parked car, drove the vehicle forward into the forest.

———————————

The car rocked from side to side as Sabrina slammed the door. "Damn! Now what do we do?"

This was the first time I'd seen her where she didn't appear to have complete control of everything. Her face was flushed red, and she looked as if she wanted to wrestle a bear. The frustration in the air was so thick I could have chewed it.

"There's nothing else in the diary?" I said. "No other address or hint of another place?"

"Nothing. I've been through that thing a million times."

"Any other names we can call?"

"No."

"What about the flash drive?"

She shook her head. "Useless. It looks like a load of holiday snaps."

"Well it must mean something. It was locked in her safe. You went through the entire thing? Checked every picture?"

"Well," she paused, "to be honest, I skimmed through it after the first hundred pictures or so and gave up in frustration. I think you're affecting my work. It's worth checking again, I suppose. Find somewhere quiet to park the truck and I'll go through them again."

I scanned the skies but the only thing above us was the glowing afternoon sun. This feeling of being watched was becoming a regular part of my life. I hoped I'd be able to shake it once I knew for sure I wasn't going to be chased any more.

About two miles from SonicAmerica, the road wound around and down like a looped belt and ended in a disused parking lot covered by the road above it. I pulled over to one side and Sabrina booted up the laptop, plugged in the flash drive, and opened the file.

The pictures didn't seem like holiday snaps to me, more like one of those team-building exercises where bosses sent employees they didn't want to see again.

"Looks like a retreat or a hiking trip," I said, "and check out Monica. She looks older here than she does on the pictures back at her place."

Sabrina scrolled page by page through the pictures. Most of them were of Monica and a good-looking guy with the arms of an athlete and that upright military posture you noticed a mile away.

"Not a retreat," she said. "There'd be more than two people if that was the case. Maybe a vacation they took somewhere?"

"Well, we didn't see a single picture of this guy at her place, so who's he?"

"No idea. He's not hard to look at though, is he?"

I rolled my eyes. "It looks as if Monica has the street smarts to match her office smarts too. She's an outdoor type. Check these out."

A few of the pictures were of her shooting at filled water jugs with an array of weaponry; handguns, a scoped rifle, even a compound bow. There was no doubt she could take care of herself. Others showed her sitting in a plane cockpit, giving the photographer a confident smile.

As they scrolled by, the pictures of trees, paths and weapons disappeared and changed into more serious poses. There were more pictures of Monica receiving awards. She'd been very successful. The little progress bar on the side of the screen was almost at the bottom when something caught my eye.

"Stop. Scroll back up."

Sabrina clicked a button and a blur of color shot up the screen.

"Enlarge that one," I said, and pointed to a picture of Monica standing on a front lawn holding a plaque.

She clicked again and the image filled the screen. "We know she's won loads of awards, how does that help us?"

"First off, she's wearing a wedding ring, so what if Mr. Beefy is her husband? And now she's one of those power women that doesn't wear a ring. And look over the roof of the house. See that water tower in the distance?"

"Okay," she squinted. There was half a 'W' and then the letters 'ATER' painted across the side. "It just says 'water', though. So what?"

"No. I've seen that tower. It's sad but, when you drive around as much as I do, you get to recognize the most ridiculous landmarks. I assume your laptop can access Google Maps?"

"Of course, I use it all the time for reconnaissance."

"Yeah. Sure you do," I said, not even slightly surprised. "I reckon I could find that house based on the angle of the picture and the position of the house in relation to the water tower."

"How the hell will you do that? There must be hundreds of towers dotted around the country."

"Yes, but it doesn't say the word 'water' on that tower," I said. "That's only the side visible in this picture. The word is painted around the side of the entire structure, which stands outside a small town named Waterford. I've driven past there many times."

She looked at me with those hypnotic pools of brown and, for the first time, there was a hint of trust in them. "Well then, what are you waiting for? Get to work!"

I got to work.

It didn't matter if it was mile after mile of open desert, or a shit hole town in a Middle Eastern country, or a forest in the middle of America, Vince Molito was an expert at blending into his surroundings. The running joke in their old unit was that he was able to hide behind a brass pole and surprise the stripper when she swung around it.

The surprise was theirs this time.

Day after day of relentless training had ingrained in them an attitude to underestimate no one, regardless of appearance or demeanor. A woman or a kid running down the street toward you might just be a scared civilian, or they could be a suicide bomber wearing a vest lined with explosives. The small guy leaning against a bar might be a harmless sales guy enjoying an after work drink, or he might be a martial arts expert with a mean temper. You never knew.

The two guys in the lead SUV were good. Superb, even. They'd seen right through their plan. And no Federal agent ever moved with that kind of speed at the first sound of gunfire. They didn't experience enough of it in the city to develop the reflexes. The first instinct is to flinch and cower, then cover yourself. These guys were military. Trained, just like him, to drop and seek cover as soon as the shit hit the fan.

One of them, the one who appeared to be the lead, lay on the brow of the ridge and looked right at him. Molito remained motionless, unblinking, as the man scanned the surrounding terrain. His neutral clothing blended with the browns of the bush he'd chosen to hide behind. He breathed in and out through his nose, controlled and relaxed, and ensured that his fingertips maintained minimal contact with the rifle that lay in front of him.

The guy ran toward him in a zigzag pattern and stopped behind a tree, not twelve feet away. He didn't flinch. There'd been no widening of the eyes, so either he was exceptionally well trained, or he hadn't seen him and was being cautious. Molito was developing a respect for this guy. It would almost be a shame to kill him.

After a couple of minutes, the guy retreated and moved over the ridge and out of sight. Molito counted to sixty, waited for any surprise reappearance, and then snaked forward through the foliage and back to the ridge. On his stomach, he peered down to the road. One guy cleaned up the mess in the ruined SUV, the other crouched in and out of sight behind the car, presumably rifling through Bell's clothing for identification. He ducked and held his breath as the first guy glanced back up at him. No sound or movement. It was too risky to take any more shots at them, not alone. They had a rough idea where he'd fired from. If he showed himself again, they'd be on to him and it would be all over in seconds.

It took the two men a few minutes to check the scene. They moved the car off the road and climbed into an SUV and sat there for a while. Molito saw nothing through the tinted windows, but that didn't mean they couldn't see out. After a while, the vehicle drove away.

He slid down the embankment and approached his old friend's body. A perfect hole sat in the middle of Bell's forehead like an obscene tattoo. There was no exit wound. The hollow point would have rattled around inside his skull, destroying everything. His ankles were bloody and shattered too, and Molito recounted the shots fired and pieced together the way his friend had died. Anger welled up inside him, but he pushed it back down again to keep in reserve for when the right time came.

Bell's eyes stared, lifeless and glazed. Molito slid them closed and searched his pockets. As he expected, they were empty, so he moved to the car. It was cleaned out too. His spare pistol was taken from under the steering column as well as the keys.

A search of the remaining SUV and the bodies it contained proved fruitless. Molito scooped up Bell's body and laid it with precision and care in the trunk. It wasn't ideal, but the rear seat was too risky and asked for trouble. Regardless of the situation, he never left a man behind.

The time had come to call Beck. He sat in the car and pulled out his phone. The small dot still moved away from him on the GPS screen.

He ripped off the plastic casing that covered the steering column, tore away wiring, and hot-wired the car. Then he swallowed heavily and dialed the number.

CHAPTER SEVENTEEN

Having completed tours on almost every continent, losing comrades became part of the job to Kyle Beck. Men in any deployed unit lived a life a heartbeat away from death. They saw every new day as a bonus, even if it was in a sandy shit hole. Sudden charges by an enemy unit, a hidden roadside device, or an unseen shot from a mile away; there were many ways to turn out the lights.

This was different. This was on home soil. This wasn't supposed to be a war. And Bell wasn't just a comrade. The muscles in his cheeks twitched as he ground his teeth, a habit he'd picked up years ago in Iraq as a way to filter out the anger. Chew it up and spit it out. The grief would come later. For now, the plan had to go ahead. And now, with the intervention of the suits, they'd just declared war.

Beck agreed with Molito. After hearing the story behind Bell's death, these guys were not with the FBI. Federal agents went through rigorous training but they also followed rules. There were protocols for every situation. They broke a few of them.

However, two men had stumbled upon a professional ambush, read it, and reacted swiftly enough to kill one of the best operatives Beck had ever known. They'd contained another long enough to clear the scene and move on as if it was nothing but a minor inconvenience. And they'd left their dead behind. There was something about those men.

With his fingers he tapped out a complicated beat on the desk. His eyes flitted from side to side as the wheels in his head whirred and spun. Who were they? No one knew of this mission but The Consortium and he spoke with them daily. Compartmentalization kept everyone in the dark, but surely he'd have heard something if they'd employed a team to track the woman too. Still, if The Consortium wasn't aware of his team trying to acquire the drive from her, who could say he'd know that they'd deployed a team to make sure he didn't get it. Normally, he would have sent his men to find it, but if any part of the mission failed and they discovered his alternate plan, his death would be a quick one. Also, he didn't want to appear to do anything to jeopardize their trust in him, something he'd always considered absolute. Perhaps he was wrong.

He realized now that his interrogation of his wife had not been hard enough. He felt nothing for her, but for some ridiculous reason, he couldn't bring himself to harm her too severely. Presumably, she still sat in the basement at home, secured to a chair. Beck counted the days on his fingers and wondered if she was still alive. With the bar snacks in the fridge she might still be breathing.

He thought about the place they'd called home. A secure environment like that was a prison to a man who had slept in tents and dusty rooms with curtains for doors, but he tolerated it. She held valuable information and details of machinery they would be turning into legendary weapons of mass destruction. Maybe that's why a previous government failed to find any – everything they needed stood there all along, in plain sight, just waiting for the right person, the right program to flick the switch.

Molito was heading for the house since the woman had the same idea. The second drone was recalled and Beck put his trust in his man instead. Molito would get there first and question Monica in a much firmer fashion. She had to have some knowledge of that drive. There were no solid leads on its whereabouts, but the other woman traveled east in search of something. She seemed to have an agenda, an idea of where to go and what to do. Beck was certain, as long as he stayed in touch with her, he would get the drive before the launch. After all, that's why he hired her.

I'd predicted my ability to find the house in the picture with the confidence of a con artist. After twenty-five minutes of browsing and roaming the digital streets of Google Maps, I began to doubt myself.

Like the phone book, I wasn't even sure they made map books anymore. Gone were the days of tracing your fingertip along pages of colored lines like a blind guy reading Braille. Now you could fly over the rooftops and swoop down to meander through the streets as if you were standing outside the place you were viewing. They must have photographed millions of miles of streets to create the program. Someone somewhere must have been caught by the roaming camera in an act of alfresco lovemaking.

The one thing I didn't take into account when looking at the picture of Monica was that it pictured the building from ground level. Once I had an aerial view of the town, there were rows of buildings arranged like waves that rolled away from the water tower. And there were a lot more of them than I expected. And Waterford might have been a small town, but I'd always driven past it, not through it.

As I zoomed the image out again to reposition the cursor, Sabrina must have seen something. Her arm brushed across mine as she leaned in to point at the screen and, when she looked at me to apologize, I saw something new in her eyes. I'd noticed that they'd softened a little, as if us spending more time together had somehow made me more acceptable, but they sparkled more intensely now too. There weren't lightning strikes going off in them by any means, but that hardness had weakened.

"Sorry," she said. She gazed at me for a second too long, then her eyes fluttered and the moment passed. "Bring up the picture again, something just occurred to me."

I flipped the screen and Monica appeared, still standing on the lawn, still holding her award, and still looking ordinary.

"Look right behind the property, it looks like there's a row of trees in an exact straight line. That's unusual unless they designed them in that way for security or privacy. We have a rough idea where the house is relative to the tower, now just zoom in, search for the row of trees and ignore everything else."

"Good idea," I said. Dammit, why didn't I think of that?

A few minutes later we were back at street level looking at the front of the house that Monica had stood against. The tops of the trees peeked over the top of the roofline. Sabrina's idea had panned out and the darker color of the trees had looked like a racing stripe against the lighter colors around it. I noted the address on a napkin we'd taken from Burger King.

The F150 didn't have the all singing, all dancing features of the Lexus, so she typed the details into her phone's GPS and got our next route on screen. It turned out to be a good three-hour drive away. We both looked at each other with a 'really?' kind of expression. Both of our stomachs rumbled and we were feeling the effects of too much traveling.

"What do you want to do?" I asked.

"I don't know," she said, "you want to get a room somewhere so we can approach this fresh in the morning?"

Maybe it was my imagination, but our voices seemed softer, as if either we'd reached a point where we'd grown comfortable with each other and some defenses had dropped, or we were just exhausted. It helped that nothing had followed us for a while. Either way, something had changed.

"Yeah," I said. "We should be as alert as possible tomorrow. With luck, it'll be the breakthrough we need to deal with whatever is going on once and for all. Do you have somewhere in mind?"

"No. Head toward Waterford. If we can get at least halfway there, we can get dinner and find a place to crash for the night. We can rest up and start again in the morning. We're out of cash and I don't trust ATM's anymore, so I guess it's time to break out my credit cards. Pray they're secure enough."

I drove for about a hundred and eighty miles and only stopped once to pick up sandwiches to tide us over until breakfast. All the time I was driving, my peripheral vision was split between the sun dipping in the west, and the occasional glances I got from the passenger seat. Something had changed in me too. This woman sitting next to me was amazing. The first night we'd spent together was one of those nights that happened to strangers meeting in a bar somewhere. Sure she was gorgeous, and it was a great night. But what had happened since, and the comfort we'd gained from each other, was from two people getting to know each other. Getting to rely on each other. We were building trust even as I drove. She was visibly more relaxed in the passenger seat, which said much more than anything else that had happened.

About hundred and ten miles from Waterford, a small motel flashed its gaudy neon sign across the highway, beckoning drivers into its fleapit hospitality. It worked.

"Does that look good enough for you?" she asked.

"It does," I said. "I'm beat. Let's shower and rest for the night."

I parked the truck around the back, out of sight, and then we checked in to a room.

I sat on the edge of the bed and flicked through the TV channels, trying to find something that wasn't filmed in 'Snowvision', when the bathroom door opened and Sabrina's head appeared through the steam. Her hair hung around her head in rats' tails, the water dripping off its ends and running in rivulets down her neck and breasts. They were perfect, one on either side, just the way I liked them.

"There's room in here for two…you know, if you want to conserve water."

I'd learned my lesson from the bar. There'd be no walk of shame past a mirror this time. I paused for a second and killed the TV in as cool a fashion as I could muster. The remote bounced across the bed as I tossed it with complete nonchalance, then shed my clothing piece-by-piece and sashayed to the bathroom.

We left the shower clean and refreshed and climbed into bed together. This time sleep could take me when I was ready. Through exhaustion, not drugs.

CHAPTER EIGHTEEN

V ince Molito towel dried his hair and then picked at the soil still embedded under his fingernails.

He'd buried Bell as respectfully as possible in an unmarked grave far in the depths of the Monongahela National Forest. Without a spade, it had not been easy, but with a curved shaped tree limb and his bare hands, he managed to dig a hole deep enough to place Bell's body away from any of the forest's wildlife. Then he'd driven east, following the GPS, until emotional and physical exhaustion overtook him. He checked into a small motel for the night, showered and collapsed onto the wafer thin mattress.

Digging Bell's grave brought back a lot of bad memories. Along with Beck, the men had spent years together. Their trust was absolute. They knew one another like brothers and behaved that way, but without the sibling rivalry. They'd saved each other's lives more times than they could remember and they'd also buried more men than they could count. The difference this time was that Blaine Bell was a friend. And a brother.

The walk from the car to the grave, with Bell draped over his shoulder, was arduous and draining and Molito stumbled a few times. Each time he cursed the wannabe Fed with the close cropped hair and swore to his dead friend that his death would be avenged. Wartime was indifferent, each target nothing but another bag of Muslim meat to be dispatched to the virgins in whatever hell they went to.

This was different. Personal.

The flashing dot on the GPS stopped in a small town a few miles away. Molito was certain that they'd stopped close to the same location Beck had given him, his old house, but he wanted to make sure they ended up there. He still needed the flash drive. The woman was the best way to get it and she seemed to be tracking it with confidence. In a perfect scenario he would meet them at the house, get the drive and kill all of them in one fell swoop.

Tomorrow, everything would come together. He steadied his breathing, closed his eyes and dreamt of warfare.

Once again, I woke up in an unfamiliar room. This time I woke up to an unfamiliar sensation too, and not because I wasn't on the sofa. Warmth radiated down one side of me, an arm rested across my chest, and a weight nestled in the crook of my arm. I rolled my head to one side and got a mouthful of fragrant hair. Sabrina still slept with her body pushed right up against me. I had no complaints.

Last night was everything I'd read about in books and seen in movies. I had no need for wiseass comments or witty comebacks. The blue numbers on the digital clock by the bed told us it was two in the morning by the time we rolled apart, spent but satisfied. Now they said it was 8.10.

After a brief struggle, I managed to extricate my arm without waking her. I rubbed it to encourage the blood to flow back into my fingers, then crept into the bathroom and took a solo shower. When I walked back into the bedroom, Sabrina had woken. She looked up at me, her head resting on folded arms. Her face wore a smile of contentment that made me want to stay in this room with her forever, even though we had important work to do. Part of me still expected our flying friend to find us at any moment. Like Sabrina, I just wanted this whole thing to end, even more so now so we could explore where we went from here.

Like the first time, which already seemed like a lifetime ago, there'd been little talking last night. Unlike the first time, there was no frantic effort or assumption that it was just one night. I don't know why, but I felt as if we didn't need to talk about it. We could just ride the wave and find out what happened next.

She propped herself up against the headboard and smiled. "Morning, General."

Despite the arousing affect her smoky morning voice had on me, I had to laugh. I had made a smart ass comment last night after all. During a brief moment of conversation, I may have confessed to having promoted my gentleman's equipment from Captain to General based on its excellent performance. Part of me had hoped she'd forget I even mentioned it, but from the look on her face, there was a chance it would run forever.

"Morning. Did you sleep okay?"

"Oh, yes." She stretched and a toned leg appeared as the covers moved. "You wore me out. Seems I needed a good night's sleep." She pointed to the coffee maker by the TV. "Now, are you going to make a girl a cup of cheap coffee or what?"

"Of course," I said.

She showered while the coffee sludge filtered through the strainer and, within an hour, we were back in the truck and on the road. The drive itself was uneventful in that nothing followed us, at least that we saw. In terms of our behavior, it seemed as if a dam had collapsed and the water had gushed over the crumbled sides and flowed freely. We both swam in it.

I opened up about my marriage and how I blamed myself for its failure. I told her about Kacie, my beautiful daughter, and how she pushed me to become a more trusting person. In turn, she told me about her life. It was a tragic story, I already knew that, but I learned how she dropped out of school before all the tragedy struck and met a guy named Max. As much as she loved her parents, she thought they didn't understand her. He took her in and taught her how to survive. It turned out she excelled as a pupil and her education evolved until it sounded like she studied at spy school. Max was her mentor, and he seemed to mean a lot to her. She said at one point that I should meet him. I took that as a positive sign that something good had happened between us and not that I needed to learn how to pick a lock.

After a couple of hours, we reached our destination. I turned a corner, stopped the truck a couple hundred yards down the road from where we thought the house would be, and pulled into the curb. We walked the rest of the way, found the road easily and approached the building.

"Okay, I'll check around the back," said Sabrina, "you take the front. Walk by as if you're familiar with the area and make sure there are no neighbors twitching the curtains. Then double back and see if you notice any movement. I'll meet you down the side of the house in about five minutes and we'll go from there."

"Got it," I nodded. "I hope she's home."

"Me too," she said. "Be careful."

I squeezed her hand and we climbed out of the truck and headed our separate ways.

CHAPTER NINETEEN

C al Lennon and Eric Weston knew the process of grief. It's dealt with in stages. First, there's the shock, the realization that something was lost. Denial follows and, to combat the denial, next comes a simmering anger. Sometimes there's guilt and the search for a reason. But then the human spirit kicks in and the mind gains new strength and hope and adjusts to the loss. It doesn't forget. It never forgets. It adjusts.

They were the exception in their team. They had got to know each other even though they were aware that it was dangerous. It was a bond that could be severed at any moment. Despite this lapse in controlled emotion, they remained cold, trained to ignore the process and to harness the start and the end of it. Retain the anger and adjust.

The journey through the rest of the forest and on toward the town had sapped the remaining energy they had. When the GPS dot on the phone stopped moving, they agreed to stop too. They'd been driving for days in a state of heightened alert. Muscles ached, the senses dulled and the previous night's sleep was interrupted. They needed to get a night of solid rest and pick up the chase in the morning. Both knew the risks of going into a dangerous situation when not operating at one hundred percent.

Both of their alarms sounded at 8:00. They woke refreshed, showered and ate a light breakfast with the captive phone on the table in front of them, plugged into an outlet to charge. Just after 9:00, the screen illuminated. She was on the move again. They moved too.

Lennon focused on the road ahead and wondered whether Platt and Sullivan had forged a bond too. Being in the other vehicle meant that he rarely communicated with them, other than to relay orders or questions from SD1. As required by their company, neither of them had family or friends to miss them. Still, he felt like a surgeon who had lost a patient on his table. Someone died on his watch. Worse still, the shooter was still out there.

"You think he has a phone too?" he asked.

Weston snapped out of his somber reverie startled and glanced across at his colleague. "Huh?"

"The shooter. Do you reckon he has a phone like the one I took from his partner, and he's tracking the same GPS?"

"Depends if they worked apart, I guess. We should assume that he does and be ready to meet him when we get there. I'm ready to meet him. I've got a shitload of payback built up. I fucking hate snipers."

"Hey, I can relate to that," said Lennon, "but remember, he's just like us. He's doing a job. We mean as much to him as he does to us and don't forget, we took out his partner too."

"Yeah, well I don't give a shit about him. I don't like not knowing what we're really doing. I've always followed orders, but something's not right about this. It started as a tailing job with no urgency and now it's a life or death 'get the job done now' thing? It doesn't make sense. What changed?"

"I wish I knew," said Lennon. "Either way, I'm sure we're coming to the end of it now. This tracker's been very consistent. We just need to follow it until we're parked on the dot."

It took two hours for the dot to stop again. Once they caught up with it, they pulled into a wooded area and parked the SUV two blocks away.

CHAPTER TWENTY

W hen Sabrina mentioned I should check for neighbors, I didn't expect the nearest one to be a mile away. I'm sure she just meant for me to be vigilant.

I'd parked against a curb that curved around and dissolved into a dusty trail. Just inside the tree line, the trail morphed into a gravel drive that meandered for quite a distance and ended at a single story bungalow with a wraparound porch. The property sat on about two acres of well-kept land. It had louvered green shutters that hung on either side of each window and a row of fluted columns that held up an overhanging roof. A Stars and Stripes hung by the door and fluttered in the breeze. I expected there to be an old woman knitting in a rocking chair on the porch, but other than a couple of sparrows perched on the gutter, the place looked to be deserted.

My first pass by produced no results. I glanced up at the house as if it was interrupting my walk and I didn't expect it to be there, and then I scanned the windows. Nothing moved other than the tips of the trees behind the house that we'd used to find it in the first place. The windows were closed, which surprised me. It was a warm day and I could just hear the insect-type buzzing of an air conditioning unit running around the back.

On my walk back in the other direction, I thrust my hands into my pockets to appear nonchalant and trudged up the gravel drive to the front of the house. The steps up onto the porch creaked like old bones and the sparrows chirped their disapproval and flew away as I moved to the windows. The kitchen was on the left. It looked like a rustic farmhouse, with pine cabinets and lots of glass doors. She must have loved the glass look. The other window revealed a seating area that had two sofas with blankets draped over them and cozy footstools.

Nothing moved inside the house either, so I edged over to the front door. As I drew back my hand to knock Sabrina hissed, "What the hell are you doing?"

She peered around the corner and beckoned in some kind of crazy semaphore. I didn't understand it, so I ducked underneath the window and scrambled to join her at the side of the house.

"I didn't say you should knock and introduce yourself. Don't get me wrong, I hope she's home but, I don't know, even if she is she might not be happy to see us. We need to maintain the element of surprise. I assume you saw nothing out front since you were about to say hello. There's nothing at the rear either, other than a top of the line grill. It all seems too quiet, though. I'm beginning to fear the worst. We should check inside, but come around to the back of the house and keep watch. I'll check out the door."

I took up sentry duty while Sabrina, once again, rifled through her bag of goodies and produced the pouch I'd seen at the other house. She eased open the screen door and turned the doorknob. It mustn't have moved because she pulled familiar instruments from the pouch and picked the lock. I did understand the motion she made when she put her raised finger in front of her lips and pushed open the door, one careful inch at a time. It opened silently, so I kept quiet too and followed her into the house.

This time it wasn't a ringing phone that got her attention but the dull thud of footsteps. There'd been no knock at the door. She didn't even hear it being opened, but someone walked around in the house over-head, trying not to make a sound. They were failing.

It was Kyle's idea to dig out a basement or, as he called it, a storm shelter. A crew spent weeks digging through the upstairs floor, shoring up the sides, and pouring drum after drum of concrete to form fresh walls and a new base. When it came to replacing the upstairs floor, they laid plywood sheets over joists and then installed hardwood on top of that. With no insulation between the two levels, any noise upstairs sounded twice as loud down below.

Kyle knew this and anyway, since he was the one who'd secured her, he didn't need to walk on the balls of his feet. She worried that he might come back for her, but the more she considered his behavior, the more she doubted he would.

Once he'd tied her to the wooden chair, he questioned her about the flash drive. The drive was no mystery, but she didn't know at first how he was aware of its existence. Her team at SonicAmerica produced a product that turned everyday machines into a means to wreak devasta-tion if it fell into the wrong hands. Just as every man-made virus had an antidote, so did every project that SonicAmerica worked on. Kyle wanted the antidote. Her problem was that her drive was stolen. She had no idea where it was so she was entirely honest with him. The drive he knew about was in her bag, and her bag was stolen.

He pushed her harder and harder for answers. After his absences from home and his furtiveness, she suspected he was involved with black ops. Maybe still on the front line, or he had already paid his dues in the field and now commanded his unit. Either way, this meant for sure that he'd taken life. She had no doubt her husband was a killer, but when he'd raised his hand she didn't flinch. She didn't provoke him either. It would have been like poking an angry bear with a sharp stick, but she held his gaze and found the strength to hold her head up. Despite what she suspected, one other thing became apparent to her. Kyle Beck did not hit women unprovoked. It didn't matter whether it was in his upbringing or his genes, he wouldn't hurt her. The only fear that remained was that he might send someone else who would. Still, she suspected a colleague of his would also forego tiptoeing across the floor upstairs, knowing that she should be tied to a chair in the basement.

She reached for the corkscrew and held it as a weapon once more. Since no one else knew of her situation, the person upstairs had broken in, perhaps with the intent of robbing the place. They'd look around for a while and then notice the bolted door. Locked doors normally had valuable things hidden behind them.

Or, Kyle had sent someone to finish her off.

The stairs to the upstairs level ran up the side of the far wall, held in place by tall posts and a sturdy rail. The space beneath the stairs was empty. She turned the stool to face the bar and looked around the room. If she hid under the stairs the room would appear to be empty. Then, when the intruder descended, she could reach between the treads and trip them. After that, she would have to see if she possessed the mettle to do what needed to be done next.

She switched off the light and crouched beneath the stairs. It felt like forever, but after a while the metal bolt behind the door grated against the loops holding it and a shaft of light staggered across the treads. She held her breath and waited.

CHAPTER TWENTY-ONE

I'm not sure who the glass-wrapped country property we broke into a couple of days ago belonged to, but I knew this house belonged to Monica Bridges. A lot more pictures were dotted around, and the SonicAmerica logo appeared on folders in the office and on a calendar magnet stuck to the fridge door. The athletic looking guy we'd seen her with showed up in more of the pictures too, although he never appeared alone, always with Monica. She also looked older in the pictures in this house.

As we suspected, we were alone. There was no sign of Monica. There were no dishes in the sink or half eaten dinners on the table like they always find on television, although the place seemed a lot cleaner. It wasn't blanketed in a layer of dust either. For whatever reason, we still crept around and opened doors and drawers to see if we could find any clues to her whereabouts. I began to draw the same conclusion Sabrina had – something untoward had happened to Monica and I thought back to the land that surrounded the country house. Was she lying in a shallow grave somewhere?

This house felt different from the other too. The country house belonged to a young person; modern and full of life. This was more like a farmhouse, as if there should have been an older couple living here, retired and growing old together. Everything was warm and welcoming with blankets thrown over scattered furniture and over the queen-sized bed that took up most of the only bedroom.

When we entered, I turned to the left and Sabrina went right. Both sides of the house were open plan, separated by a hall down the middle. We circled through each side and, after we'd checked around, we met back in the hall.

"Nothing," I said. "I don't think anyone's been here for a while, although the milk in the fridge is still in date so we're not talking weeks."

"I agree," said Sabrina. She frowned and pointed to the far wall. "But check this out. This side of the house doesn't appear to be as long as the other."

I didn't understand what she meant so we walked down the hall. She stopped where the right side ended. I walked on a further three feet.

"You're right. Does it end in a flat wall?"

"No," she said, "there's a small door on the left that opens on to a closet filled with cleaning materials. Now I'm looking at it from here, though, it's nowhere near big enough to take up the entire wall."

We walked back around to the wall and I opened the closet door. Sure enough, there was a collection of mops and buckets and a small shelf with detergent on it. Even though the inside shone with white paint, the right side of the closet was shrouded in darkness. I stuck my head through the door and took a closer look.

"Hey, there's another door back here." I looked around the closet and found a light switch behind the door. The small room burst into light as I flicked it to reveal a sturdy looking wooden door with a black iron bolt closed across it. We looked at each other and shrugged.

"Wait here," said Sabrina. She walked off into the kitchen and came back with a knife that could gut a lion. "You can never be too careful. A locked door is not always a good sign."

"I agree," I said. "So let me go first." As I moved toward the door she restrained me with a strong hand.

"I'm not a wimpy girl," said Sabrina and fixed me with a glare that confirmed it. "Also, I have the knife so you stay behind me."

I considered getting a knife of my own, but she breezed past me, slid back the bolt and pushed open the door.

The beam of light cast through the door lit up a wooden staircase that led down into darkness. I didn't remember seeing any basement windows from outside the house. Sabrina turned to me. Her eyes said the same thing. She fumbled across the wall until her fingers found a switch. As the room below was bathed in light, she crouched to look into it. I ambled up alongside her.

Downstairs turned out to be a nice looking bar area. A long oak countertop wound its way toward us from the far wall like a wooden river. Four matching stools lined up in front of it. Small pendants hung stationary from the ceiling and provided the light.

Cool air washed across my face through the open door. It was musty and tainted with something else I couldn't quite place. She looked at me again and mouthed, "Blood?"

I hoped she was wrong, but after a while I placed the scent. A tiny hint of that cloying copper smell drifted up to us. I nodded in agreement.

Sabrina rose and walked one by one down the stairs, each planted foot making no sound. I began to follow but, as she reached the third step, she let out a cry. I caught a fleeting glimpse of a bloody hand as it retreated under the stairs and saw four red finger marks streaked across Sabrina's white socks. Then she stumbled, lost her footing and pitched forward.

Lennon and Weston turned the corner and looked at the magnified land ahead of them through binoculars. The dot on the GPS screen was still stationary and they were standing on top of it.

"That has to be it," said Lennon. He nodded toward a tidy looking house in the distance. "There's no sign of life, though. No people. No cars. Nothing."

Weston scanned the surrounding area. The only thing that moved was nature. "I think it's safe to assume they did the same thing we did and parked a distance away. Chances are they're in there right now, and the shooter is either close by or in there with them."

"Okay, well I say we plan for three bogies to be sure. I see a door at the front. We need to check out the back and make sure we can cover any other exits. Assuming there's a back door too, we can split up and contain them. Waste the shooter by all means, but try to keep the woman alive. I want to know what's going on and we still need that flash drive."

"What about Howard?"

"Honestly," said Lennon, "I don't give a crap about Howard. If he gets in the way take him out, but he's just a civilian caught in the middle of this. One less body is one less thing to deal with, and he can't identify us."

Weston nodded. "Seems fair to me."

Both men checked the rounds in their silenced pistols, swept their binoculars across the surrounding terrain once more, and made their way toward the house.

CHAPTER TWENTY-TWO

Sabrina was slipping.

As she fell she dropped the knife over the side of the stair rail. I lunged forward and grabbed at the collar of her t-shirt and snagged it but my nails raked through the fabric as she slid away from me. Buttons popped and bounced happily down the staircase and, almost in slow motion, Sabrina fell away from me and tumbled down the stairs after them. As her head hit the floor I heard a clamber beneath me and saw a whirl of motion. In no time, someone shot out from the shadows below and rushed around to the foot of the stairs. She looked disheveled and her hands dripped with blood, but we'd found Monica Bridges.

She dived onto Sabrina and took advantage of her disorientation. Within seconds, she had Sabrina in a headlock with the wrong end of a corkscrew pushed against her neck. The smooth skin that covered her artery turned white and dimpled as Monica applied pressure.

"Monica! Stop!"

As I shouted her name, she froze and stared at me. She made no attempt to hide her surprise. She looked like a cornered animal, muscles tensed, ready to rip the crap out of whoever came anywhere near her to take away her catch. Then she crab-legged into the corner of the stairwell with her arm wrapped around Sabrina's throat.

"How do you know my name? And that I was here?" she hissed. "Do you work for him? Have you come to finish me off?"

"Him? Who?"

"Kyle. Kyle Beck."

I had no idea what she was talking about and her panicked state scared the crap out of me. "Who the hell is Kyle Beck? And please calm down, we mean you no harm. Please don't hurt her."

"Don't you fucking play with me or I swear to God I'll slice her neck open."

"Don't! Don't do that. We're not your enemies, I swear."

I held my hands out in front of me, thanking any deity that would listen that I wasn't holding a weapon of any kind. "Please, just let me talk. I won't move, I promise. I'll sit on this step, but let me explain why we're here. Like I said, we mean you no harm. Please, I'm begging you, don't hurt her."

Tears welled up in my eyes and threatened to leap out and rappel down my face. They were genuine, and it seemed Monica sensed it because she relaxed a little and spoke in a calmer voice.

"If you're not enemies, why did she have a knife?"

"There are people looking for us. She was being careful because we had no idea what was down here. Hell, we didn't even know there was a 'down here'. Someone is chasing us because of something she took from you. We need to ask you about it."

I regretted the words as soon as I said them. Monica tensed again and Sabrina's head lolled against the arm wrapped around her throat. Monica frowned. The wheels in her mind were spinning as if she was deliberating our fate.

"She had no idea what she was getting herself in to," I offered as a weak defense. "She did a job for someone and didn't realize how badly this was going to turn out. Please, would you check her? Is she okay?"

"I can feel her pulse against my arm," said Monica. "She's fine. So this was who Kyle sent to get the drive."

"She had to get a drive, yes, but the name Kyle means nothing to me. Who is he and what do you know about that drive?"

Monica relaxed the pressure against Sabrina's neck, but kept the corkscrew within striking distance.

"I can tell you everything about that drive. I helped make it. Now it's your turn. Please tell me you have it and he didn't get it because, if you really aren't my enemies, I'm going to need your help. This is going to sound ridiculous, but we have to stop him and save the world."

The two men parted ways.

The house sat as proud as a castle in the middle of open ground, surrounded by a moat of lush green grass. Trees ringed the property but, once inside the tree line, nothing but open space lay between their position and the house. It was wide open. There was no way to approach without the risk of being spotted. The windowless sidewall seemed to be the safest option.

Weston waited by the road and watched through binoculars as Lennon made a wide circle of the property and ran in a crouch to the side of the building. He paused and waited to see if his run drew a response. When none came, he edged to the rear of the property and stopped behind the wooden railing that surrounded the house. He curled his fingers over the ledge and pulled himself up enough to peer through the window. A shake of the head confirmed that all was quiet inside. He stayed low and moved to the right and once more looked through the other window. Another shake of the head.

The left side of the porch had a small seated area that had its back to the property. It faced a large, well-used grill in the corner. Old metal teapots and kettles with flowers growing out of them cluttered the right side of the porch, dotted around like land mines. Lennon crept through the opening in the railings, went left, and knelt beside the entrance. He reached for the storm door and grimaced as his shoulder connected with one of the cooking implements hanging from the grill. It clattered into the utensils hanging next to it. Weston heard nothing from the road, but the look on Lennon's face meant it must have sounded as loud as an out of tune wind chime. He froze and braced himself to deal with anyone inside who came out to investigate.

A few seconds passed and still nothing moved. Lennon reached for the storm door again. Inch by careful inch he pulled it toward him, waiting for a squeak that never came, then leaned inside and slid back the catch to hold it open. Then he reached for the door handle. Weston grinned at the surprise on Lennon's face as the door opened. It was unlocked.

He pocketed the binoculars and moved toward the front of the house. Once Lennon had the back door open, Weston had three minutes to position himself outside the front door. If anyone inside tried to leave he would apprehend them.

If the shooter appeared, there would be no apprehension. Just a bullet.

CHAPTER TWENTY-THREE

Molito watched the entire thing unfold through the high-powered scope mounted on his rifle. He swung it back and forth from one man to the other, and back again. They worked well as a team. From their actions, they must have considered the house to be occupied. The guy he wanted most hid behind railings at the rear entrance while his colleague had taken up a similar position at the front. It was an obvious shakedown. One went in to flush out the occupants while the other waited at the only other exit until they emerged and popped them. Stings like this lasted a matter of minutes. Molito knew that he didn't have much time.

The guy at the front seemed to be more vigilant. Molito elected to move toward the side of the property behind them to take out the guy around back first. He was the one who'd killed Bell. A rifle shot would have been easier, the target was a literal sitting duck, but it would spook the others inside the house. Both men had to die, along with whoever else remained, and he couldn't afford to have multiple targets running. Also, he wanted to look the man in the eyes as his life left his body.

He pressed himself against the sidewall until he knew he'd cleared the distance undetected, then laid the rifle in the grass as if it were his baby. It was useless at close quarters like these. The gun was bulky and took too long to reload. It was time to go old school with surprise and brute force. He moved along the wall until he reached the railing and peeked around the corner. A large gas grill blocked his view, so he crouched lower to see beneath it. An exposed back and a pair of boot heels lay in front of him, almost close enough to touch. The guy was crouched, oblivious, a few feet away. Molito rose to his full height, placed a foot between two posts and grabbed the top rail. Just as he tensed and gripped the rail to hoist himself over, the guy opened the back door and slipped inside the house.

Molito relaxed his grip, cursed, and moved around the railing to the porch entrance. The screen door was propped open, but the back door had swung shut with a whisper. His enemy might have heard his approach. He could be ready and waiting for him on the other side of the door. Shiny metal glinted in the light and caught his eye. A row of cooking implements hung from hooks on the side of the grill like a torturer's armory. He grabbed a sturdy two-pronged fork, ignored the back door, and made his way across the side of the house and around to the front.

At the other corner, Molito held his breath and glanced around the wall's edge. Looking through the wooden slats was like looking through prison bars. The other guy knelt in his cell. He hadn't moved and still mirrored his partner's pose, crouched beside the door ready to deal with whoever came through it.

The fork felt solid. Its shaft remained rigid as Molito gripped it and flexed it to test its resilience to force. In one fluid move he leapt over the railing, clamped his hand across the man's mouth, and plunged the twin forks into the back of his neck. There was a moment of frenzied panic as realization sunk in. Boot heels and a dropped pistol clattered against the wooden floorboards. Metal ground against bone as the blades forced their way through muscle and between the cervical verte-brae. Molito held him close and pushed harder and, as the spinal cord was severed, the man's body went limp and collapsed into his arms.

He threw the lifeless body over his shoulder and dumped it over the railing, then vaulted over after it and dragged it around to the side of the house. The greasy blood slicked his hand. He wiped it against the dead man's jacket and made his way back to the front porch. The door was locked, but at least now he had a pistol.

It was time to check in with Beck. He made his way back to the rear porch. Part way across the sidewall, he paused and took out his phone. It was too risky to talk, so he texted four words.

Found them. One down…

The other guy with the close-cropped hair would take much longer to die. He'd pay for what he'd done. Molito pocketed his phone, checked the chamber of the pistol to make sure it contained a round, and made his way to the rear entrance.

To my relief, Sabrina had regained consciousness much quicker than I expected.

She was lying in a prone position, groggy and in a headlock. A corkscrew glinted in the light inches away from a major artery, and the look in her beautiful eyes said that she was going to kick Monica's ass. Part of me didn't doubt she could. Still, you only get one chance with a major artery so I spoke in my best salesperson tone and attempted to mediate.

"Sabrina, lie still baby. You might have hurt yourself falling down the stairs." I added the 'baby' to try to elicit some empathy from Monica, but to be honest, saying the words felt good too. "The person behind you is Monica. We found her, but I haven't told her who we are yet. She doesn't trust us so stay cool and let me explain everything. We might need to work together."

Sabrina tilted her head back a fraction of an inch to address her captor. "I'd say hi and shake your hand, but I feel like you're about to pop my cork."

"You can say hi from where you are," said Monica. "Do you have my drive?"

"No," said Sabrina. "I looked everywhere, but…"

"That was you in Chicago? You took my purse, right?"

"That awful fluorescent thing? Yes," said Sabrina, "but I didn't find a drive, just your notes. And I'm sorry for stealing your purse. I was just doing my job."

"Is it with you?"

"Yes. At the top of the stairs up there in my work bag."

I made a move to get up from the step and Monica tensed again and moved the corkscrew back toward Sabrina's neck.

"Whoa, take it easy, Monica. I'll walk slowly backwards and reach back for the bag and slide it down the steps to you."

"What's the point?" said Sabrina, still as stubborn as ever. "I emptied the entire thing. It's not in there."

"When I say it's in the purse," said Monica, "I mean it's actually 'in' the purse. Get it and slide it down here. Slowly."

I walked to the top of the stairs and reached around the frame until my fingers snagged the strap of the bag and then dragged it onto the stairs. The thing weighed a ton. It slid with a metallic clunk down the first three steps and got caught up in the carpet, so I nudged it with my foot.

"Okay," said Monica, "this isn't going to work. Take out my purse and toss it over here."

I did as she asked and the gaudy looking thing landed at Sabrina's feet. Monica relaxed her arm again and pushed Sabrina upright.

"We'll soon see if you're telling the truth. Slide my bag back to me with one hand, and slide that knife you dropped back with the other. One false move and…"

"Yeah, I get it," said Sabrina. She slid the items back and pushed them behind her. "Don't worry. Like he said, we might be on the same side. What did you mean about working together?"

"One thing at a time. Brace yourself upright; I'm going to move out from behind you. I'd be grateful if you'd stay put for a little while longer."

Monica stood, picked up the purse and the knife, and walked to the bar as Sabrina moved back into the corner. She pointed up the stairs to me.

"You have me at a disadvantage. You know my name. What's yours?"

"I'm Paul," I said, "and that's Sabrina you were just holding."

"Okay Paul, please come downstairs and join Sabrina, would you?"

Again, I did as she instructed. As I crouched next to Sabrina she edged past us, picked up Sabrina's kit bag and moved up the stairs.

"I'm going to leave you two here for a moment while I grab something from upstairs. If you can behave, I promise I'll come back and we'll talk."

"Like we have a choice," said Sabrina.

"Well, you really don't, but you've been true to your word so far. You'll get the same from me."

She went through the door, closed it and slid the bolt.

At least she left the light on.

CHAPTER TWENTY-FOUR

At first he thought that there was a TV playing somewhere. Lennon heard muffled voices. They sounded as if they came from the other side of the house but, based on the building's layout, the voices should have been bouncing off the walls toward him in clear tones, not drifting around as if under water. He crept along the hallway, moving every time the voices sounded to mask his footsteps, but, when he reached the other end, he found no one. The sounds got louder, though, and appeared to be coming from a cleaning closet sunk into the wall at the far side of a country style kitchen.

The small room was shrouded in shadow. He approached it with his pistol leading the way, but then turned and scurried back to the rear rooms, as a familiar sound grew louder in front of him. Someone was climbing a staircase. The sound of the footsteps soon stopped, replaced by the faint grate of sliding metal. Baffled, he peeked around the wooden doorframe as a woman exited the closet.

He was confused. This couldn't be the woman they'd been tracking. Lennon had expected someone more exotic looking. He knew she was able to take care of herself but this woman looked as if she'd been in the fight of her life. Her bloody hands dropped a couple of bags on the floor as she opened a cabinet door. She knelt and rummaged around for a moment and then stood, clutching a handgun, which she placed on the counter top. The faucet squeaked as she ran water over her hands and wrists, turning and rubbing them with the care of a children's nurse. The water ran red into the sink below it. Her body jerked and her shoulders shook in silence while she dried herself. Then she wiped her face with the towel, picked up the gun and the bags, and moved back into the closet.

Once more, metal grated and footsteps descended.

Lennon inched forward toward the opening, wary of her return, and took a moment to look for Weston through the far door. Since there was no sign of him, Lennon assumed that he'd hidden himself and the exit was secure. As he approached the dark opening another voice spoke, this time male. He moved as close as he dared to the doorway. After a deep reassuring breath, he entered the darkness of the closet, leaned in to the open door and listened to the conversation that drifted up the stairs.

Monica seemed to walk down the stairs with more confidence than she did when she'd walked up them. This time she carried a pistol along with the bags and a knife. She was kitted out ready for a war I didn't realize we were fighting. The look in my eyes must have tipped her off.

"Don't worry. Not that I'm a good judge of character based on my earlier choices, but you two don't seem as if you're here to do me any harm. Still, I'd appreciate it if you'd keep your distance for a while. Why don't you come and sit at the bar while I take care of this."

We moved from the corner to the stools at the front of the bar while Monica moved behind it to take care of whatever it was she'd mentioned. She left Sabrina's bag on the floor at our feet, maybe as a test, while she placed the Vera Bradley purse in front of her on the oak top next to the pistol. She unclipped the shoulder strap from one side of the purse and slid the bulky shoulder pad off one end and laid it flat on the bar. Then she forced the knife between the stitching and cut through the fabric with a sawing motion. She created a cut wide enough for her to slide two fingers inside the pad. They emerged with a small piece of black plastic. The flash drive.

I felt Sabrina's body deflate as she realized that the thing she'd been chasing across the country was with her the entire time. She mumbled 'shit' under her breath and, for the first time, Monica smiled. The two women looked at each other and as Sabrina shook her head, Monica pulled the purse toward her again.

"That's not all," she said. "I assume you've had people following you?"

We nodded in unison. Monica hefted the knife again as if she was about to fillet a fish and cut away at the base of the purse. Once she had cut from one side to the other, she fumbled around inside the fabric and pulled out a small metal object that looked like a bronze colored quarter.

"Is that what I think it is?" I asked.

"That depends. If you think it's a tracking device then yes, it is," said Monica. She laid it on the bar top. We stared at it as if it might perform a trick.

"Well, aren't we supposed to step on that or something?" I said. "I mean, shouldn't we assume they're still following us?"

"We could do that," said Sabrina, "or we could do this." She held out her hand, testing to see if Monica would pass the knife. Monica paused for a moment and then spun the blade around on her palm and presented it to Sabrina. We seemed to be making inroads in the trust department although the pistol was still lying there. Sabrina picked up the tracker and slid the knife into a small crack along its outside edge. With a slight twist of the wrist, the thing popped open to expose a small circuit board and a compact jumble of wiring. She pushed the knife under the wires and levered out a tiny battery, then pulled it from the device and tossed it and the knife back on the bar.

"Done," she said. She looked up at Monica. "So, how did you know about that tracker? I don't know about you, but I think perhaps it's time we compared stories."

"Yes," said Monica. "Yes, it is, and in the spirit of building trust, I'll go first. It turns out that my wonderful husband is not the man I married. He reckons he's untouchable, though, like all greedy psychopaths. They think they can do whatever they like to whomever they like. There's a program antivirus on the drive. He had me call into work and get one of my team members to delete the office version of the program and then tender my resignation. Then he locked me down here and left me to die. He didn't have the balls to do it himself although that doesn't stop him from sending someone else along to finish the job. That's what I thought you'd come here for."

"We're here to find out about that drive," said Sabrina, "because ever since I took that damned purse I've been shot at and trailed halfway across the country. I guessed the two were linked. At least now I know why the purse was so important. The drive was in it all along. But we meant what we said. We're no threat to you."

"Kyle hired you to get the drive from me because he considered himself to be too high profile and didn't want to risk being spotted. He said you were one of the best at what you do."

As impressed as I was, Sabrina laughed it off. "You'll forgive me if I'm not too flattered."

"Of course," said Monica. "He also stitched the tracker inside my purse so he could keep an eye on my movement. It's great he had no idea how close he was to the drive."

"How do you know all of this about your husband?" I asked. "I don't see why someone who has all kinds of resources would give up so much information."

Monica laughed. The more we spoke, the more at ease she seemed to get. For the first time, I thought we might actually get out of this without being shot. As if she read my mind, Monica picked up the pistol. My stomach lurched, but she lifted the back of her shirt and tucked the weapon inside her belt.

"Kyle tied me up here to interrogate me. I wasn't as forthcoming as he expected and, when he got frustrated, he flipped out and had a Scooby Doo moment."

It was my turn to laugh. Sabrina frowned and looked between the two of us as if we were crazy. Monica explained. "At the end of every episode of Scooby Doo, right after they pull off the bad guys' mask, he would always say 'If it wasn't for those pesky kids' and then give a full confession. It's a shame it doesn't work that way for law enforcement. It would be so much easier to get a conviction."

"So why has he gone to such lengths to get that drive? What exactly was his confession?" said Sabrina.

Monica took a deep breath as if she was about to unburden herself to a listening priest. "When I said I might need your help to save the world, I wasn't joking. You've heard of drones, right?"

"Oh yeah," said Sabrina. "We have one in the truck."

Monica missed a beat for the first time since we began talking but quickly rallied. "Of course you do. Well, did you know that there are over six hundred air based drones in use around the world by the U.S. alone? And that's just American drones. The English have them too, and the Chinese. All the larger world powers rely on them for information gathering. The thing is, some of them are armed, and armed to the teeth. And these are only the drones in the sky. There are more swimming around in the oceans and others digging below ground. They use SonicAmerica's tech, which is why Kyle was interested in me. He knew I'd have access to the information he'd need. No one knows the total number of drones out there because some countries are a little more private about releasing that kind of information. It goes without saying there are thousands of them. And they're everywhere. The people Kyle works for have created a program that will seize control of every last one of them around the Middle East. Whenever they decide to, they can strike. Every drone within range will unleash its arsenal at the Middle Eastern region simultaneously. There will be complete devastation. Whole cities will crumble. There'll be bodies everywhere; men, women and children. And what do you think will happen afterwards?"

I was having a hard time taking this in. I looked at Sabrina, probably with the eyes of a ten-year-old faced with a serious algebra problem. Monica didn't wait for an answer, though; she was on a roll.

"Retaliation. The Russians and the Chinese will point fingers right away, and both in the same direction. None of the superpowers ever dared to press the big button, the one that would start the next big war.

If we were seen to be attacking on such a large scale that would be all the reason they'd need. It would be the start of World War Three, and probably the end of the world."

Three days ago I'd had the night of my life. Since then, I'd been chased by surveillance drones. Twice. Then I'd driven around the country and broken into property. Also twice. I was sure I'd lost my job, or would at least have some major explaining to do if I wanted to keep it. Now I was part of a conversation concerning the end of the world. I couldn't see how things could get any worse.

Then things got worse.

CHAPTER TWENTY-FIVE

Monica's head snapped to one side and looked past me up the stairs. Her eyes widened, either in shock or surprise, and then a male voice spoke from somewhere behind me. "Nobody move a muscle. I don't want to hurt anyone."

I recognized the voice but, for the life of me, I couldn't put a name to it. The stairs were just out of sight in the room reflected in the mirror behind the bar. Regardless, I didn't move a muscle. I did see Monica move her hand around her hip to the gun tucked in her belt. Sabrina shook her head a fraction of an inch from side to side, enough to signal 'don't be stupid'.

"You should pay attention to your friend," said the voice. "A few days ago, my response to that action might have been different, but after listening to your little story, I'm intrigued enough to hear you out. This drive has caused me nothing but trouble, not to mention significant loss. Then you mentioned it was enough to start World War Three. I've fought in enough fucking wars and I didn't go through all this bullshit to sign up and start another."

There was a pause as he made his way down the stairs. He still wasn't visible in the mirror, but I sensed him to one side of me.

"Okay, you two on this side of the bar, Howard and the woman.

You can spin around on those stools with your hands out where I can see them."

As soon as he said my name I remembered his voice from the hotel. The FBI agent that helped me to search the bathroom. I swiveled on the stool. It spun and grated on a cheap mechanism that could have learned a lot from the door at SonicAmerica. He had a gun trained on us which, to be honest, was getting old. He didn't even look at me. With his cropped, light colored hair and his gaze fixed on Sabrina, he looked like an owl that had spotted a stray mouse. At least he nodded when he said my name again.

"Mr. Howard. We meet again as they say. And you," he said, still looking at Sabrina as if he'd discovered a lost Picasso, "you must be the woman I've been trailing for fucking miles. I think I'm pleased to meet you – at last."

Sabrina said nothing and just glared at him.

He pointed the gun past us toward the bar. "And you, who are you?"

Monica walked out from behind it and stood next to me. She stared at Lennon with impressive defiance. "I'm the one you want to be talking to if you want to know more about what the hell is going on here. And that drive won't start World War three by the way, it'll stop it."

"Fair enough," said Lennon with a shrug. He looked over at the bar. His eyes flickered as he noticed the drive sitting there next to Monica's purse. To be fair, he played things very cool. "Why don't we grab all our crap, go upstairs and get to know one another. Let's see what's going on here."

He beckoned us toward the stairs so we grabbed our crap and made our way, single file, to the upper level. I trailed behind the ladies in a feeble attempt to offer some masculine protection but, all along, the phrase 'out of the frying pan and into the fire' rattled through my mind.

CHAPTER TWENTY-SIX

1 4:02:47.

The clock continued its count down, precise and relentless, the red digital figures folding in on themselves to create a constantly decreasing number. In less than a day, all of the pieces would be in place. Beck knew the end result; devastation of the Middle East and a new world order, or untold riches and the means to engage his private war.

He studied the maps of each region displayed on the screens hung around the room. Green dots peppered each one. Each dot represented an unmanned drone, either swimming, flying or buried underground, all occupying the route that they'd been programmed to take. Right now, most of them were harmless chunks of metal and wire, circling and waiting or moving into position. When the program ran, every one of them would be armed and instructed to unleash their payloads at specific targets. Blanket devastation, much like carpet bombings he'd witnessed in many war zones, but with much more power and precision.

In the hunt for the drive, the antidote to The Consortium's virus, Molito was proving his worth. He already had one bogey dispatched and the others about to follow. In hindsight, Beck knew that he'd underestimated his foe. He'd sent the best-trained men he had, but for something as important as this, they were insufficient. Still, if he'd sent anything more obvious, more substantial, watching eyes would have been alerted. Questions would have been asked, the kind that would be answered during a brief meeting in a dark alley with a couple of hollow point .22 rounds. He couldn't second-guess earlier plans. They were dust in the wind now. There was nothing else they could do but plan for the future.

Jones was still sitting in the same seat. He looked tired, but the dark rings below his eyes lifted as he offered a positive wave and a smile that Beck mirrored. A full day in the dark room had taken its toll on the young soldier, but the payday he'd been promised would make it all worthwhile. He had no idea what the countdown related to, or what would happen when the flashing numbers reached zero, but Beck assured him that he was safe.

Beck subscribed to the point of view that, if you paid peanuts, you got monkeys. Jones earned a lot of money. Just as he had in the Gulf, he did his job and he asked no questions. When the time came, Beck would rely on him to operate one of the two workstations and turn the other key required to run the program. Once the program kicked in, it would be a matter of seconds before fire rained down. Hundreds of missiles would dance through the air, falling from the sky or breaking the surface tension of the oceans to rise from the seas. Heavy machinery fitted with SonicAmerica's technology would cut through and level whole cities further inland, in the areas beyond the range of the missiles. Then the new world would begin. Power would shift and Beck would become a king amongst men.

He blinked and broke the hypnotic hold of the myriad of flashing lights and shifting patterns on the screens. Despite the losses incurred in the build up to this day, the finale was almost here. His adrenaline surged as he clenched his fists against his sides to control his emotions. In less than one day, one way or another, millions of people would perish and the Middle East would cease to exist.

He could hardly wait.

CHAPTER TWENTY-SEVEN

W e sat around the kitchen table. Sabrina and I sat back in our chairs while Monica hunched forward. Her blouse concealed the pistol's bulge in the rear of her belt. Lennon moved to the front door, glanced around, and returned as if he'd misplaced something. He went to peer through the kitchen window.

"Something's wrong," he said. "Look, I'll explain later but right now I need you to know that I'm not the enemy. I had a partner outside guarding the front door. Now, he's gone."

"What, gone because he was bored, or gone because he's dead?" I said.

"He wouldn't leave his post. There are no signs of a struggle or blood, though. Something happened to us a while back. Those guys that were chasing you? They tried to ambush us in the forest."

"Hang on," said Sabrina, "I thought you were chasing us. Those drones weren't yours?"

"I don't know about any drones," said Lennon. He nodded in my direction and pulled a cell phone from his pocket. "We were following your phone signal until we lost it. Then we were ambushed. They left this behind."

He waved the phone in the air and then passed it across the table. I swiped the screen to reveal a GPS map. I recognized the region right away. A red dot hovered in the center of the screen. It might as well have been sitting at the table with us.

"Wait, we've had two groups tracking us?" I asked.

"It seems that way, although I had no idea until we bumped into them. Listen, can we leave the back-story for a moment and find my partner? We need my partner and trust me, if I was a threat to you, you'd already be dead by now."

"And you say that in such a reassuring tone," I said, "but you have a point. So what are you saying? There are more bad guys out there?"

"Just one, I think," said Lennon. "A sniper. He killed two colleagues of mine. I killed one of his. It's safe to assume he has a phone like the one you're holding. In which case, he's outside. Weston, my partner, was keeping watch on the front porch. Now, he's not."

"We have no weapons," I said, stating the obvious, "so what would you like us to do, curse him to death?"

The three of us looked at each other as if we expected one of us to turn into a Navy Seal. I didn't want to mention Monica's pistol in case he was talking crap, although he seemed to be genuine. He'd already let down his guard more than I expected. Wooden floor legs scraped across the floor as Monica stood.

"I have weapons," she said. Monica was our Navy Seal.

"Good," said Lennon. "Let's see what you've got."

"They're in a safe behind the closet door," she said. "You okay if I move back there to open it?"

"Go ahead," said Lennon. "Now would be a good time for us to start trusting one another. I'll go first. My name's Lennon, by the way."

Monica moved around the table and walked into the closet's shadow. I leaned forward and watched her through the crack in the door. A tall gun safe was built into the drywall behind the closet door. She pressed her thumb against the small glass window of a biometric scanner. The door's locking mechanism clicked, the sound barely audible in the kitchen. As she reached for the handle a louder, abrupt noise broke the sound of comfortable chatter.

Then all hell broke loose.

"Everybody, hands in the air!"

Monica froze in the darkness of the closet, as the claustrophobic confines shifted around her. Panic rose in her throat, her head swam and she lost her balance and began to fall toward the door. She thrust her arm out into the shadow, snagged the handle of the safe door and steadied herself, then peeked through the crack of light into the kitchen.

At first, she saw the same three people sitting at the table with their hands at shoulder height. The first couple looked ashen faced with shock and fear. The new guy looked pissed off. A tall man in a black tee shirt and denim jeans sidled into view, and side stepped with precision until he stood with his back to her. She could still see the second man, Lennon, but the other two were now hidden. The tall man spoke.

"That's it? That's the piece of shit drive all this crap is over?"

Lennon said nothing, his face impassive and stone like. One of the others must have reacted.

"Toss it here. Now."

Someone threw him the drive. He slid it into the back pocket of his jeans, and then pivoted to his left in order to face Lennon.

"And you. You're the fucker that killed my partner. I'll save you for last. All of you get up and move against the wall."

The girl spoke in a voice so defiant that Monica braced herself for a shot. "If you're going to kill us, at least grow some balls and do it like a man. I'm not kneeling for anyone."

The tall guy laughed. "You're not Beck's wife, that's for sure. I checked up here, so I assume she's still tied up downstairs. She can listen to you begging for a while. It might soften her up."

Monica tensed, both scared and insulted. So this guy knew Beck. She reached behind her back and pulled out the pistol, then slid her feet into a more comfortable position. It was clear to her that he was the enemy. The couple and the new guy were at the very least the enemy of her enemy, which made them her friends. She watched as he swung again to the right and his shoulders bunched as he lifted his arms. He was about to shoot.

All of her training told her to aim for center mass. No risky head-shots or incapacitating shots to the legs. Aim for the part you couldn't miss. The irony of it all was hilarious. Kyle had taught her how to shoot and she had become very proficient. His training would be the thing that stopped him, at least for now. She pulled back on the hammer of the gun to fire a round. As it clinked, the guy spun to face her. She panicked, but got off her shot before he made a complete turn and hit him directly in the butt. He frowned for a second, right before he collapsed like a sack of potatoes onto the kitchen floor.

CHAPTER TWENTY-EIGHT

I sat frozen like one of those street performance artists as he turned to face me. In a split second I forgot how to breathe, although my heartbeat did its best to remind me. The perfect black circle of the business end of a gun barrel pointed right at me. It looked like a cannon.

The guy came in through the back door but, over the noise of our conversation, none of us heard him. Before we knew it, he stood in front of us. We were at gunpoint, all seated and all unarmed. Monica had just left to get something to arm us with. The Karma Gods hated me.

He looked like the kind of guy that went through school with no friends, with a face frozen in the snarled position. I could tell he didn't care for me and he hardly glanced at Sabrina. When he looked at Lennon, hatred swam around in his eyes like oil on water. It wasn't rocket science; this was the sniper he'd mentioned.

There was a brief conversation and, as the grim reaper sharpened his scythe and I braced myself to see my life flash before me, the guy reacted to a scuff behind him. None of us moved, but he spun and almost faced the closet before his hip shot forward and he folded in on himself and collapsed. I swear he bounced twice on his ass.

Lennon leaped out of his chair as if it was electrified, leaned over the guy, and punched him squarely on the jaw as his head lolled from side to side. It was a punch befitting a heavyweight champion, and the guy went limp right away and lay crashed out like a corpse. The closet door swung open in slow motion, and Monica appeared from the darkness, the color drained from her face. She shook and held a pistol out in front of her. Sabrina took it from her and laid it on the table. Lennon let out a nervous laugh and clapped Monica on the shoulder.

"That's the first time I've seen a shot in the ass take a man down," he said. "What the hell were you packing?"

He knelt beside the prone body, rolled the tall guy over and reached toward his back pocket, then jerked back as if his hand had brushed against a snake. The feathery tuft of a dart bloomed from the guy's butt. Lennon plucked it, held it in front of his face, and stared as if he'd discovered a new species of insect. Monica stepped out into the kitchen, took the dart from him, and placed it next to her pistol on the table.

"Tranquilizer dart," she said. I could tell that she was forcing her voice through a wavy filter of nerves, trying to make it sound stronger than it should have. "Kyle had them formulated. They can take down an elephant in a minute, so a regular guy will drop like a stone instantly. When he first broke in, it was the only gun I could get without spooking them. Plus, I don't know if I have it in me to shoot another human being." She glanced at Lennon. "Nice punch, though. If this doesn't make us a team, I don't know what will."

Lennon shook his head and stood upright. "What the fuck have I got myself in to?" He wiped his hands, all business, and moved back to the table. "Okay team, we need something to tie this guy up with. Oh, I almost forgot. The drive."

He stooped once more, rummaged through the man's rear pocket, and slowly produced a pile of broken plastic and metal. He shook his head again. The drive was smashed.

"It's useless. Now what do we do?"

I glanced at Sabrina. She looked crushed.

"Didn't you say that the drive is the only thing that can stop the violence your husband has planned?"

Monica opened her mouth to answer but stopped when, somewhere on the guy's lifeless body, a cellphone rang.

We all looked at one another, and waited for someone to step up and take the lead. Sabrina stood and moved to the center of the kitchen. She looked at Lennon.

"Well, don't just stand there. Don't you think that someone should answer that?"

In their entire time working together, Bell and Molito always checked in with Beck with trained military precision. They never missed their appointed time.

Kyle Beck walked the rounded corridors of the control center again. Bell had already checked in for the last time. Molito was now thirty minutes late. Protocols demanded that Beck wait for the call or assume the worst, but losing his friend and the pressure of the ticking clock had him on edge. He walked past the center room and carded his way into the next section of the facility.

The doors in this section remained open to all the facility's occupants. Through the first door he reached lay a kitchen. It looked like it belonged in a prison, decked out with steel tables bolted to the floor. Pretty close, thought Beck.

No one would get very far, even if they managed to open one of the outside hatches that allowed access onto the circular path he was walking. Two men leaned against a buffet bar at the far end of the room and watched a video on the screen behind it. They'd probably seen it a hundred times already. Beck knew the video from start to finish. Cartoon characters explained the value of the work they did here, the research into the Earth's resources and how it benefited the planet they all loved. It kept up morale and worked to allay the effects of claustrophobia that came from working in the submarine-like conditions. The video didn't mention the control room, or Dave Jones sitting in the central room surrounded by the circular wall of screens with the maps and the green dots. Or the digital clock that was still counting down time. Few keycards opened that door.

The room next to the kitchen was filled with storage racks designed to hold a year's supply of food. They were lined up in rows that rose from floor to ceiling like roof supports. A door in the side-wall opened into the kitchen to allow a chef access to both rooms. Beck stepped into this room and closed the door behind him. His gold-fish bowl of an office was too visible for this phone call. He palmed his phone and pressed a speed dial button. The dial tone chirped in his ear.

Molito was efficient and not prone to time wasting. He answered his calls as soon as the ring tone began. The tone dialed again. And again. No answer. Beck's stomach tightened with each ring but, just as he was about to give up, the call connected. He said one word.

"Report."

Silence, followed by an airy echo. Then a woman's voice spoke.

"Who is this?"

Beck froze. The wheels in his head turned at double speed and he considered disconnecting the call, but realized that it would achieve nothing. He was safe where he was, and besides, he needed information.

"You first," he said. "It's only fair since I called you."

There was more silence until a different woman's voice spoke. From the echo, he could tell that he was on speakerphone.

"I'd recognize that accent anywhere. You bastard! You left me to die!"

Beck also recognized the voice at the other end of the line. He laughed.

"Oh shit, it's the wife! I'm sorry babe. You shouldn't take it personally. Anyway, you should've got shit faced on wine and shuffled off in style. I have to say, though, I'm impressed. How did you get Molito's phone? You shag him and then stab him while he slept?"

"You've put me off men for a while, you worthless piece of crap. I figured you'd send someone to finish the job. Hate to break it to you 'babe', but he's lying on the floor in front of us. His days of working for you are over."

Beck fought the urge to unleash a torrent of abuse. His team was finished; so retrieving the drive was no longer an option.

"Us? So I have an audience, do I? Hello everyone. Come on then, what you done to my mate? I'm guessing he didn't get the drive?"

Another voice joined the conversation, a male voice.

"The drive's destroyed, you piece of shit."

"Oh. Hello. Well, that's a shame mate. It would have been useful. Still, we move forward regardless. Where there's a will there's a way, onwards and upwards and all that. So, who might you be?"

"I'm someone that's going to take you out. Let me hazard a guess – you work for The Consortium, right?"

Beck was caught off guard, for a moment, at the mention of his employers. "It doesn't matter who I work for. You can shove your confidence where the sun don't shine. It won't be long before you're living in a different world to the one you're dreaming in now. In the meantime, I'll be on an island living off the interest. Now, as you Americans say, go fuck yourself and have a nice day."

Beck disconnected the call and placed the phone on a wire shelf, then spun and slammed his fist into a huge bag of flour. White powder plumed into the air as he screamed at the wall.

CHAPTER TWENTY-NINE

We sat and stared in disbelief at the silent phone sitting on the kitchen table. Sabrina looked different, now dressed in one of Monica's blouses to replace the one I'd torn trying to prevent her fall down the stairs. She looked up at Monica and spoke first.

"So, that was your wonderful husband?"

Monica shrugged her shoulders and pulled a face that said 'What was I thinking?'

"Well," she said, "soon to be ex-husband."

"Okay. Well, I have to say, your soon to be ex-husband sounds like a complete dick."

"To be honest with you, since I've got to know him better, I've come to the same conclusion. He is a complete dick, hence the soon to be ex part."

"Ladies," said Lennon, "I hate to break up the marriage guidance discussion, but why don't we secure this guy. Then we can get our heads together and try to work out what's going on here?"

"Drag him downstairs," said Monica. "He can take my old seat."

Ten minutes later, the tall guy was zip tied to a chair, while we leaned against the bar and shared a bottle of wine. If I'd seen this on

TV, I'd say this group of people gelled way too easily. The reactions of each person, to the situations we'd been through, showed we were on the same page. Trust was earned, not given.

I was the first to state the obvious. "So, without that flash drive we can't stop what's going to happen, right? Can we contact a government office or law enforcement or the Feds?" I glanced at Lennon. "The real Feds. No offense."

"None taken," said Lennon.

"There's good news and bad news on that count," said Monica. "You already know the bad news. The people Beck works for, The Consortium, are powerful and far-reaching. They've got people in all walks of life working for them. They're in the military, law enforcement, they're politicians, judges. And they're all faceless. We can't trust anyone but ourselves. That's the bad news. Now for the good news."

She pushed herself up from the bar and grabbed a stool, carried it over to the far wall and placed it against a large wine rack. I looked at the others and they looked back at me, each as baffled as I was. Monica clambered up onto the stool, swayed for a moment, and used the wall for balance. She wiped away a spider web that hung across the top corner of the rack, pulled out a bottle and reached in with her other arm. When she pulled her arm back out, she turned with a smile and showed us a small object gripped between thumb and forefinger.

She had another drive.

"Lesson number one kids," she said. "Always, always back up your important information."

She placed the drive on the bar and sat down again. "Okay," she said, "let's compare notes. I learned quite a bit from Kyle's Scooby moment. I've mentioned The Consortium. They're all seeing, powerful and control way more than one group should. They figure that a new war in the Middle East will cause a massive rise in the price of oil. You won't be surprised to hear that there are oil barons in The Consortium. Oil prices and the price of fuel will skyrocket. It's like a monopoly, they can charge as much as they want since we can't do without it. Politicians and governors will rake in the tax dollars too. Don't forget the military is pulling out of Iraq and Afghanistan. Those boys and girls will be right back in there, keeping the troops occupied and the arms sales constant. At the next election, the politicians seen to be doing something about the war will win votes and extra terms in office. And The Consortium will pull the strings and make sure their people are in all the right places."

"And drones will cause all of this?" I said.

"Don't underestimate how many of those things are out there. Just the devices that control the equipment using our programs can cause a ridiculous amount of damage. The panic alone would cause so many casualties I can't bear thinking about it. One knee jerk reaction and it's all over."

"Okay," said Sabrina. "So these drones are everywhere and your husband has a program to turn them into Decepticons or something. We have a program that can plant a virus to stop it. The big question is where do we plug the drive in to plant the virus?"

"Well..." said Monica, and then she paused. She looked around at us and continued. "This might sound crazy, but I think he's on a ship in the Atlantic Ocean."

I reached into my pocket and pulled out the business card I'd found on the hotel room floor what seemed like a lifetime ago. I placed it on the bar next to the drive.

"It doesn't sound crazy at all. This belongs to you, right?"

Monica looked at Sabrina again with narrowed eyes. Sabrina held up her hands. "Sorry. Again."

"Do you guys have anything else of mine?" asked Monica.

"Well," said Sabrina, "let's not get off track. I'll explain everything later."

We hadn't mentioned the country house yet. We owed Monica an alarm panel, a jewelry box, and another flash drive. She owed us an explanation. I interrupted to get the conversation moving again.

"I ran those numbers as coordinates," I said, "and it placed them a couple hundred miles off the east coast. Where did you get them?"

"Kyle was always secretive when he was on the phone at home and it made me curious. He jotted those numbers down on a note pad one night and hid the page when I walked in on him. He did it like he was hiding an affair or something. The pressure of the pen left an impression on the page underneath. I scrubbed it with the blunt edge of a pencil, like when you're doing rubbings, and wrote them down on the first thing I could find."

"That's very Girl Scout of you," said Lennon. He pointed to the card. "What are the other numbers, a safe combination?"

"That was my first thought too, but I have no idea," said Monica. "I've typed them into search engines so many times they're burned into my mind now. I don't even need the card anymore. So, that's it. You know what I know."

Sabrina spoke next and mentioned her efforts at trying to work out what the numbers meant. I had nothing to add since I'd just been tagging along with her. We all turned to Lennon. He planted the palms of his hands on the bar as if he was steadying himself for a big confession.

"I suspect I work for The Consortium too, not that I knew about it. I was never told any more than was needed to complete a mission. There is one thing I do know. We don't have much time. They've brought everything forward. I'm sure this whole thing is going live tomorrow. Since we have nothing else to go on, we might as well assume that those numbers are a secret location. Which begs the question; how the hell do we get from here to the Atlantic Ocean by tomorrow?"

Vince Molito heard every word of the conversation. The ties that bound his hands were tight and dug into the skin around his wrists, but he fought the urge to writhe and move. Instead, he sat slumped with his eyes closed and listened. Someone would say something he'd be able to use once he broke free.

There was a moment when one of them moved to within inches of his seat and retrieved an object from a shelf or something beside him. He kept his eyes closed, but from what they said it sounded like another drive. Since he felt no pressure in his butt pocket, he had to assume that the original was gone. A replacement would be good enough to get to Beck. His wrists may have been tied, but both ankles rested loosely between the legs of the chair. The urge to stand and barge into them with it almost overwhelmed him, but his discipline held out. The sucker punch to his ass was just as humiliating as the one to his chin. Someone would pay. Also, he still had a score to settle with the guy who claimed to work for The Consortium. He just had to wait for the right time.

Most of the conversation was old news, but the mention of the Atlantic came as a shock. Despite the trust that existed between them, Beck never mentioned his location to anyone. Molito hadn't even known where he lived, until he received the coordinates to come here for the woman. He'd never heard Beck mention a ship of any kind either, although he knew from experience that Beck was an expert swimmer and diver, just at home under water as he was on land. The whole idea seemed too far-fetched to be true, but they'd pieced together enough of the other facts to plant a tiny seed of doubt in his mind.

He opened his eyes a fraction of an inch and moved them enough to view the room through the blur of his eyelashes. They'd secured him against a huge wine rack while the others sat across the room at a bar. A staircase ran up the far wall, presumably the one they'd dragged him down after the cheap shot in the kitchen.

Beck's wife sat behind the bar, facing him while the others sat with their backs to him. Two men and two women. How sweet. None of them seemed to be armed. With the element of surprise, he could take care of them and get the mission back on track. He needed to be patient and wait for the right moment, for them to leave the room and go upstairs so he could look around and find something to cut his ties.

They'd taken him by surprise earlier and he was outnumbered. But he had something they didn't. They'd left him alive, so these people lacked the coldness it took to kill the enemy. They'd pay for that.

CHAPTER THIRTY

We sat around the kitchen table and hammered out a crude plan. It was hard not knowing what time The Consortium would unleash their drones. We knew we had ten and a half hours until midnight at the location of the coordinates, so we made that our deadline. Ten and a half hours to get to the east coast and then, as Sabrina put it, borrow a fast boat, get to those coordinates and find that ship.

I had this image in my mind of a huge warship anchored offshore. Its turrets pointed at the sky in defense, with a control room above it bristling with technology and a large red button, isolated and waiting for Beck to press it. Lennon pointed out that with the vast array of satellites spinning around above us, he could be sitting in a little rowboat with a laptop. Either way, I had to find a way to tell everyone the one thing that concerned me more than the size of Beck's ship. I hated water. I could barely swim. There'd better be water wings where we were going.

Monica was full of surprises. As soon as she mentioned that Beck owned a single prop plane, I remembered the picture on her flash drive of her sitting in a cockpit giving the camera the thumbs up. Once her parents passed away, she lost herself in all kinds of outdoor pursuits to focus her mind and work through her grief. She earned a pilot's license and had the basic ability to fly the plane. We just had to get into a local airfield to get to it.

"And you're sure you can fly it all the way to the east coast?" I asked.

"I'm sure I can get us airborne, and I can program the GPS. The main problem will be getting into the hangar. I'm sure there's more going on there than meets the eye. They have security everywhere, and it's not like we can crash through the gates Dukes of Hazzard style. The longer we can keep everything quiet, the more chance we have of reaching our destination before the bad guys are onto us. We'll need to take weapons too. We won't get those past regular guards."

That was when Lennon stood and flashed his FBI badge. It turned out to be a cheap tin replica, but it fooled me earlier. Predictably, it hadn't fooled Sabrina.

"Any personnel worth an average paycheck would see right through that," she said. It was clear that she was still annoyed at his earlier behavior.

Lennon smiled. "Some of the security guys at these small airfields are like rent-a-cops. They relax after a while because most of the people passing through are local folks. Just be confident and act the part. This badge carries more power than you'd think, tin or not. I'll get us in and Monica can get us to the coast. After that, the real fun starts. We need to get a boat with a decent GPS to find Beck's ship. That begs the question, how do we scour a harbor for a sufficient boat without attracting attention?"

We batted ideas back and forth before Sabrina stood and walked to the door. "I have an idea. Be right back." She ran outside and returned with her bag of tricks and the drone she'd commandeered a couple of days ago in West Virginia. "If I can reprogram this thing, we can stay out of sight while we take a look around for suitable transport."

She pulled various tools from the bag and then called her 'mentor'. After the briefest of conversations, she linked the drone with her laptop and followed his instruction. We stood around dumbstruck like a group of medical students watching their first autopsy. With the help of one of Beck's Xbox controllers and some technical wizardry, they re-configured its software to give her full control of it. It only took five minutes of shaky test flight in the yard outside before she'd mastered the controls. It buzzed around the property like an angry wasp with its camera beaming the image of our waving arms back to her laptop in the kitchen.

The whole plan hinged on too many 'what ifs' but, since we had no alternative, we plowed ahead anyway. We kitted ourselves out with Monica's weapons, some of which fired real bullets, not tranquilizer darts. Then I asked the group to give me a moment. I needed to make an important call.

There was never a time when I would win the Father of the Year award. I married my ex-wife right out of college and gained the added responsibility of a baby girl within a year. When we married, I thought that marriage should be a team effort, a limited company of two dedicated employees. Once we were working together, I found that I preferred to be the manager and delegate everything. Don't get me wrong, I always put food in the fridge, the bills were paid on time, and the family never went without. I gave them everything they could want. Except a partner and a father.

I never sat on a grassy bank with other parents to watch my daughter run along a field with an egg balanced on a spoon, or jump across the same field while standing in a flour sack. I never heard the teachers say how well she did in her lessons, or how she mixed with the other kids. She never sat on my knee while I read her a story before bedtime, and she never handed me her cute paintings after school. I only saw them taped to the side of the fridge when I got home every Friday night. My life was work, work, work. And avoidance. Work was much easier than parenting.

It didn't take long for my absences from home to drive my wife into someone else's arms. The fact that those arms belonged to my best friend didn't make things any easier. It's amazing how much a mind can wander when there's nothing to distract it. Suddenly, in one hotel room or another, I had plenty of time to kill. Plenty of time to think. And I thought about my daughter.

I made a conscious effort to reconnect with Kacie. For a while, I called every other day to check in on her schoolwork and whatever else she was up to. Every other weekend we went to the park or to the movies. Then work got busy and the same thing happened again.

Kids are much smarter than adults in some respects. A serial cheat will make the same mistake repeatedly. Gamblers and alcoholics grow addicted to destructive lifestyles and fall in love with the very thing that will destroy them. But you can only wrong kids once. They learn the heavy stuff first time around.

I'd spent the last twelve months trying to win back my daughter for a second time. It turned out that the distrust she had of my efforts taught her to recognize my distrust in pretty much everything in my life. As a result, our conversations always got around to my single status. She'd reached the age where boys would be a factor, although I hadn't yet plucked up the courage to broach that subject. Still, it gave her the confidence to broach the subject with me. After a while, she pointed out my stupid excuses and the obvious roadblocks I'd throw up every time I mentioned someone in particular. She became my therapist and make me pinkie swear I'd let her help me get over my 'affliction' as she called it.

While Sabrina sat at the table in Monica's kitchen to perform surgery on her drone, I looked at the motley crew sitting with her. It occurred to me that, if this went wrong, no one around the table had anyone to miss them. Lennon and Sabrina both had jobs that left them isolated, and Monica was an only child. I was the only one who might be missed if anything extreme happened. Whilst running around like a crazy person, being chased from state to state, I hadn't taken a moment to consider how dangerous the past few days were. I could have been shot at any moment and I hadn't said goodbye to my girl. The next few hours were about to be even worse, but if I wanted a decent world for Kacie then I had to be involved.

As a group, we decided that no one was chasing us anymore, at least not for now. I excused myself and stepped out onto Monica's porch, pulled out my phone and called my daughter.

CHAPTER THIRTY-ONE

"Hi Dad, what's up?"

I jumped. Caller I.D. is something I doubt I'll ever get used to. There's a whole generation that will never feel the anticipation, or the dread depending on your lifestyle, of picking up that huge brick of plastic to answer an old fashioned, screwed into the wall telephone with no idea who was calling. And there was no sending any unwanted calls to voicemail either.

"Hi baby, I'm just checking in. What are you up to?"

"Just getting ready to go for Sunday lunch with Matthew. You okay?"

My father's 'boyfriend-sense' started to tingle. That was a new name. A new male name. "Oh? Who's Matthew?"

"You don't have to worry Dad," came back the world-weary sound of a teenager who was expecting such a question. There were things that every generation did know. "Mom is going with us too."

"Okay, that's cool. How's your week been? School okay?"

"Everything's the same, Dad. Same old same old. What's up with you? You sound different."

Damn, she was so observant. I wish I knew my daughter as well as she knew me. I shook my head as years of passed opportunities tugged at my stomach and a jumble of lost moments forced a watery blur into my eyes.

"Well, I'm going on a trip, honey. Do you remember when we watched that movie Armageddon? The one where the little boy sees his Dad doing something heroic on TV, even though all along he didn't think he'd amount to much?"

Silence.

I had to get this out of me before I lost it. "Well, I've stumbled onto something important. I'm with a group of people who are going to try to stop some bad people from doing some awful things."

More silence, and then, "Dad...have you joined a cult?"

Trust a kid to bring things down to ground level. "What? No honey, I didn't join a cult. I can't give you too many details, but I've realized that I don't talk to you enough. We need to spend more time together. I mean to make that right as soon as I get back and I wanted to tell you how much I love you."

I heard Kacie's breath catch in her throat. "Dad, you're scaring me. What's going on, really?"

"Well, hopefully you won't see me on TV going into space," I said with as much humor as I could manage. "I'm sure everything will be fine, Kace. I'm with a group of people who are very good at what they do. When I get back we're going on vacation together, okay? Somewhere hot and sunny."

It was the first thing that came to mind, but once I'd said it I wondered why I'd never said it before. No more taking life for granted. It was too short. Kacie sounded like she wished I'd said it years before too.

"That's a cast iron deal, Dad. I'm holding you to that."

I caught a blur of movement through the windows. The group in the kitchen was gathering around the table again.

"Honey, I have to go. I love you, okay? I'll talk to you soon. Go and give your Mom a hug for me too, will you?"

"Of course I will Dad. What happened to you, did you drink something weird?" She burst out laughing before she sang 'Byeeeeee' down the line. It was music to my ears, but I tried to speak through it anyway.

"Take care Kace. Love you. I…"

The innocent chiming of her laughter ended abruptly as she disconnected the call. I ran my fingers through my hair, wiped my eyes and went back inside to join the others. Everyone looked up at me as I walked into the kitchen. I must have looked like I'd walked face first into a heavy wind.

"You okay?" frowned Sabrina.

"Yeah, I'll be fine," I said with a wave of my hand. "What did I miss?"

"Not much," said Lennon. "We were debating which vehicle to take to the airfield. We figured we'd better take Monica's since mine is bound to be tagged, and yours - well it's not really yours, is it?"

"That's a good point. Do we have everything we need?"

"No. We need the FBI or the police, but we'll make do with what we've got." He beckoned toward the kitchen closet. "Before we leave, we should check on the bastard tied up downstairs. We don't want him giving any advance notice of our little trip to the bad guys. I could just kill him. Be much easier."

"No more killing," said Sabrina. "There's been enough of that. I know people who can take care of him and make sure he doesn't bother us but let's get some distance between us first. Come on, let's check his ties."

We followed her down the stairs and kept a close eye on Lennon. He wanted revenge and didn't attempt to hide it. The guy was still trussed to the chair although now he was wide-awake and glared at us with contempt.

"You're all dead," he spat. His eyes flitted to look at each of us. "It's just a matter of time."

"Yeah, yeah, whatever," said Lennon. "You're on a death list yourself as it is, so just be grateful these people have more compassion than I do. I'd like nothing more than to slit your throat and listen to you choke on your blood."

The man spat in our direction and thrust his chin in the air in defiance. "Choke on that."

I grabbed Lennon's arm as he lunged forward and pulled him back. He yanked his arm away from me and stomped like an angry teenager over to the bar. "You check him. I'll break his fucking neck if I get near him."

Sabrina observed everything with interest while Monica stayed back behind her. I could tell she hadn't had much experience with serious confrontation. You can shoot at as many targets as you like, but unless they shoot back you'll only know attack. Not defense.

I strode with purpose toward the guy in a desperate attempt to show no fear and knelt beside the chair. He sat there as if he was getting ready to enjoy a beer. I checked the zip-ties around his wrists. They were still locked tight. Had it been me in the chair, my wrists would have been chafed or cut to ribbons. His showed no signs of distress as if he hadn't moved an inch. He was either very calm or he was well trained. Neither thought filled me with glee. I was just glad he was tied to a chair. He watched me with complete indifference. The bar lights glinted in his cold eyes. He looked confident that he'd stand up and walk out of the house as soon as we left. Their corners tilted at the smallest hint of a smile, even though the rest of his face was frozen in a mask of hatred. A shiver ran through me as I stood and turned to face the others. Something had changed. Someone was missing from the group.

Lennon had vanished.

CHAPTER THIRTY-TWO

Anger is an emotion that is dealt with in different ways, by different people. The best way to deal with it is to not get into a position where you'd experience it in the first place. However, if left with no choice, it's not an emotion to leave festering. Anything that continues to heat unchecked will either burst into flames, burn dry, or boil over. Cal Lennon knew his limits. He was about to boil over, so he left the house and stepped outside onto the front porch.

It wasn't about the men he'd lost this week. Other than Weston, he'd never gained an attachment to anyone. He had to assume that Weston was dead; otherwise the guy downstairs would be lying outside in a pool of blood. Weston was as close to an attachment as he'd formed in years. Even then they were like office coworkers that spent eight hours a day in separate cubicles, not two men that covered each other's backs and depended on one another for life.

It wasn't the group of people he'd fallen in with either. For a bunch of civilians, they seemed to be switched on. They had a decent combination of attributes he could command, to give them a slight chance of pulling this mission off. It also seemed that both women were made of sterner stuff than Howard, but then Howard had stepped up to check on the bastard downstairs.

And there it was. The bastard downstairs. The cause of his anger. Not the man himself, but that this man got the upper hand on him. Twice. If it weren't for an opportune shot with a tranquilizer dart, he would have been bested once at the ambush in the forest, and again here in the kitchen. The guy was good, but he had an arrogance that demanded to be smashed out of him. It was all Lennon could do to walk away.

Sabrina was right, there was enough killing, although he knew they might have more to do. People with plans as large as these would stop at nothing to make sure that, win or lose, they saw them through to the end.

He stepped off the porch and walked around the back of the building away from the road. The house sat on beautiful land. If he survived long enough, he could retire to a place like this, away from people and the hassles of city life. As he turned the corner, he stopped short. His eyes followed the line of the wooden deck boards that stretched away from him in perfect formation. Trinkets and flowers dotted along its length, but at the far end of the porch, bundled into the opposite corner, something broke the line. A huddle of clothing. He recognized the huddle and the sandy hair that lay among it and began the somber walk to confirm his fears.

There was no pooling blood, which meant Weston's death was quick. His heart had stopped beating soon after the fork than ran through the back of his neck had disconnected the signals from his brain to his torso. Anger rose again as he saw the disrespectful hand marks swiped across his colleague's jacket, his body painted with his blood. Lennon lifted his head and screamed. He felt the veins in his neck stretch and pop as he tried to vent the anger and frustration from his body. Then he stood and rushed toward the front door in a seething mass of fury.

Howard and Sabrina met him at the corner and grabbed him.

"What?" said Howard. "What is it?"

Lennon pointed back at the porch. They glanced past him and grimaced.

"Your partner?" said Sabrina.

He nodded and pushed against them. They held firm until he relaxed a little. Sabrina placed a hand on his arm. "Please," she said, "no more killing. Let's pay them back by stopping them."

"She's right," said Howard. "Look, I'm not stupid. I'm sure we have tough times ahead of us. Channel the anger and use it to our advantage. The guy downstairs is worthless. He's just a tool. Save your anger for when we get to the ship. Save it for the big guy. Then we'll be right behind you and you can let it all out."

He looked between the two of them and, as his eyes misted, he shrugged himself clear of his captors and slouched to the vehicle parked outside the house.

Monica's ride turned out to be an SUV, black, sleek and kitted out with more gadgets than a stealth fighter. It was like home for Lennon, from one imposing vehicle to another. He looked comfortable as we left him to calm down behind the tinted glass.

The two back seats dropped flat and gave us plenty of room to load the hardware we each had, which was enough to carry out an Ocean's Eleven heist. As I turned to head back to the kitchen, a flash of light caught my eye. I stared at the house. Nothing appeared out of place, but when I turned back, the flash blinked again in the same place. Sabrina walked toward me with her laptop and the drone.

"I saw something at the side of the house," I said. "Hang on here while I check it out, would you?"

She nodded and loaded her items in the trunk as I walked over to the building. Still nothing appeared to be out of place. Monica did a great job of maintaining the property, which reminded me to ask her about the country house we'd 'visited' earlier. She was going to find out sooner or later, I might as well broach the subject and tell her we owed her an alarm panel.

As I grew closer, a sliver of black peeked out at me from under the bottom of the railing. At first I thought it was a snake, but when there was no movement I crouched and slid it toward me. The flash was the sun reflecting off the glass lens of a riflescope. The scope's cover must have been dragged off when our friend downstairs slid it under before coming into the house. I hoisted the gun onto my shoulder and made my way back to the SUV. I was still a distance away before a car door slammed and Lennon jogged toward me.

"Well, that confirms what I suspected," he said as he reached me.

"What would that be?" I asked.

"The guy we've got tied up downstairs. He didn't just kill Weston. He was the sniper that killed my former colleagues. He must've hid this before he came inside for us." He shook his head, but I couldn't work out if it was in disgust or admiration. "One guy took out my entire team. Mind if I take a look at that?" He pointed to the rifle.

I handed it over to him, ready to grab him again if he made a move to get back into the house. "Sure, with pleasure. It weighs a ton."

He hefted it, testing its weight and feel. I was surprised he wasn't more upset as he balanced the stock against his shoulder and looked through the scope.

"So that's the gun that…"

"Yes, it is. Nice gun."

"You don't seem too bothered by it," I said. "You know, if it…"

"Like you said, save the anger. I'm trained to close doors quickly when it comes to loss. When one thing ends, another begins. Close the door and move on."

"Damn, I hate to think how your high school dates went."

"They went better than this," he said, and walked back to the SUV with the rifle. He placed it with something akin to reverence in the trunk with the rest of the arsenal and climbed back into the vehicle. I got in beside him.

Sabrina buckled herself into the passenger seat as Monica appeared on the front porch. She pulled the door closed behind her, then lifted a bundle of keys and searched through them. Then she paused, laughed to herself and walked over to us.

"Doesn't seem to be much point in locking the door," she said. "Every man who visits can pick the damned lock anyway." She shook her head and then frowned. "You know, I had a moment where I doubted I'd ever see this side of that door again. Thank you for finding me, regardless of how you did it." Just as quickly, a smile lit up her face again. "Thinking about it, having a highly trained serial murderer tied up in your basement has to be as good as having a Rottweiler running loose inside, right?"

She bounced into the seat behind the wheel and pushed the key into the ignition.

"About the lock thing," I said. "When we get on the road I have something to tell you about your other property."

Her head spun around Exorcist style. "How do you know about my other property? What did you do?"

"All in good time. Don't worry. It's in good shape. Pretty much. We'll talk when we're rolling. So what's the plan?"

She resigned herself to wait and breathed a deep sigh. "Okay, we need to fly from here to a small airfield in Virginia Beach. It seemed to be the closest airfield I could find to the coordinates we have. That is, if we want to travel as the crow flies. Once we get there, all we have to do is probably fight a small war, commandeer a half decent boat and follow the GPS. How hard could it be?"

"Yeah," I said, "I've heard that before. First things first, we need to get onto the airfield at this end and then you have to get us to Virginia Beach in one piece."

Lennon grabbed a headrest and pulled himself forward. "Don't worry about the airfield, I'll get us in. You be sure to adjust your flaps or whatever you do when you're flying. And anyway, if push comes to shove, I saw a nice stun gun in the trunk. If I can't kill anybody I can at least zap a few folks."

CHAPTER THIRTY-THREE

Lights flickered and danced in the same places. Dave Jones still sat like a robot in the same seat. The green dots on the TV screens still floated like plankton in the ocean, drifting into their assigned positions, and the red digits of the clock continued their relentless fall to zero. Kyle Beck observed it all from the doorway and felt something he hadn't felt since his high school prom.

He remembered walking through the school halls and out onto the grounds, the loud beat of the school band drowned out by the whisper of a prom dress riding up and down the thigh of his date. She led him by the hand past his friends and the chaperones, past the lockers where he kept his text books, and past the main doors of the building and out into the school yard, then around the corner of the building and onto the football field. She dropped to her knees and reached for him, watched only by the dark, unlit floodlights, as his mind tried to convince his body that everything would be perfect. He didn't feel love, or lust, or even excitement. He felt anticipation. The promise of something unknown.

It was amazing.

The clock read 11:26:22.

The red neon digits morphed from twenty-six to twenty-five and still the numbers tumbled. Nothing stopped time. It constantly took and never gave back. Anticipation swooped and flapped like a swarm of butterflies in Beck's stomach, as the deadline grew ever closer. His best plan was finished. It had taken a while, but he had accepted that now. No team meant no drive, and no drive meant that the launch went ahead as planned. There was nothing left to stop it.

He had mourned his team and raised an imaginary glass to them in his mind and toasted their safe trip to whichever hell they were headed. Now it was just a matter of letting the numbers tumble and ensuring that not just the stars, but the drones were aligned at the right time.

Few men could say they had helped to form a new world, a world free from prejudice, from disputes over borders or disagreements over religion. Once the remaining superpowers had launched their weapons and countermeasures, there would be nothing left. Nothing but the new world, stripped of power, a world owned by the people that created it.

The Consortium would be the new kings and queens of every country and, since every country would have no means left to defend themselves, their power would be absolute. Everything would be theirs.

Money brought power. Power brought corruption.

And Beck understood corruption.

"You did what?"

We were traveling toward the local airfield that housed Beck's plane when I plucked up enough courage to mention our visit to Monica's country house. It turned out to be a bad idea, although there'd never be a good time. The SUV swerved as she turned to face Sabrina, but she wrestled with the wheel and returned it to the correct side of the solid lines in the road. Still, given the severity of our mission, it felt good to have a distraction.

"I may have smashed your alarm panel a little bit while we were trying to find you," replied Sabrina, "but it was a necessary evil. And look at the good it did. It did a lot of good. We found you."

The rise in the tone of voice at the end of her sentence did little to allay the wrath of the woman in control of our transport. Her body tensed like a spring. I didn't want to be in the way if it snapped.

"Okay ladies," I said, "let's talk about this. Monica, we looked all over for you. Don't forget, we weren't aware you were a prisoner in your basement, but at least we did everything we could to get to you. And we might've had to, you know, damage a few things to do that."

"So you didn't just smash my alarm panel, but you broke into my safe too? And took my jewelry box? And snooped through my pictures? What happened to privacy?"

"Hey," said Sabrina, "in our defense, we thought you were the bad guy. And, I might add, if we hadn't looked through your pictures you'd still be sitting downstairs at your house. That's assuming, of course, your wonderful husband hadn't already sent someone to kill you. We could have turned up to find your dead body."

I glanced across at Lennon. I'd been concerned about him. I'd only known Sabrina for a few days but, in truth, the other half of our team was even more of a mystery. To see him grinning at the exchange between the two women allayed a few fears. I might have been mistaken, but he may have even had a gleam in his eye when he looked at Monica. It was reassuring to see the death of his colleague hadn't completely derailed him. And somewhat unnerving.

"Okay," said Monica, "I'll give you that, as morbid as that sounds. And I'll admit I appreciate everything you've done so far. I suppose everything can be repaired if and when we get this done."

"So," I asked. "The other house. You own that? It's a beautiful property."

"Thank you," said Monica. "It's my escape. When I took the job at SonicAmerica I was still single, just me and my parents. The company paid me a ridiculous amount of money to do that job. God, I hope I can get my job back after this. Anyway, that house was my first splurge, my escape from being penned in the research facility. I didn't tell Kyle about it, like it was mine and no one else's. Maybe, deep down, I knew something was wrong with him. I did tell my parents. I didn't share it with anyone but them. After they both passed away, I went there less and less. I liked to sit outside and listen to the stream, but there ended up being too many memories I didn't want to deal with."

Lennon leaned forward and placed a hand on her shoulder. "I'm sorry to hear that," he said.

Monica jumped at the unexpected physical contact, but then her shoulders relaxed. Lennon gave the smallest of squeezes, as if offering his support, and sat back in his seat. The weirdest things happened to people in times of extreme pressure.

"My nest egg is there too," she continued. "When you work for these large corporations you get too many eyes peering into your business. Add that to the fact that Kyle began behaving erratically early on in our marriage. I'm sure you can understand why I'd try to get some savings behind me. Since the place is my secret, or was, I thought it would be safe there. I shouldn't have put the address in a notebook. That was a stupid thing to do. I had to write it somewhere though, so I could remember the details while I was sorting out the paperwork. I should have burned that book. And anyway," she said with an accusing glance, "I didn't expect someone to steal it."

Sabrina blushed at the accusation. "I'm sorry," she said. "Like I said before, I was only doing my job. And your nest egg is still safe, locked away. I'll make sure you get everything else back and I left the other place locked. I'm sure it will be fine."

Monica continued the drive in silence as if she'd accepted what happened, at least for now. She turned off the highway and on to a smaller side road that wound for miles down to an even smaller side street that terminated at a fenced in compound.

"Here we are," she said. Her body seemed to shudder. "In this new light it seems kind of foreboding."

We craned our necks to look through the windows at the land ahead of us. A couple hundred yards away, a double gate broke up an otherwise endless wall of tall wire fencing that ran off into the distance as far as we could see. It was topped off with aggressive looking razor wire. The gate was closed with an intimidating lock and also crowned in the deadly wire. A concrete drive rose up and over the brow of a small hill. Shadows moved beyond it.

The top half of one solitary control tower was visible. A red metal radar dish spun smoothly on its roof, casting rhythmic shadows across the backlit windows beneath it. There wasn't a single sign or notice to be seen. It didn't seem like an ordinary airfield.

"Looks more like a P.O.W. camp," said Lennon as he leaned forward again to gaze through the front window.

"It's weird how time and perception can change everything," said Monica. "The last time I was here, I was all laughs, nerves and handshakes. Now it's just nerves."

"Do you know where we're going once we get inside there?" I asked.

"I think so," said Monica. "Once I see the place, we'll be okay. I'm sure of that."

Sabrina reached for her bag of tricks and then looked at each of us in turn. Her eyes burned with a determination I'd never seen before. "We know what's at stake here, right? What we have to do?"

We all nodded in unison.

"Okay. Our journey starts here," she said. "One way or another, this ends in the next few hours. Get what you need from the trunk. I'll get the lock and then let's stop this bastard."

CHAPTER THIRTY-FOUR

A mateurs.

Molito was grateful that his captors seemed to be rushing. They'd tied him to a crappy wooden chair that creaked every time he moved. And he could see light through the door at the top of the stairs. The woman had left it open.

As soon the tires outside rolled away into the distance, he rocked the chair backwards and onto one leg and bounced his weight onto it. The glued wooden joints creaked and groaned as years of stress were brought to bear and their construction weakened. As it loosened, he leaned forward and shifted the weight to the leg at the opposite corner and began the process again. Small cracks sounded as the old joints gave way and wood grated and squeaked against wood. One last round of punishment was all it took before he collapsed to the floor surrounded by the broken limbs of his conquest. He stood and gathered the flailing armrests in front of him and then gripped one of them with both hands. The solid oak edge of the bar didn't budge as he smashed the wooden limb against it. After a few blows it cracked and he snapped the weakened piece in two over his knee. Within seconds, the chair littered the bar floor like kindling.

He made his way up the stairs and paused at the top to listen for any sound. The house was silent. He crept into the kitchen and looked around. Nothing had changed from when he'd stood here earlier. An expensive looking knife rack sat at the side of the sink. He helped himself to one of the mid size knives. The larger hatchet type knives might appear more fearsome but were too bulky to use quickly. This smaller knife was well weighted for swift movement.

His captors had taken their belongings with them. He searched through the house and found what he was looking for in the hallway. A small plastic box, mounted to the baseboard with a narrow wire looping away from it and around the corner. It ended at a good, old-fashioned landline, one of those plastic phones that emitted a dial tone every time you pushed a button.

Molito had one phone number stored in his memory. He dialed it and waited. It rang a few times before Beck answered. As expected he said nothing, but his breathing whispered on the line, calm and confident. He'd be wondering why this number had called. Molito spoke first.

"Reporting."

After a quick intake of breath, Beck spoke. His voice was good to hear but sounded suspicious. "Molito?"

"Yes, sir. I'm alone. The woman was here with three accomplices but they left a few minutes ago."

"You're okay?"

"Yes, sir. Just embarrassed. I got sloppy."

"It's in the past now mate, don't worry about it," said Beck. "They indicate where they were going?"

"I overheard them mention a plane and a ship but I'm not sure of their significance. They seem to have a fair bit of information."

"Yeah, you're not the only one that got sloppy. I underestimated that bitch. The plane, I knew about. The ship? I don't know what that is. Did it sound like they had access to one?"

Molito thought back to the parts of the conversation he'd heard. "Not sure, Sir, I don't think so. They're on a mission though. They're coming for you, wherever you are."

If Beck spotted his attempt to glean his location, he gave nothing away.

"Yeah, it sounds like they're getting ready to make a trip. I'll give you some directions, mate. Find a pen and something to write on."

"Okay," said Molito. "Hang on."

He laid the receiver on the side table and rummaged through the small drawer that hung beneath it. As expected, it held a phone book and a pencil. He positioned them on the table and wrote as Beck relayed directions turn by turn.

"Now get going," said Beck. "Break a few speed limits. I'm sure she'll remember where that place is, but they'll be driving at a legal speed. If you don't catch them at the plane, we might not find them again. I doubt they can get to me here, but they've come this far. I'd be stupid to underestimate them again."

"Will do, Sir."

"And mate?"

"Yes, Sir?"

"Don't mess about this time. Shoot on sight."

Molito replaced the receiver with a grim smile. It was time to go car shopping.

Cal Lennon shifted his weight to better spread himself across the tree's branches. The rest of the group milled around about fifteen feet beneath him while he scanned the compound through the scope attached to the rifle that Howard had found. It felt good to put the weapon to good use although he had no intention of pulling the trigger unless he had no choice.

The rough bark dug into his arms as he swung from one side to the other, but it was worth the discomfort to see what lay ahead of them. They'd seen shadows moving at the top of the entrance ramp and the additional height brought the cause of those shadows into full view. Two guys leaned against the wall of a small corridor formed by two large buildings, talking and laughing with one another. They seemed relaxed, which came as no surprise. It's not every day four desperate people, armed to the teeth, storm the private airfield where you played rent-a-cop.

Beyond the first block of buildings was a large asphalt cross made up of two intersecting runways. They ran almost the entire length of the compound, one from north to south, one from east to west. Each had its smaller parallel road, which Lennon assumed would be for emergency vehicles or taxiing. Each parallel road had another road branching off it, which ran up to rows of tall, wide buildings, presumably hangars. The control tower sat in the middle of it all like a huge pepper pot, surrounded by a parking lot littered with a few vehicles. One solitary plane crawled along one of the roads toward a runway, ambling forward like a stunned fly.

Other than the two guys at the gate and flashes of silhouetted movement in the control tower, there didn't seem to be anyone else home. The buildings were so tall and wide it was impossible to estimate how many more people were milling around amongst them. They would have to get up close and personal to determine what was happening in the belly of the airfield.

A whisper below startled him and he peered through the branches to see Monica staring up at him. Everything had moved so quickly since Lennon realized what The Consortium was doing. He'd had no time to assess how the events over the next few hours would change his life. He knew one thing for sure; there was no going back now. Years of non-attachment had left him cold and distant, and he liked the independent life, but there was something about this woman he found intriguing. They shared the same persona and she gave off an air of assured detachment that some might find aloof. He found it attractive. She was pretty, but not in a 'girl next door' kind of way. She was confident and capable too. Lennon liked those qualities in a woman. He had no patience for whining and handholding. There also seemed to be chemistry between Howard and Sabrina, even though he'd seen nothing obvious. He shook his head. No emotional attachment during a mission. It left everyone vulnerable and softened their approach. There was nothing but the mission. Always.

He leaned over the main branch of the tree. "What?"

"What's out there?" she whispered. "How many bad guys? Sabrina's getting ready to approach the gate."

"Tell her to hang on," he said, "I'm coming down."

They regrouped by Monica's SUV. Sabrina wrapped up a phone call as he reached the vehicle.

"Everything okay?"

"Yeah, I just arranged for a friend of mine to send some guys to release our prisoner back at Monica's place."

Lennon bit his tongue and pushed away all thoughts of revenge, then explained the layout beyond the fence.

"It looks quiet. There's not much movement other than two guys at the top of the drive and a small plane taxiing at the other end. Those two guys look pretty relaxed, but you can never be sure that's the case. Also, I can't see the front of the two buildings ahead. There could be someone either on the other side of them or inside them. To be sure we need a distraction while Sabrina gets the gate open."

Monica tossed her keys between her hands. "I can take care of that, and I'll do it alone. It'll be more convincing. Give me a couple of minutes and then be ready to go."

"Okay," said Sabrina, "but how will I know when to go?"

Monica smiled. "Don't worry, you'll know."

CHAPTER THIRTY-FIVE

While the rest of the group stayed huddled behind the trees, Monica reversed her SUV and then drove parallel to the fence about a hundred yards. She applied the parking brake and took a moment to gather her thoughts.

Something in her had snapped when Beck tied her to the chair. It would catch up with her at some point but, for now, those feelings galvanized her and drove her forward. Despite everything, she had to smile as Dirty Dancing flashed through her mind and Patrick Swayze said 'Nobody puts baby in a corner'. Well, no one puts Monica Bridges in her basement either. She'd taken a great leap of faith to allow someone into her tightly controlled life and he'd taken advantage of her. Now it was time for payback. Whatever happened during the next few hours, she prayed for a solitary minute of face time with her soon to be ex. Regardless of the men and animals he might have met in the Middle East, he couldn't be prepared for a thoroughly pissed off wife.

Then there was Lennon. She'd only just met him but she sensed something had begun to stir in him. She'd noticed the discreet squeeze of reassurance he'd given her back at the house and the way he stole quick glances. It had probably been a long time since Lennon had even thought about a woman, so she knew better than to read too much into it. Also, her track record with military types wasn't exactly littered with cute ponies and gold stars. Hell, she didn't even have a track record. Still, he was quite good looking.

The wire fence sat in front of her. She took a few deep breaths, checked her pockets, tugged at the seat belt and released the parking brake. Logic dictated that the best place for impact would be the exact center between two posts. That way the momentum of the vehicle would work with the stress of the wire to uproot them. In theory. She stamped the accelerator into the carpet and the two and a half tons of metal and glass leapt forward.

It was all she could do to keep the vehicle straight. It bucked and bounced like a rodeo bull as the smaller branches whipped across the windshield. She reined it in and rode the changes of direction and braced herself as the SUV plowed into the fence. A metallic scraping sound assaulted her senses as the wire mesh grated across the front of the hood. The fence stretched to its limit and the car slowed, stopped and sprung back as the engine stalled. The impact shook her in her seat. Surprisingly, the air bags didn't deploy, and she sat there stunned until distant shouting jolted her back to attention.

Through the side window she saw the two guards running toward her. She reached into her pocket, lowered the window and sagged through it as if injured.

"What the hell, lady?" shouted the closest guard. He was a young-looking guy, mid twenties, soft in the middle.

She lolled her head, opened the door an inch and leaned into it until it swung into the guard. "Oopsh, I'm sorry," she said, slurring the words. "Think I took a wrong turn shomewhere."

The older guard arrived, out of condition and breathless. He took one look at Monica and laughed. "Shit, dude, she's plastered. Damn, she trashed the fence."

The three of them gazed at the damage. The SUV hadn't managed to breach the fence, but it lay almost flat with its two supporting posts still firmly attached at ground level but bent back at a severe angle.

"Damn," slurred Monica. "Good fensh. I should get me one of those."

"Come on," said the older guy, "let's help her out of the car. We'd better radio this in."

The young guy moved to the side of the SUV and pulled the door wider as the older guy leaned toward Monica. As he leaned forward she raised her hand and touched the twin prongs of a small stun gun to his neck and pressed its button. A few thousand volts of electrical charge zapped through him and he squeaked, wet his pants and fell twitching to the floor. The young guy reacted with impressive speed and reached for the weapon holstered to his belt. Monica was quicker and lunged at him, connected with the prongs, and sent the guy to the floor to twitch and jerk with his colleague.

With the gun back in her pocket, she yelled a petulant "Ha!" at the two men. She retrieved cable ties from the SUV, rolled the stunned men up to the fence, secured them both to it, and zapped them once more for good measure.

She whispered, "Sleep tight boys," as she grabbed their pistols and climbed back into the truck. Against all her expectations it started right away. She reversed away from the fence and drove back toward the gate.

As soon as the rending of metal screeched through the air, we knew that was our sign. I glanced at Lennon.

"That sounded as subtle as a sledgehammer to the head."

"Yep, let's hope it worked. Let's go!"

The three of us ran to the gate, hunched over like a Special Forces unit. It felt like Sabrina and I were pretending. Lennon was the real deal.

The lock on the gate was a weird rectangle of metal that slid over the two thick bars that bolstered its center. Sabrina knelt for a closer look and reached into her bag. She pulled out two jump leads.

"We can't do a thing until the truck gets back. I've come across this type of lock before. It's locked electronically so there's no picking it. That friend of mine modified these cables for me. Once Monica gets back, I can override the lock."

As if on cue, I heard the rumble of the truck and Monica reappeared and rolled up the driveway. The front of the truck looked as if it had just finished a Nascar race, but she had a big beaming grin on her face.

"That was fun, although the truck will need a paint job. What's up? Can't you pick it?"

"I can," said Sabrina. "How long do we have?"

"As long as you like. Those boys won't stop twitching for some time and, even then, they're tied to the fence."

"Twitching?" I said.

"Tell us later," said Sabrina. "We don't have time to mess around. Drive the truck as close as you can to the gates and pop the hood."

Lennon waved Monica forward until she was inches away from the gate. The button clicked to release the hood but nothing happened.

"The impact must have damaged the release. Try it again." I slid my fingers under the metal sheet as Monica pressed the button again. I felt the catch release and pulled with my fingers. The hood grated open until it caught on the safety clip and, after a small amount of fumbling, the hood lifted. Sabrina propped it open and attached clips on the ends of her cables to the battery terminals and pushed the modified ends into the lock. She twisted and pushed the cables until a small wisp of smoke drifted into the air, then disconnected the cables and lifted the metal box up.

Once the cables were stashed back in her bag she sashayed up to the gate. She turned, swooped her arms open like a ballet dancer, sang a tuneful "ta-daaaa" and gave it a bump with her hip. The gate swung open an inch and she gestured with her arms. "After you."

As he walked by me, Lennon turned and said, "That was cool. She makes it look easy."

"You have no idea," I said, shaking my head. I followed them up the ramp and into the airfield.

The driveway ran between two large buildings. Their backs were covered in sheet metal that angled back into the fence, leaving us no way to sneak around the sides. The brick sidewalls created a corridor that we had to move through to reach the inside of the compound. A strong smell of diesel drifted in the breeze and the only sound was the distant drone of the small plane. It was either still taxiing to take off or it had just landed.

Lennon took the lead and had us fan out against the wall. Sabrina followed behind him. It was fascinating to watch them move together, like parts of a well-coordinated pantomime horse, first one moving forward and the other falling into position behind it. They looked like a veteran team and a small pang of jealousy nipped at my stomach. As if reading my mind, Sabrina turned to face me and placed a hand on my arm.

"You doing okay?"

"Yeah," I said, "I'm cool." The flush I felt spread across my face probably told a different story but, if she noticed, she did me the courtesy of ignoring it.

"How about you?" she asked Monica.

Monica looked as if she was on one of those adventure weekends outdoorsy people take, kitted out with a tranquilizer rifle and grinning like a mad woman. All she was missing was the face paint. "Oh, I'm ready for this. Have been for a while."

"Stay back and don't get too excited," said Sabrina. "I'm sure you're itching for revenge, but we have to get there first. Take it easy and follow our lead."

"Will do," said Monica. She pointed across the compound. "The hangar we want is on the other side of the airfield. We'll have to skirt around and go across the first runway."

Lennon shuffled back across the wall toward us. "How will we know which one belongs to Beck?"

"That's easy. Most of these buildings aren't hangars. They're huge storage units for all kinds of stuff. I think one of them is an illegal distillery."

"Well, as tempting as it is to raid that one first," he said, "let's stick to the task at hand."

"Of course. Sorry. Well, the hangars are the first row of large buildings down each side of the far runway. Becks is number thirteen."

"Thirteen," I said. "How nice. Lucky for us, huh?"

"I'm not superstitious," said Lennon. "A hangar's a hangar, the number makes no difference. Wait here while I check around the corner. I didn't hear anything, but I want to be sure."

We nodded our agreement. We wanted him to be sure too. Lennon and Sabrina could take care of themselves but I doubted Monica and I could fight our way out of a kindergarten. Lennon inched back along the wall to the corner, glanced right and left, and then vanished around it. He seemed to be gone for ages, but just as we began to get concerned he reappeared.

"These buildings look to be some kind of receiving offices. There's a couple of paper pushers in each one, but it all looks harmless. Still, we don't want to arouse suspicion. The windows are high off the ground so we should be able to sneak under them. Keep your weapons low so the rifles don't drift across the windows like periscopes."

I took Sabrina's bag so she could concentrate on carrying the drone and covering us. I'd forgotten how heavy it was but I hoisted it onto my shoulder, ducked as low as possible without falling forward, and took the rear and followed them around the corner.

We were wide open and exposed as we shuffled beneath the window. I saw no one in the expanse of land to the side of us, but that didn't make us invisible. I breathed a little easier when we reached the other side and I could stand upright against the side of the building. No one moved while we waited to see if the door around the corner would open and an innocent office worker would blunder into us. After a few seconds of total silence, we huddled together again to plot our next move. Sabrina stopped short, reached into her back pocket and pulled out her phone. Now I heard the faint vibrating.

"Hello?" she whispered. She listened intently for a few seconds.

"Shit. Okay, thanks. Yes, will do. Okay, thanks again."

She slid the phone back into her pocket and turned to face us.

"We may have a problem. The guy you tied up in your basement? Do you reckon he heard our conversation?"

Monica looked baffled. "I don't know. He may have. Why?"

"Because my guy is at your house. He's not in the basement any more. He escaped. If he heard us, he's bound to have contacted Beck, and you can bet he'll be coming for us."

CHAPTER THIRTY-SIX

Vince Molito shook his head and laughed aloud as he turned the small car onto a narrow road and followed Beck's directions.

People were not that trusting these days. He'd waited almost half an hour for someone to respond to his thumb at the side of the road. At least a dozen cars and trucks had blasted by, ruffling his hair and his temper in their slipstreams. Just as he considered carjacking someone, a beige colored box on wheels swerved over to the side of the road. The driver beckoned him over through the side window. Molito climbed in with a smile.

Once they reached the town's outskirts, he pulled out the knife and had the driver pull over to the side of the road. During the brief conversation, he learned that the young man was a high school teacher. He had every ounce of Molito's respect. Anyone that could control a room full of teenagers deserved a knighthood, not a paycheck. Kids these days were a pain in the ass. No respect for authority, just a feeling of entitlement that was nowhere near justified and, if you tried to give them a good slapping, they ran off crying to Child Protective Services. Teaching and parenthood were both a chore, one that Molito was glad he never entertained.

The teacher wore a wedding band. A simple white gold thing that didn't say money or status, just that someone at home waited for him. Someone who depended on him. Maybe even more than one person. Molito left him at the side of the road. Even though the guy bitched and whined like an old woman, he resisted the urge to kill him and sped away. Teacher had no idea how lucky he was. Molito didn't leave witnesses as a rule, but this guy was no threat.

Beck's directions were perfect, and so it didn't take long to steer the small vehicle on to the narrow road that led up to the driveway entrance to the airfield. The gate he'd mentioned stood wide open. Molito parked the car a distance away and climbed onto the roof. The extra height showed nothing new, so he slid down the windshield and moved toward the entrance. The knife wouldn't be much good in a gunfight, but its feel in his hand provided a small degree of comfort and reassurance. Up close, not many people on the planet would beat him in a knife fight. The only downside was that, in a knife fight everyone got cut regardless of how good they were. And in a gunfight, they were pretty much useless.

He cleared the entrance to the airfield and found no security, which meant the people before him had cleared them out. The runways and open ground before him were also clear, which meant the group was well on its way to achieving its objective. It also meant he would find them across the airfield in hangar 13.

Molito hefted the knife, partly out of habit but also because it gave him a measure of control. He slid it into his waistband, turned the corner and walked into the office. The heads of both occupants snapped around as the opened blinds rattled against the door. They were probably more used to security showing people in here, than having visitors arrive unannounced. He squared his shoulders and marched up to the desk.

"Reggie Wayne, Airport Security Services. I'm here to check your permits."

The two men glanced at each other as Molito strode behind the counter and approached the biggest guy. He looked like the typical bagman, not enough sense to run the operation but ambitious enough to try. The one who also had a nice looking sidearm strapped to his side.

"We don't need any permits. Where're your credentials? Hang on, Airport Security Services? ASS? Are you…?"

He fell silent as Molito slammed an elbow into his face. The other guy retched at the sound of snapping bone and cartilage. Before he could compose himself, Molito stripped the gun from the unconscious guy's belt and cocked it ready to fire.

"Toss your gun over and get on your knees. Now!"

The smaller guy complied and fell to his knees with a thud. "Come on man, I have a family. We've got no money here. Just take what you want and leave us alone."

Molito picked up the second discarded pistol. "I have what I need. Close your eyes."

The guy closed his eyes and whimpered. Molito silenced him with a blow to the back of the neck. He tumbled forward unconscious as Molito stepped over him and left the room.

He checked the clips in both guns, secured them in his waistband, and set off around the perimeter.

It took quite a while to reach the far end of the compound. We skirted the entire place and moved in a crouch close to the fence to avoid the eyes in the control tower and any stray people that might wander about or use the compound. A few hundred yards along the first stretch we heard moaning and came across a damaged fence. There were two guys tied to it. Both twitched and shook as if they were recovering from a night of heavy drug use.

"Is this your work?" I asked Monica.

She nodded, sheepish but proud.

"We heard the racket you made, but why didn't you tell us you leveled the fence? We could have shimmied over this instead of going through that entire 'get past security' thing we just did."

"I'm sorry," said Monica. "I got distracted."

"What the heck would distract you at a time like this?" said Lennon.

"Oh, that's easy. Watch this."

She knelt by the guys and zapped them with a stun gun. They screeched and twitched in unison as the electricity coursed through their bodies. Monica watched them with a morbid fascination. She was beginning to concern me.

"I can see how that might be distracting," said Sabrina, "but you should give them a break. They're probably innocent and have nothing to do with this."

Monica shrugged. "I needed to vent my anger," she said. "These guys were in the wrong place at the wrong time." She leaned over the two as they writhed against the fence. "Sorry again, guys."

"Come on," said Lennon. "We're wasting time. Monica, what's the lay of the land over there?"

"Okay. These rear buildings are the storage units I mentioned," she said and pointed across the compound. "We should be vigilant, but if there's going to be anyone around I'll bet they're behind those buildings at the front by the runway. Hangar 13 is on that first corner."

Between the fence and the first building lay the runway, the parallel road, and a patch of well-maintained grass. Everything here was straightforward. It didn't have the maze and slapdash look of a large airport where lines and multicolored lights intersected and crisscrossed with a pattern understood, it seemed, only by pilots. I estimated the open distance to be around a hundred yards. A hundred yards of total exposure, where one sighting from the control tower, one furtive glance from the offices, or one random person wandering amongst the buildings could ruin everything. Once we were airborne I didn't care who saw us. Until then, we had to maintain our cover.

"What do you think?" I asked Lennon. "Run across there one at a time, or all of us make a break for it together?"

He looked at our surroundings. I sensed a thousand calculations firing in his head. The benefits of military training.

"The sun is to our right, so anyone in the control tower has to squint into it. It does mean we'll cast shadows though. Monica's right, we can't plan for anyone moving around the buildings, we'll have to hope that good luck is with us. The folks in the offices should be too busy working to even bother focusing this far. I say we run in a solid line, side by side. Just run hell for leather and hide between the first two buildings."

"I'm with you," I said. I turned to the ladies. "Ready? One quick burst of speed and then dive for cover?"

They nodded together. I half expected them to hold hands. Instead, they shuffled between Lennon and I until we formed a rough line, hunched over and tensed like sprinters on starting blocks. Lennon did one more scan of our surroundings and braced himself.

"Ready?" he said. "Okay. Three, two, one... go!"

CHAPTER THIRTY-SEVEN

Claustrophobia. Cabin fever. Stir crazy. Submarine Syndrome. There were so many names for the same symptoms, symptoms that Beck had never experienced. The desert, his usual haunt, presented the grandest theater of all, a vast expanse of nothing that ran from one horizon to the next. Row after row of dunes littered with the occasional camel and palm tree, with as much space to move in as one man could ever need. Being trapped in this facility drove him insane. He had to get out of his confines and at least move around a little.

The room still buzzed as operators monitored drone movement and issued smokescreens of information to outside agencies that noticed their deviations. Shifts in weather patterns, accommodation for other air transport and seismic activity were some of the reasons given to explain why drones owned by building corporations, military agencies, and even the weather stations had behaved against their owners wishes.

Beck left the room and headed toward the central control station. Everything looked reassuringly similar, other than the clock, which counted off more time and now read 9:50:45. He turned left, walked past his office and up to a door he hadn't opened in days. A wave of his card against the panel opened the metal door to reveal a corridor different to the one behind him. It had the same curved form with the same cold lights set into the ceiling, but this corridor had small vents built into the bottom of the walls, designed to monitor the water content of the air. His footsteps echoed as he walked, but didn't bounce about, as if the surfaces were denser to help absorb the sound.

He followed the curve of the wall until he reached another door. There were only two of these in the entire building. Neither opened from the inside without the card that hung around his neck. Again, he swiped his card and the door clicked inward with a hiss. He opened it wider to face another identical door. The small entrance lobby between them was an eight feet square of solid metal with no panels, handles or buttons. Nothing more than a metal box with a vent in the ceiling. He stepped inside and closed the door behind him. The second it latched shut; another hiss sealed it and the door in front of him sprung open.

Beck thought back to when they'd built this facility. Men had lost their lives in this tiny room. As one door closed, the opening mechanism had failed to activate the other. The vent pumped in no oxygen, leaving them to suffocate in the vacuum of an airlock. Their twisted faces and bulging eyes had disturbed most of his colleagues. He'd seen it before in the aftermath of chemical warfare. A much more painful death, but with the same result.

The second door opened onto a platform. He stepped onto it and slid his fingers across the top of the handrail as he descended below the main floor. His boots clanged against the metal steps. The air changed. The temperature had dropped, and it held a crisp, clean smell, not sanitized like the offices. This staircase led to his favorite place. No curved concrete walls, no cold lighting and no claustrophobic confines. The walls on either side of the upper door angled away to the sides of the room to create a cavernous space. The staircase hung in midair through the middle of it and led to a huge metal concourse of slatted aluminum that led off into the distance. It ended in a pair of huge double doors. Either side of the concourse, water pushed against the walkway. Beck had no idea how deep it was, but it handled the submersibles that transported people and supplies with ease. A row of small vessels waited at one side and sat unmoving with no current to disturb it.

The two sides of the giant room were made entirely of glass, which gave the whole place the feeling it was one with the ocean. Only the down lit ceiling and the back wall destroyed the illusion. Shoals of marine life floated by in bursts of color or bumped idly against the walls like punch-drunk boxers. The activity outside the glass was a stark contrast to the relaxed serenity of the interior.

Beck stood in the center of the concourse and spun slowly around, his arms hanging at his sides. The sensation was like standing in water, suspended in a massive bubble of air. Tension flowed out of his body like the liquid around him as he gazed into the depths of the ocean.

The exact reason for the existence of this facility was lost to time and red tape. He'd heard the rumor they'd built it years ago as an underwater government research facility. Then, as presidents and priorities changed, so did the funding. And as the money dried up the place was evacuated and closed. It remained vacant for a while until high-level Consortium members learned of its existence. They redesigned the interior and refilled the ballast rooms to keep the whole thing stationary in the water. It was repopulated under an umbrella of non-disclosure agreements and an intensive and exclusive recruiting procedure.

Beck turned back and walked toward the staircase. As his foot touched the first step, his phone chirped and vibrated. He palmed it and swiped the screen.

Molito was calling.

I stared at the expanse of open land ahead of me and, for a moment, tried to imagine how the troops must have felt. You can pick an era. Either the soldiers from World War One, who raised their heads from flooded trenches to check out the way ahead, before they made the charge across the sludge of no-man's land through a hail of gunfire to the next one. Or the poor souls trapped in the slums of East Germany, who gazed across through the razor wire and guard posts to the other side of the Berlin Wall, and wondered whether to make the almost certain fatal dash to reach an isolated family or a better life.

Either way, despite the churning in my stomach, I was fairly sure that on my dash I wouldn't be shot at, not like those folks. The thought offered little comfort though, and I still squirmed in the line-up like a kid on the first day at a new school. I remembered something my daughter Kacie had said once she'd accepted her mom and I were not getting back together. In one of those ways that made her more of an adult than me, she said, "Dad, one day you'll meet someone who will change your life. You should be sure to give them a chance."

Well, that had happened. I glanced at Sabrina. I'd known this woman for a little over three days now. Sure, she was a professional thief, but she had a good heart. And she was stunning. However, other than the pleasure and amazing feelings and adventure and exhilaration, she'd brought me nothing but trouble. Lennon stood next to her. I didn't know him at all. A few days ago, he'd lied and told me he was an FBI agent even though he worked for a shady covert organization and, before that, he'd been shooting at Sabrina. Next to him was Monica. I didn't know her either, and I'd found her locked in a base-ment where she'd attacked Sabrina with a corkscrew. Damn, you couldn't make it up.

But I gave them a chance.

Lennon's voice broke my train of thought. "… two, one… go!"

I bolted forward in an explosion of energy I didn't realize I could muster. Sabrina's hand found mine, squeezing and empowering. Every step felt like wading through thick mud. My eyes were squinted half shut, waiting for the crack of gunfire or the whistle of a projectile. The backpack bounced behind me, its contents stabbing and prodding and making all kinds of noise. I ran, keeping my head down and pumping my knees to power me forward. No shots sounded and no projectiles whistled and, after what seemed like a lifetime, I slammed against the wall of the building. My overworked heart banged against my chest wall, trying to work its way out into the light for relief. My breathing seemed heavier than everyone else's and I rested my hands on my knees while Lennon shimmied across the side of the building to check behind us.

"Everything looks quiet," he said with no effort. "I think we're good."

"Good might be overstating it a bit," I said as my heart tried to settle back into its usual pattern. "Damn, I'm out of condition."

"We can work on that later," said Sabrina with a sly smile. "You did good. And I appreciate you carrying my bag."

Monica stepped forward, hands on hips. "Come on kids, no time to waste. We can cut through the middle of these buildings behind me and then move left. That'll avoid the tower. Then we can work our way around to the hangar and we should be home free."

"I don't know about free," said Sabrina, "but it's a step in the right direction."

We stood between the first two buildings in the closest row of four. Behind the front four, three more rows were stacked three deep from front to back, moving away from us toward the runway.

Twelve huge hiding places.

I didn't expect to bump into any enemies, but we still needed to get out of here without being seen. I looked back for Lennon, but he'd vanished. The man was like a magician. Or a ninja. Seconds later, his head appeared around the corner and he beckoned with a hand. "Come on, the coast is clear."

We followed him around the corner and into the maze of tall buildings. Monica and Lennon moved confidently as if they had some kind of internal compass. Sabrina and I followed them like well-schooled sheepdogs, until we reached the front row. One more corner, then past two buildings, and we were home and dry.

Monica stepped up to Lennon and whispered something in his ear. It was too faint to hear, but he stood back and let her take the lead. Something was definitely happening between them. A chemistry or some sort of partnership was forming. She walked out into the open and marched to hangar 13 as if she owned it, her arms swinging and her chest out, the epitome of confidence. In a way, I suppose she did own it. A faint clang and a rustle sounded behind me and I froze.

Sabrina heard it too, but nothing moved. All the buildings were closed. There were no open doors or signs of activity. Monica continued her walk past the huge sliding doors until she reached the small side door that led into the hanger. She grabbed the round metal handle and twisted it. It was locked. She turned to Sabrina with a grimace. Sabrina turned to me with a smile. I turned and passed her the bag of tricks and she marched over and joined Monica by the door.

Sabrina pulled out the lock pick set, knelt and got to work. As her knees touched the ground and the two small pins entered the lock, I heard movement again. This time right behind me. Before I made a full turn a tree sized shadow passed over me and a man mountain strode past me and out into the open. He towered over us and looked us over with obvious distrust. Then he saw Sabrina and spoke in a voice that would have parted the sea.

"What the hell do you think you're doing?"

Sabrina turned with the lock picks still dangling from her fingers, wearing a look of disgust that she'd been interrupted. Lennon was right behind her. He turned in surprise, amazed that we'd been spotted. I jumped, then froze in shock, and then completed my turn in slow motion to see who had crept up behind me. Only Monica reacted.

The guy must have been a mechanic working on a plane in one of the hangars. His spade-sized hands were caked in grease and held a shiny metal wrench. The red flannel shirt and bib overalls he wore covered a body that was built like a lumberjack on steroids. He was easily six feet five inches tall and almost as wide, which made Monica's jump all the more impressive. While we stood as if we were ankle deep in concrete, she leaped past me, pirouetted, and landed a spinning kick against the guy's jaw that would have unhinged a gorilla. He stumbled backwards and dropped the wrench to the ground. It cartwheeled behind him, but through its clang and clatter, I still heard the blows of the follow up punches she planted on his disoriented chin. Every one of them rocked him backwards and within seconds he was flat on his back and unmoving. I looked at Sabrina, whose wide eyes matched mine. Lennon grinned like a teenager who'd been handed the keys to the family car. Monica turned to look at us and, in an instant, the tough persona melted and the woman we'd met earlier today faced us.

"Oh my God, do you think he'll be okay?"

She stepped back as I knelt over the prone whale of his body to check his neck for a pulse. I could feel it beat steadily through his beard.

"Yeah, he'll be fine. Shit Monica, what the hell just happened? Are you one of those programmed killing machines they talk about on late night TV?"

"Hey, you don't think you can spend five years with a military man and not pick up a few tricks?"

I held up my hands in defense. "I'm sure you'd out-box me but let's not find out, okay? Sabrina, get that door open so we can get this guy out of sight."

Sabrina shook her head in disbelief and turned back to the job at hand. Lennon sidled up to Monica while I rifled the guy's pockets to make sure he wasn't carrying anything else that might hurt us. Or him. He had a driver's license and credit cards, which led me to believe that he was a regular Joe and not an emissary of Monica's soon to be ex. An innocent casualty she'd probably call collateral damage. I was grateful he was only unconscious. Actually, I was very grateful he was unconscious.

Sabrina murmured a "yes" of triumph and pushed open the small door. Monica stepped past her and entered the hangar. Footsteps echoed behind the massive metal doors as she walked around the interior. A faint click carried through the metal as a beam of light illuminated the entrance and then her head reappeared through the door. "Well, don't just stand there," she said, "come on in."

She dipped back inside the building. Another clunking sound and the whir of a motor bled through the doorway and the huge hangar doors shuddered and inched apart.

I nodded to Lennon. "Help me grab Goliath. I don't want to hurt the guy; he was just in the wrong place at the wrong time. Let's make sure he won't bother us again until we can get out of here."

Lennon grabbed his feet while I took his wrists and we dragged

him into the hangar with minimal gravel burns to his ass. I tied him up
with thin rope and left a box cutter just out of reach so he'd be able to
cut himself free when he came around.

The inside of the hangar was like The Doctor's Tardis from Doctor
Who. It seemed much bigger on the inside and was made entirely of
corrugated metal, held in place by steel studs and huge metal trusses.
Equipment and tall tool chests lined the back wall. The place was
kitted out with everything needed to maintain a fleet of planes, not just
the single prop parked inside. Psychopathic killers must get paid a lot
more than pharmaceutical salespeople. I was in the wrong business.

By the time we'd secured our sleeping prisoner, Monica had
rummaged through a cabinet, found what she needed and was getting
comfortable in the cockpit. I could just make her out as the lights
suspended overhead reflected off the curved glass. She reminded me of
Kacie, years ago at the funfair, when she sat in one of those models
planes that spun in circles if you paid it a dollar. She looked excited,
moving around and adjusting the seat. Not for the first time, concern
crept into my mind. She seemed to be enjoying everything a little too
much as if she was at summer camp on one big adventure. That being
said, she'd saved us twice already. Maybe I underestimated her. Still, I
made a mental note to remind her of what was at stake. We might be on
a mission to prevent the next major war, but right now I was distracted.
I was about to allow myself to be taken thousands of feet into the air in
a metal box, controlled by a woman who bounced around in the
driver's seat like something off The Muppet Show.

CHAPTER THIRTY-EIGHT

Molito held the phone to his mouth and whispered into the mouthpiece. It was a pointless exercise, and the irony was not lost on him. He was skirting an airfield in the open, a steady afternoon breeze blew and the leaves on the trees surrounding the facility rustled their dry song. Still, old habits die hard.

"No sign of them yet, Sir. They're here somewhere though. I caught every word they said back at the house."

"Yeah, she's there all right," said Beck. "I swear mate, if I hadn't just had a piss I'd feel it in my water. How close are you?"

"I'm about to follow the fence to the far corner and then I'll move over and sneak around the back of the hangar. Five, ten minutes max. You said it was on the edge of the runway, first corner unit, right? I can see the side of it from here, but it's too far away to tell if there's any movement."

"Be wary. She's surprised me at every turn so far. Now there's a team of them. Enough's enough. Take them out. Oh, and mate?"

"Yes, Sir?"

"Try not to put any holes in my plane. That fucker cost me a hundred grand."

"Will do, Sir," said Molito.

The wind dropped and the tree boughs sighed and rested. Through the quiet he heard a faint groaning sound and the clinking of metal links.

"Sir, let me call you back. I'll report in as soon as I have details."

He pocketed the phone. He already held one pistol but he pulled out the other, crouched low and edged along the fence line. Surely they weren't this close, they had too much of a lead on him. Still, one of them might have picked up an injury, which would explain the lack of progress and the moaning sound.

The ground rose and fell like grassy dunes and Molito followed the contours exactly, molding his shape to the landscape. He hadn't gone far before the angle of the fence changed and sloped inwards. He ducked even lower until he reached the point where it laid almost flat, then stopped. There were two guys zip tied to it, writhing around on the ground. They looked up at him with wide eyes filled with panic and embarrassment. He raised the pistols he was carrying and they panicked even more, thrashing against their ties.

"Hey, come on man, help us out would you? We've done nothing wrong. We just want to go home to our families."

Molito looked down on them. Their ties were solid. They wouldn't be going anywhere. He shook his head and moved past them. "Fucking amateurs," he said to himself. "I'm almost falling over them."

The whining voices faded into the distance as he continued to move along the fence line. He reached the corner and looked across at the buildings. Still no movement. Crossing the open space would leave him exposed but, by the time anyone reacted, any confrontation would be over anyway. It was now or never. He sprinted across the distance and moved toward the hangar.

CHAPTER THIRTY-NINE

Monica was back on solid ground and scurried around the plane like a mouse around a trap. Despite my reservations, she seemed to have a good grasp on what she was doing. I'd already watched her check the fuel levels in each wing and disconnect the lock that tied the plane's tail to the hangar floor. Two things I would never have considered. I'd have destroyed us before we even left the building. She checked the wing flaps and tail rudder and shrugged her shoulders.

"I don't have time to do anything close to a full system check, but the essentials seem to be okay. Everyone load up and climb aboard."

She sounded confident enough, so we piled what we had through the door, slid the drone between two seats and boarded the plane. Lennon moved up front to sit in the cockpit next to Monica while Sabrina and I buckled ourselves into the seats behind them. One of the plane's wings was right outside my window.

"I'd do one of those safety demonstrations," I said, "but I figure, in the event of an emergency, just put your head between your legs and kiss your ass goodbye. If we don't make it out there, it's as good as gone anyway."

Wry smiles spread through the cabin as Monica flicked switches and pushed a button to the side of the steering yoke to prime the engine.

"Everyone ready?"

She turned the key.

The engine whirred and sputtered and burst into life. The propeller on the front of the plane spun and went from looking like a daisy into a blur in a matter of seconds. It looked much smaller from inside the cabin than it did from outside. I hoped it would get us off the ground. I resisted the urge to cheer as she disengaged the parking brake and pushed the throttle to move the plane forward. Its nose eased out of the hangar and small squares of light drifted through the cabin and across the seats as the afternoon sunlight flooded in through the windows.

"Okay, for obvious reasons I didn't file a flight plan, so keep your eyes everywhere and let me know if you see anything coming. I'll fly as low as I can to avoid any collisions. That should also keep us off radar, so the control tower won't send fighter jets after us."

I gulped and spoke for everyone. "Yeah, it would be nice if you could make sure all of that happens. Especially the fighter jets part."

Without a word and like a well-oiled machine everyone took a window and scanned the runways and the surrounding sky. We were turning into a decent team. The more time we spent together, the more we seemed to gel. Maybe we could actually pull this off.

The plane bumped as we reached the runway and Monica turned it to face the long stretch of concrete ahead of us. It looked nowhere near long enough for us to build up enough speed, but our fate was in her hands now. She made a few adjustments and the plane jolted to a stop.

"Looks straight enough to me. Buckle up and hold on tight folks. Here we go."

She checked a few dials and then pushed the throttle forward. They must have read okay because the engine screamed and then my head snapped back into the headrest as the plane lurched forward. Butterflies swarmed in my stomach and my palms began to sweat. As I pulled my head out of the leather behind me, I caught a movement outside my window. I assumed it would be shade thrown from one of the tall buildings around us, but as I turned my head and looked out the window, I saw him. The guy from Monica's basement. He was running after the plane. His arms pumped back and forth beside him to gain speed, his teeth clenched in determination and his clothes fluttered in the wind as he sprinted toward us. He had a pistol in one hand and he was gaining on us.

"Er, I know you're concentrating Monica, so I don't want to bother you, but we seem to have a bad guy chasing the plane. Can you go any faster?"

Everyone, including Monica, craned their heads to look past me.

"Damn," said Sabrina, "you just can't keep a bad man down."

The plane was increasing in speed but not quickly enough. The cabin rocked as he caught us and jumped up onto the edge of the wing. He glared at me through the window. His face looked like he was sucking on a lemon, contorted in anger. The wind stretched his skin and buffeted his hair as the plane rolled quicker still, but he was able to clamber up onto the wing.

Inch by inch he worked his way toward me on his hands and knees until he was outside my window. His face twisted again as he slid his torso up the side of the fuselage, this time into an evil smile. He raised his arm and aimed the pistol right between my eyes.

I tried to sink into the seat, but in the ultimate of ironies, the safety of the lap belt held me tight and in place. The bumps in the runway did enough to stop the guy getting a perfect aim, but he jostled about and managed to get his arm rested against the side of the plane. I closed my eyes and waited for the gunshot. It was the longest few seconds of my life, but the shot never came. I opened my eyes again. He seemed to have had a change of heart and had moved forward toward the cockpit window.

"Monica! Wiggle your flaps or whatever you do to move the wings. He's coming your way."

Lennon hadn't realized what had happened and looked at me as if I was just out of high school as Monica glanced back and over her shoulder.

"I can't move the flaps," she shouted. "They raise and lower the plane. Plus, we need to get off the ground and we're running out of runway."

I looked up through the cockpit window and, sure enough, the thick wire fence at the other end of the runway was growing larger by the second.

"I'm going to try to shake him off. Hold on to something."

She pulled the steering yoke a fraction to one side. It was enough to swerve the entire plane toward the grass that ran along the edge of the runway. The guy must have expected the change in direction and he shifted his weight to balance himself. She turned the other way and he slid across the wing. As he reached the edge he jabbed his boot heel into the metal along a row of rivets. It was enough to halt his slide, but the movement forced him to drop the pistol. It bounced and skittered across the wing and fell off the edge and out of sight. I heaved a sigh of relief. He grimaced, reached around to his back and pulled out another, then edged forward again.

Sabrina looked over my shoulder. "Monica, he's moving toward you again. You better do something."

"We have more pressing concerns," she replied. She strained against the yoke. "After all of these distractions, I didn't watch our speed. I'm not sure we'll be fast enough to get the lift to clear the fence. I have none right now."

The tires below us continued their constant rumble against the concrete and the whine of the engine and rush of the wind across the nose and wings of the plane increased by the second. The distance between us and sweet oblivion decreased at the same rate. Our predicament was not lost on the guy outside. He stared at the end of the runway, the wind causing tears to flow from his eyes, across his cheeks and into his ears. I could almost hear his brain making the calculations; jump and be torn apart by the impact with the runway, or hold on for dear life and lose it in a ball of fire when we reached the other end of the compound. He chose option B, lay flat against the wing and wrapped both arms around its front edge.

I wasn't sure if the guy was brave or stupid but my attention snapped back to the cabin when Sabrina shouted, "Pull on the handle. Pull the damned thing, Monica!"

Monica screamed and nodded at the steering yoke. "You see this? You see it? You see me pulling it?" She extended her arms to their fullest extent, leaned back into her seat and pulled.

The rumbling of the tires suffered a minor interruption. Then concrete. Then another interruption.

"Is it lifting?" I screamed.

"I'm pulling the fucking handle," screeched Monica. She sounded as if she'd caught her hand in a car door. "I'm pulling it. We're going to make it!"

The fence was feet away now. The guy on the wing had tucked his head behind one of his arms as if it would protect him from the impact with a fence and the resulting fireball.

The tires jumped again and then, at last, the only sound was that of the engine. No more tire rumble, just glorious flight. Gravity played with my stomach as the plane lifted. The fence vanished below the cockpit window and I swear I heard the wheels bump once more as if they'd run across the top of it. Then we were free and climbing into the sky. Free that was, except for the bad guy holding onto the wing right outside my window.

Cold air bit into his fingers and the tendons in them stretched to their limits. Molito curled his hands around the front edge of the wing and held on for dear life. It took immense effort, but he pulled himself forward and looked over the wing. The features on the ground below were growing smaller by the second as the plane gained altitude and he regretted his decision to stay put. As the plane cleared the fence he should have jumped onto the grassland beyond it. He may have suffered a little, a few broken bones, but he'd still be alive. It was a matter of time before his fingers gave out and he plummeted to his death. Even if he held on for a decent amount of time, the higher the plane climbed the thinner the oxygen became, and the temperature would drop quickly. If he didn't suffocate he'd freeze to death anyway. Still, his instinct for survival held him firm. His instinct for revenge whirred away in his mind as well, and soon overrode the other.

Could he reach the propeller without falling? And if he did and he threw himself into it, would the plane be destabilized enough to cause it to plummet to the ground, or would he simply be shredded like ground beef? He glanced across at the fuselage and through the side window and saw them watching him. They were bouncing about looking panicked, even though they were safe and warm inside the cabin. The guy in the nearest window said something to the pilot, and he saw her nod in the cockpit.

The plane banked to the left. His legs splayed out behind him and the shift in weight tore at his fingers. He arched his back and dug the toes of his boots into the wing for added grip and hung on like a fly on a windshield. The wind whipped into him and chilled his body. As he settled into his new position, she banked right and then left once more. His body rocked from side to side and finally the movement beat him. His right hand flew back from the wing and his left followed a split second later. The rushing air flowed beneath him, scooped him up and threw him off the back of the wing.

He made no sound as he tumbled downwards. His body tossed and spiraled like an Olympic high diver. There was no deep pool beneath him though. There'd be no splitting the surface tension of water. He'd be landing on the finality of solid ground.

He knew his death would be instant. There'd be no pain, no funeral and no one to mourn him. There was no God to make peace with and no confession to give.

There would just be the nothingness of death.

A look of pure evil washed across the guy's face before his grip surrendered and gave up the fight. He flew off the wing like a bundle of rags and disappeared behind the plane. There was no panic or fear, just hatred. He'd remained so calm it scared me. The wind had torn and

clutched his hair and clothes, as it fought to claim him. When he'd
vanished, he'd looked like a circus puppet floating in a wind tunnel and
someone had cut its strings. In that sick, morbid way we have, like
rubbernecking at a wreck on the highway, we craned our necks through
the window to watch his rapid descent. He was out of sight in an
instant. And I was grateful I missed the end of the show.

There was a huge possibility this wouldn't be the last glimpse of
death I'd get before we were done. We were dealing with people that
lived different lives to us with a warped set of morals. Based on the
desperation we'd seen they would stop at nothing to achieve their goal.
I wasn't sure I could sink to that level, so I figured I'd better stay
behind Lennon if and when the time came. I reckon he'd sink pretty
quickly.

"Everyone okay back there?"

Monica's voice startled me. I was grateful for the intrusion. Sabrina
leaned forward and looked over Lennon's shoulder. "So how high are
we? You said you were going to stay low, but how low can we fly
without hitting something?"

"I leveled out at one hundred and fifty feet," said Monica. She
spoke with the confidence of a veteran pilot. She showed no outward
sign that our close encounter had bothered her, but her shoulders
hunched up around her ears as if she was stressed beyond belief. "That
should be low enough to get us out of range of the radar at the airfield.
Still, I need to be wary of any others we might fly by. The folks in the
tower back there must be freaking out by now. Hopefully, they didn't
pick up our direction. I'll have to stay away from populated areas at
this height, so I may deviate off course from time to time. I also turned
off the transponder so the towers can't communicate with us. They use
this send and receive thing where they can ping the plane to get information. With no transponder, the ping should, well…just ping off into
nowhere. I don't dare get any lower than this, and if we come across
something I can't get around, we'll have to climb so be prepared. As
far as obstacles ahead of us, I'll keep looking through the window. It's
a learning curve. I've only flown alone a few times."

She said the last sentence with a smile. Reassuring.

I swallowed down my nerves and curbed the desire for a good, strong bourbon. "How long will it take us to get there?"

She glanced amongst the many dials and buttons. "GPS guesstimates about three and a half hours based on projected wind speeds. We've got to find somewhere to land and then we have to find a boat. That'll leave us what, three, three and a half hours to midnight? Cutting it fine."

"No kidding," I said. "Well, we can only work with what we've got."

We sat in silence for a while. I wondered if the wing guy who took a flight had a family. I'm sure the saying went something like 'every boy is someone's son'. Sabrina reached over and placed a hand on my knee. I must have looked pensive.

"You okay?"

"Yeah, I think so," I said. "I've never seen someone fall like that before. Hell, I didn't even see the guy die. He just vanished. But you know what I mean."

"Yeah, I know what you mean," she said. "To be honest, even in my line of work I'm in the same boat as you. I try to stay away from life or death situations. They're dangerous."

I glanced across at her. Damn, I could drown in those eyes. It seemed like forever since that first night. She wasn't dressed in the red that had first caught my attention at the bar any more. Now I looked at her, I saw it wasn't what she'd worn that had drawn me in. Her eyes were hypnotic, and she had a smile that could settle trade disputes on its own. Her face was placid, as if she didn't have a care in the world, but after what we'd been through I knew differently. She looked relaxed; despite the buffeting the small plane was taking from flying at low altitude. Her trust issues must have been tearing at her insides like barbed wire. She just smiled through it. My respect for how she handled everything grew by the second. Maybe it was what she did for a living, but she was clearly much tougher than me.

"How do you like Monica's flying?"

She laughed. It was a musical sound that was a pleasure to hear. "Surprisingly well. I think spending these past few days with you has helped me a lot. Well, other than the danger and the violence. I haven't left my fate in someone else's hands for a long time and I've adapted much quicker than I expected. It's mostly because of you. Thank you."

I shrugged away the compliment, as only someone who never gets them can. "Nah, it's a team effort. We make a good team, don't you think? I hope we make it through this. I'm interested to see what's next."

She squeezed my knee and flashed that perfect smile. "I'm done with this shit. Retirement might be in my not too distant future. I don't need the money anymore, but I'll still need something to keep me busy. I enjoy taking risks and I'm not used to taking them with someone else. I'm usually responsible for me. No one else."

I placed my hand on her knee and reciprocated the squeeze. "Oh, I'm definitely a risk," I said, "but I'll try to make it worth your while. And I promise to keep you busy."

CHAPTER FORTY

"Have you spoken to your daughter lately?"

I'd been staring into space to take my mind off the tips of the trees that flitted past a few feet below us. Despite the view, the ebb and flow of the plane battling against side winds relaxed me. Sabrina's words made me jump. She gave me a grim smile that said she knew I was nervous as hell but trying to hide it. And I didn't need to.

"Kacie?" I said. "Yeah, it's all good." I nodded, knowing so many things were left unsaid. So many things I should have said a long time ago. Or while I was still could.

Lennon and Monica were having their conversation in front of us. Despite being seated inches behind them, I tried my best to tune out their words and not eavesdrop on their discussion. I was so wrapped up in my little world that Sabrina's voice threw a noose around my attention, or one of those shepherd's crooks that appeared at the side of the stage and yanked a performer off into the wings. I turned to look at her. She looked back at me with an expression that made me feel like a prisoner on death row, about to take the long, final walk to the chamber.

"Paul, you realize how dangerous this is, don't you? We're not

dealing with a couple of muggers. This is life and death stuff. Chances are, not all of us will make it back. These people are not boy scouts. They control whole organizations. If we get in the way, they'll kill us and think nothing of it. We'll be like ants on the sidewalk. If you like, when we get to Virginia Beach, we can let you out. You can still go home to your family. This isn't your fight."

Hearing the words out loud sent my stomach on a cruise to depths unknown, but my mind already knew the facts. I'd had a while to work them out. And I'd had time to speak to the people in my life that meant something. By a weird twist of fate or alignment of the stars, one of them sat right next to me. The ones that didn't were still front and center in my mind.

The truth was I didn't have a choice. A tiny part of me thought that maybe Monica's beliefs were exaggerated, that she read way too much into this whole thing. If that were the case, we'd fly to Virginia Beach, 'borrow' a boat and sail out into the Atlantic. Once we got there, if nothing transpired, no harm no foul. We'd be embarrassed, but the world would go on as normal and we'd all go home. But Lennon's statement backed her up. The plot was brought forward. Regardless of which shadowy corporation he worked for, he believed something serious was happening too. That was fifty percent of a good team. I liked and trusted those odds.

So, if something serious was going to happen, I couldn't leave that world for my daughter. I couldn't have Kacie growing up in a world fighting the next Great War, a war that might send missiles or suicide bombers to her city. To the stores she shopped in. Or to her school. Someone had to take a stand. Someone had to stop these people before our loved ones had no world left to grow up in.

"No," I said. "This actually is my fight." I sat taller in my seat. "Too many people are standing around while this crap is going on. I hear stuff all the time about small teams that go into places and perform heroic acts to save hundreds of people, yet you never see it on the news. I want to be part of one of those teams and I don't care if no one knows. My daughter needs to live longer than I will. Isn't that why we're on the earth, to move the population forward? To give our kids a better life than we had? Well, fuck 'em. Fuck the bad guys. I'm in. One hundred percent. My daughter will have a future whether I see it or not. If I die securing a better world for her, then so be it."

Sabrina looked at me as if she'd found the Holy Grail. The churning in my stomach was replaced by a nice, warm fuzzy feeling.

"And anyway," I continued with a broad smile, "after the night we spent together, if I'm going to go out, then at least I'm going out on a high."

Monica massaged the back of her neck, squeezing the tendons and kneading them with her hand, and looked again through the curved glass at the front of the plane then again at the instrument panel. She used the two aids to paint a picture of the ground ahead and to plot a course that avoided as many obstacles as possible. Her eyes felt dry as if she'd been wearing contact lenses for a week. She blinked to wash away the imaginary grains of sand that scratched at her and looked again at the landscape ahead.

They'd already been flying for an hour, the trip smoother than she'd expected. There were two instances when she'd needed to divert from her route. Each time she banked the plane, she sensed the anxiety of the people around her increase. This was how it must feel to drive a school bus, with the responsibility of transporting little people from A to B, ensuring they reached their destination in one piece. Except when this group reached its destination, there'd be no disembarking for a nice, easy day. They'd be walking into danger. She blinked once more and craned her head forward as if the extra inch enabled her to see a mile further ahead.

"Isn't there an autopilot or something on this thing?"

The sound of Lennon's voice made her jump. Oncoming blurs filled her vision, any of which would destroy the plane if she clipped them. She'd focused so hard on avoiding them she'd forgotten he sat next to her. They'd had a brief conversation earlier, just small talk, and then he'd withdrawn as if he'd realized she didn't want to be distracted. Her blinking must have been more frequent than she realized.

"Yes, but he never showed me how to use it." She lowered her voice and leaned toward him. "To be honest, I've never flown this far alone. And definitely not this low. I have to concentrate. There's too much at stake for me to mess this up. Our lives don't mean that much compared to what might happen if we fail."

Lennon followed her lead and leaned into her until their shoulders touched. Goosebumps spread across her arm. "Your secret's safe with me," he said, "but for the record, I'd still appreciate it if you got us there in one piece."

Monica smiled and enjoyed the way his warm breath washed across her face. The last time warm breath had hit her she'd been tied to a chair, and it was mixed with spit and threats. And it came from a voice she'd trusted. Was it the situation they were in that created these feelings she had, that she could trust this man she'd just met? And that there was a possibility he might even like her?

"I'll get us there in one piece," she said and grimaced, "or I'll die trying." She turned to him and gave him the biggest smile she could muster. It felt good to smile. The positive energy reinvigorated her. She shook her body and shuffled back and sat upright in her seat.

Lennon looked at her and shook his head, his face fighting a smile of his own.

"What?" she said.

"I've never met anyone like you," he said, "although I got signed up right out of school, so it's safe to say I've never really met anyone. You know, other than for, well…"

"Yes," she laughed. "Or at least I think I do. Wait until you see me deal with Beck, then make your assumptions. You might be surprised and run a mile. Or you might surprise me."

"Now you have to get us there," he said. "I'd pay money to see that meeting."

"I'm sure you would," she said. "It'll be emotional for sure." They were quiet for a moment. She wanted the conversation to continue. "Tell me more about you, something no one else knows."

He frowned and stared for a moment. "Okay. Well, like I said I signed up out of school. Did the military thing. After a while, a guy who promised me the world approached me. You know, money, glory. The things guys dream about coming out of high school."

"I always thought guys dreamed of ways to get into the girl's locker room without being spotted."

"Oh, they do," he said, "but the other ten percent of the time we think about money and glory."

"Whatever," she said with a shake of the head. "Carry on, glory boy."

"Well, they trained me, a lot, and then turned me loose. I never saw who called the shots. I followed orders and got the job done. I don't want to sound arrogant, but I was good at it too. I hope I'm as good when we get to where we're going."

She turned again to look at him, ignoring the landscape that flew by through the windshield for a second. "I promise to get us there, if you promise to take care of business."

He nodded and placed a hand on her arm. "I promise," he said.

She looked ahead once more. "How about a lighter topic; tell me something about you."

He chewed his bottom lip for a moment. "Okay," he said in a whisper, "my name is not really Lennon."

"Well, given what you've told me so far, that's not much of a surprise to be honest." She didn't push for more information and continued to look out the window.

"Everyone here knows me by that name, so let's get through this and not confuse things. When we come out the other side, I'll tell you my real name."

"Okay," she said, "I'll try not to be distracted by your air of mystery."

A tension hung in the air between them. Lennon seemed uncomfortable and she had no idea how to lighten the mood. She regretted the sarcasm. His gaze turned toward her again. More secrets?

"There is another thing," he said.

She braced herself. Watch him turn out to be married.

"When I was stationed overseas I had a cat."

"That's it?" she said. "No one else knows you had a cat?"

"Oh no, everyone knew about the cat, but I told the boys I'd named him Savage. He was a small tabby that wandered around the alley outside base. He was skeletal and couldn't bite his way out of a wet paper bag, so I adopted him. The thing is, I didn't call him Savage when we were alone. I never told anyone his real name."

"Okay," she said, "so what was his real name?"

"Stevens. Cat Stevens. It was almost Cat Benatar."

She burst out laughing. "And you're here to help me save the world?"

"Yep. Absolutely."

She shook her head again. "Oh boy."

As we got closer to the east coast, the knot in my stomach wrapped around itself and pulled tighter. It wouldn't be long before my intestines were garroted. It was still a blessed relief when the first sliver of the ocean appeared on the horizon.

The sinking sun reflected off the rolling Atlantic like a shower of amber jewels. Its colorful magic show in the distance was beautiful, not just because it was a stunning sight, but because open space lay ahead of us. I swear we'd clipped treetops more than once but Monica assured me that, if we'd clipped anything, we'd know. She mentioned something about a fiery ball falling from the sky. I'm allergic to fire. And falling from the sky.

Since they sat right in front of me, I couldn't help but catch snippets of a conversation she had with Lennon. Earlier today, I'd been concerned that she was a loose cannon that could go off and jeopardize everything we were trying to do. Now, I felt much better. I didn't eavesdrop but I overheard enough to put my mind at rest. She was invested in what we were doing, and it also seemed that, the more time she spent with him, they were forming a sort of partnership.

"Okay team," she said, "we need to find a place to land that won't be a million miles from the water. And we still need to find a decent boat, so I'll climb higher to give us more of a view. If you spot a marina or a boat yard, speak up."

We each took a window, just like when we'd taken off, and began the search. Monica flew us up to the coastline and then turned and flew parallel to it for a while. I saw nothing but beach houses I'd never be able to afford, and a couple of run down shacks I probably could. After a few minutes, when none of us had seen anything of use, she banked the plane inland again and flew back in the opposite direction. A few slips reached out into the water, constructed in rows that looked like crocodile teeth taking a bite out of the ocean. They were either empty or had small boats moored that wouldn't get us half the distance we needed. It seemed like we flew for ages.

"Hey Monica," I said, "don't forget that the further north we fly, we..."

"We're flying south, Paul."

So much for my manly sense of direction. "The further south we fly, the further away we get from our best 'crow flies' place to launch into the ocean, right?"

"Yeah," she replied, "well the further south we fly, we might find a boat that will take us the hundred and eighty miles it is to our objective. Unless you've earned some kind of superhero swimming badge you didn't tell us about?"

I nodded and slumped back in my seat. "Yeah, you got me there. Let's keep looking."

We rounded a curve that housed a tranquil bay lined with palm trees. The tide washed inland and the white of the surf lapped onto the beach. Every time it receded it left a perfectly formed mustache on the sand. The view was breathtaking, but I'd concluded that boats were not moored directly on the ocean. I moved across the aisle behind Sabrina and gazed back inland. Small rivers threaded through the land like veins and ran past properties with built in swimming pools and helicopter pads. Maybe it was just me, but why would you want a swimming pool with the ocean outside your door? I followed the trail of one river that ended in a larger body of water, its green a deeper shade than that around it.

"Stop," I said, "I see something."

"That would be a bad idea," said Monica. "If I stop the plane it'll stall and we'll die a fiery and horrible death. We already talked about fire. What did you see, Paul?"

I cringed. Monica was getting too smart. I took a closer look at a carpet of real estate that rolled out into a large lake. The river continued to snake away from it and wound around buildings and land until it reached the ocean. "It looks like a marina. There are two decent sized boats moored there and, if I'm not mistaken, fuel pumps too."

Lennon looked over his shoulder. "And? What are you thinking?"

"Well, if the boats have to stop to refuel, their owners have to get out of them and go into the store to pay for the gas, right? Wouldn't that be a good time to, you know..." I glanced at Sabrina. "...borrow one?"

CHAPTER FORTY-ONE

B eck lifted his shirtsleeve with a finger and glanced at his watch. Four and a half hours had passed since Molito had last called. Earlier in the day, when he first thought his team was decimated, he'd written off the guys and prepared himself to follow the mission through alone. Molito's call, out of the blue and unexpected, had awoken the warm buzz of comradeship he was familiar with; the team spirit from the battlefront, the 'us against them' mentality that got them through so many seemingly unwinnable situations. Now, it seemed he was alone again. There was no way Molito would go this long without contact.

Against protocol he palmed his phone, speed dialed Molito's number and held the device to his ear.

Silence. No service.

The pulse in his cheek ticked again, then grew tendrils that spread up into his temple. He massaged the twitch with his fingertips.

By his reckoning, everything would kick off in about five and half hours. The Consortium chose Dubai as its central target so the city's time zone was built into the calculations. It was the hub of the Middle East, packed solid with businesses and civilians, its skyscrapers reaching up into the heavens and its ports teeming with transport. It was eight hours ahead of the local time, which meant when everything went live, the time there would be noon on Monday. Lots of rag-heads milling around: grabbing lunch, or praying, or whatever the hell they'd be doing on their last day on Earth.

The thought rejuvenated him. He reached into a drawer at the side of his desk and pulled out a bottle of scotch and a shot glass and placed them next to his keyboard. He spun the bottle until the black label faced him. Glenfiddich 30-year-old single malt. There were older and more expensive variants out there, but years ago on a miserable night in Baghdad, after a brutal skirmish that cost many lives, the bloodied core team of Beck, Molito and Bell had huddled together in the pouring, filthy rain to toast their futures with this exact drink.

He filled the shot glass with a steady hand, put the bottle back in the drawer, and twirled the glass around in his fingers. It was amazing they'd all survived so many wars together. Wars that came with crude roadside devices that showered passersby with nails and screws, and with attractive, smooth talking women sent to seduce them and murder them in their sleep. With hundreds of thousands of unorganized and crazed locals that knew nothing more, from one generation to the next, than to kill the foreign infidel. And who seemed to turn up at a moment's notice in panel vans and trucks at the slightest rumor. Wars fought by much better trained mercenaries, armed with their profiles on cellphones and the promise of a big payday for their heads. They'd survived all that, yet were taken down by his ex fucking wife and her bunch of goons.

Sometimes life dealt you shit. All you could do was play your hand. He turned his back to the control room and raised the small glass to his chest.

"To my mates," he toasted. "Raise a shit storm in Hell and treat them down there like you did up here. Rest easy, you'll be avenged."

He swallowed the liquid with one gulp and allowed its heat to spread from his throat into his stomach, then replaced the glass and smoothed out his shirt.

"You'll be avenged. Mark my words."

CHAPTER FORTY-TWO

Monica had tasked us with finding somewhere to land. Somewhere with no trees or power lines and enough flat earth with enough room to safely stop the plane. Night was closing in, but apparently, landing wasn't rocket science. We just had to find a decent strip of concrete. I hoped she knew how to work the brakes better than how she worked the accelerator when we took off.

On one side of us, the endless ocean flowed and rolled until it blended into the horizon. There were no twinkling lights of transport ships to break up the blue mass, just a jumble of persistent tourists milling around near the shore trying to live every minute of their vacations. Patchwork squares of greens and grays lay on the other side, the fields and valleys mixed in with the town lights and commercial areas. Amongst the mix of color, I spotted a stretch of road that appeared to be unused, hidden behind a clump of trees, about two inches away from the marina. When Monica translated that to ground level, I'd actually found a stretch of road hidden behind a mini forest, about half a mile from the marina.

She banked sharply and sent us sliding in our seats, then steadied the plane until she appeared to be dead level on approach with the road. As impressed as I was with her flying ability, my stomach still lurched as she lowered us into a dive, and we approached the asphalt at what appeared to be a thousand miles an hour. Perception has a weird way of playing with you when you have no control over events, especially in the gloom. I glanced at Sabrina. She held onto the lap belt, her knuckles white and her eyes closed. I don't think she was praying, but I couldn't read her mind. I reached over and clasped her cold hand in mine.

Everything on the ground grew larger way too quickly for my liking. Monica remained calm and steered the plane between the trees and buildings, and dropped us lower until it looked as if we were at the same level as the road. The odd street sign whizzed past the windows, completely unreadable, and the dotted line in the center of the road became a solid line as the black surface rushed up to meet us. I closed my eyes and remembered the fireball conversation we'd had earlier, and jumped as the wheels screeched a protest against the asphalt. The plane bounced back up into the air. My stomach followed it until it caught in my throat. The wheels made contact again, this time a little firmer. A deep rumble drowned out the sound of rushing air as they found solid ground. Gravity did its thing and dragged the plane down and we rolled and swayed along the road as Monica slowed us to a halt.

She looked over her shoulder like a school bus driver. "Everyone okay?"

Lennon looked like he'd taken a thrill ride on a rollercoaster. Sabrina was deathly pale but nodded anyway. I was grateful we were on the ground again. We sat there, surprised we'd come this far and were still alive.

I pushed open the door and jumped out onto the road. We'd landed in the middle of a sprawling commercial area. On either side of us rose tall, clinical looking units, all white walls and glass, each with its loading dock and shutter door lit by security lights. No one ventured out to see what all the commotion was, but then it was Sunday evening. It would probably be a hive of activity in the morning but, for now, we appeared to have the place to ourselves.

I poked my head back into the cabin. "All right, what's the plan? Where are you going to put the plane?"

"I'm leaving it right here," said Monica. "It's not my plane and anyway, one way or another, it really won't matter tomorrow, will it?"

I did a slow pirouette to get my bearings. "Good point." Across the concrete was an opening between two of the buildings. "I reckon the marina is that way. Let's load up and get going."

We did the A-Team thing and locked and loaded our weaponry and hid it as best we could. Monica emptied a few things out of her bag to make space for the drone and swung everything onto her back. I reached out my hand. "I can carry that for you, if you like."

"That's okay," she said. "I appreciate the offer, but I'm sure you've realized by now I'm the independent type. Now if I should happen to get shot or something…"

"Ha. How about you don't get shot and continue to be independent, okay?"

"Sounds like a plan," she smiled.

We hadn't got out of the area when we heard a chirping noise. We stopped and turned. Lennon reached into his pocket, retrieved his phone and glanced at the screen.

"Well, look at that. It's the boss. You think I should take this?"

Lennon swiped his palm across the screen and lifted the phone to his ear. "I'm coming for you, you son of a bitch."

There was silence for a moment, and then the same voice spoke. SD1. Calm, even, assured, still with no hint of a regional accent. "Mr. Lennon. Did someone annoy you?"

"You've been lying to me. Why didn't you tell me what I was involved in? Starting another war? You've got to be fucking kidding me."

"I've never lied to you. I may have kept some information to myself, but that was for your own good. If you'd known the bigger picture you wouldn't have done half the things you've done for us. You've done them so well too. I gather you've found what you were looking for?"

"Not now I haven't. Now, you're what I'm looking for, and when I find you…"

"You'll do what?"

For the first time since the conversations began, the tone of voice changed. Those three small words held more arrogance and confidence than Lennon had ever heard from the man before.

"You'll do what, you insignificant little man? You've got no idea who or what you're up against. Go against me and you'd better be looking over your shoulder every day, for the rest of your short life. Call the police if you like. We own them. Speak to the Feds, or your congressman. Guess what? We own them too. You want to walk out of this alive? Wait where you are and I'll send someone to pick you up. We'll take care of everything else and you'll be compensated enough to retire somewhere hot and sunny. Dip your toes in the sand."

"Yeah, until the missiles start raining down. You're a psychopath. There's only one way this ends, and it ends when this threat is over."

"And you think that would be it? Don't be so naïve Lennon. There'll be a next time, and a time after that. What the hell happened to you, did you have an epiphany? Did someone actually give you a soul? Don't forget, I know everything you've done. And if that information ever got out? Well, it wouldn't look very good, would it?"

"That information would implicate you too, you bastard. I've had my eyes closed for years but they're open now. We're coming for you. We'll find that ship and we're coming to stop you."

Silence. And then a deep breath and a sigh as if a well of patience had finally run dry. Then the usual SD1 voice returned. "I don't know what you're talking about. What ship? Whatever, you'll never find me, I hold a much higher position than you realize. Who's to say I'm even in the same country as you? But please, go ahead. Come for me. But Lennon? You'd better bring a fucking army."

I'd only ever seen Lennon behave like the FBI agent he'd pretended he was. Despite only hearing one side of his conversation, if it was between a man and wife then divorce was imminent. His face flushed red, his teeth bared, and he yelled obscenities before he launched his phone into the air. It bounced with a crunch and skittered across the concrete and slid into the curbside shattered and broken. That call was definitely disconnected.

I waited a moment longer, partially to let him cool down but also because he scared the crap out of me, and then stepped toward him. "Hey man, are you okay? If you need a minute, that's cool, but we really need to get moving."

He glared at me, his eyes wild and dangerous, as if he'd overdosed on steroids. Then he breathed, put his hands on his hips, and looked at his shoes. When he lifted his head again, the Lennon I knew stood before me. "I'll need a new job after this."

"Me too," I said. "Maybe we could go into the drug business together." He looked at me like I had two heads. "Yeah, okay." I said. "Let's go shall we?"

Nothing moved in the surrounding area. Monica had landed the plane quite a distance away from the hubbub and touristy action of Virginia Beach. I'd spotted that further up the coast and was grateful we didn't have to navigate through it. Regardless of how well we'd hidden our weapons, someone would surely have said something about four random people wandering the streets with bulges and backpacks, as if headed to war. Which I supposed we were.

Outside the commercial block, the road meandered off into the distance and faded into a row of tall trees. We skipped the winding road and walked right through the low brush up to the tree line, into a wooded area. The ground was rugged and uneven and, more than once, one or another of us slipped or lost our footing in the dark. After a while we coupled up. I linked Sabrina as Lennon linked Monica, and we edged our way forward arm in arm like a search party, until we reached the other side of the wood. A glimpse of the marina lights poked through the foliage.

The change of surroundings was dramatic. Gone was the cloying must of decomposing undergrowth, replaced by crisp, clean air blowing in off the small lake. My mouth watered as the familiar smell of pizza drifted in the breeze and my stomach grumbled in acknowl-edgment. I hadn't eaten for hours but, during the mayhem of the day, I hadn't even thought about it.

Just in front of us, outside the tree line, was a boardwalk made of concrete slabs seated into a metal frame that led the way to the small marina. It floated on the surface of the water and bobbed up and down peacefully with the water level until it reached the main area. Flick-ering torches lit up a half dozen tables scattered about in front of a small store, with faux straw tiki umbrellas sticking out of their centers. Two of them had occupants, and one of them held a pizza the size of a trash can lid. Off to one side, a fuel pump moored two small boats. Not big enough for what we needed.

I turned to the group. "What do you think? I know we're up against the clock but shouldn't we get something to eat while we can? We can sit right there in plain sight and wait for the right kind of boat to come along."

"Basic training says always eat when you can," said Lennon. "You never know where your next meal's coming from. I'm with you. Let's eat and hope something useful turns up."

A slatted wooden storage shed sat behind the store, almost hidden in shade. Despite the dark, the vivid color of life vests still showed through the slats. Sabrina was on the same wavelength as me. "We can stash everything in there until we're ready to go," she said. "Hand everything to me and wait here."

We offloaded rifles and anything that couldn't be tucked away. She took them and crept across the back of the tree line, vaulted a low fence, and carefully placed our arsenal on top of the shed's contents. She returned a minute later. We linked arms again and walked out onto the concrete walkway like two couples out for a stroll, laughing and joking at nothing in particular, and made our way to the store.

As we grew closer, the people seated at the tables looked up at us, nodded a welcome, and went back to their conversations. I could see the barrel of a rifle protruding through the side of the storage shed and stopped to tie my laces while I nudged it back inside with an elbow. Sabrina laughed.

"What?" I said.

"Just imagining what the Paul I met a few days ago might have done in the same situation."

I had to chuckle. "Not that," I said in a quiet voice. "I'm definitely not the same person I was a few days ago, but I'd like to think that change is good. Now I don't know about you, but I'm starving. Let's get some food."

Light blue paint covered the inside walls of the store. I imagined it was to conjure up images of sea life and sailing, but it reminded me of a baby boy's bedroom. It looked as if someone had tried to cram two tons of junk into a one-ton storage space. Fishing equipment and basic boat parts were scattered around in no particular order. A hand painted sign behind the counter said 'Octopus Marina'. It had a cute looking octopus in the center with his tentacles holding onto small placards with advertisements on each; diving club, treasure hunt, fishing club, scuba club, glass bottomed boats. The aquatic life might be more appealing if I didn't have a paralyzing fear of drowning. A scare in a swimming pool had left me nervous around water. Given our destination, I had to mention it to the team. I just had to find the right time.

Beneath the octopus hung another handwritten sign that said 'Scuba club meet. Sunday at 9.00pm. Drinking and planning. Snorkels and flippers welcome'. That could be useful. A clock on the wall above the sign said that the meet started in ten minutes.

A young boy and an older woman eyed us with suspicion as we sidled up to the counter. They didn't look friendly.

"What do you fancy?"

Monica's voice snapped me back to attention. "I'm sorry?"

"Food. What would you like to eat?"

"Oh." I waved a hand. "I don't care. Pizza's fine, whatever you want to get."

I took Sabrina and Lennon to one side while Monica gave our order to the boat people. "There's a scuba meet here tonight. Don't those guys usually have their boats packed full of equipment?"

Lennon nodded. "Yes they do. Who knows, perhaps we'll get lucky and not have to work too hard for a change."

Monica walked back toward us, sliding her credit card into her pocket. "Okay, we're all set. I got three large pizzas. Let's go find seats."

We sat in the middle of the marina's deck, a few tables away from the people already there. It was a beautiful night under a dark sky. The tiki torches cast tongues of orange across the lake. Small candles burned on each table and flickered in the cool breeze and a faint smell of citronella hovered around the table. If it wasn't for the horrendous day and the nightmare ahead, and the medicinal odor of the bug repellant, the whole setup might have been romantic. Lennon glanced across at me. I'd dragged my chair closer to Sabrina. He'd noticed.

"So, how'd you two get together?" he asked.

I scowled but he smiled, happy to put me on the spot. "What? We have time that we really don't have, to kill. Tell the story, Howard."

"Yeah," said Monica with devilish glee, "tell it Paul."

Telling the story killed the time it took for the pizza to arrive and cost me just as much in embarrassment as in time. Three pizzas, the size of the one we'd seen earlier, were placed before us. They were so big, they hung over the edges of the table precariously. To ease the burden, we dived into them with a mad scramble, tearing into the wedges like lions that hadn't fed for a week. Over the sound of chewing, a rumble behind us grew from a whisper to a full-grown growl and back to a steady throttle. Two boats had sailed into the marina. They eased off on the power as they passed the buoy markers on either side of the lake that instructed them to power down their engines, and drifted into dock. The wake calmed and the huge ripples outside the marina washed out onto the banks or faded into smaller ripples that lapped against the wooden posts beside us.

We glanced at each other, then focused on the boat that brought up the rear. The one in front was no slouch. It was a nice-looking vessel, maybe twenty-five feet long, and looked as if it could hold its own against a decent racer. The one behind it was a different proposition altogether. It was a good fifteen feet longer. Its nose rose proudly out of the water, and cut an easy swathe through the surface as its pilot guided it into the dock. It was sleek and painted in a swirling mix of white and burgundy. 'Ship Happens' was written along the side in a swirly font.

The first boat moved past the fuel pump, killed its engines and drifted into a small slip to the side. The second moved beside it, again ignoring the fuel pump. It was looking like we'd need a plan B, but then its owner had second thoughts and swung it inwards toward the jetty. It coasted up to the pump.

Before they reached the deck, his partner leaped out and grabbed the chrome rail that circled the boat, pulled it up to the rubber bumpers along the side of the jetty, then roped it off and walked toward us. She strode with purpose like an Amazonian warrior, all flowing blonde hair, tanned skin and toned muscles. The young guy from the store ran right by her without a glance out to the boat and talked excitedly to the boat owner. He gave the kid directions and then jogged along the jetty to catch his partner. They walked by us with an air of arrogance, noses in the air, and didn't even glance at our table. The engine was still running, so the kid jumped into the boat, turned it off, and then got back out, popped the fuel cap and jammed the pump nozzle into the boat.

This might be easier than I thought. 'Ship' was definitely about to happen.

CHAPTER FORTY-THREE

The small chime over the store entrance sounded as they entered.

I glanced over my shoulder at the closing door. "Okay, are we ready?"

Monica held up a hand. "Not yet. We should wait until the boat is fueled up, in case it's low on gas. We might have a distance to travel."

"Agreed," said Lennon. "Let's sit tight for now. Enjoy the pizza."

We carried on munching as the young guy carried on pumping. He was still working as the couple exited the store. They walked to the left of us and took a table with the owners of the first boat amongst the people already seated. This had to be the scuba meet. Hopefully, that meant their boat was loaded with the equipment for such a task.

After one more slice of pizza, the kid doing the fueling replaced the gas pump and walked back into the store. I looked at Sabrina who, once again, read my mind. She pushed her chair away from the table. "I'll get our stuff and meet you at the back of the store. Give me a sign when you're ready."

She got up and sauntered past everyone as if she was going to check out the other side of the marina.

"Okay you two," I said to Lennon and Monica, "take a casual walk over there as if you want to buy that boat. I didn't see the kid take the keys with him. If it looks like we're good to go, give us a wave and we'll go for it. I'll distract the owner."

Lennon nodded, grabbed Monica's hand and walked off toward the boat. I ambled back into the store and hung around for a moment looking at overpriced shirts and provisions. The whole place had a musty smell I didn't care for, like damp from the water was living in its framework. After a while, I went back outside and moved toward the boat's owner. He looked at me as if he'd just stepped in me and couldn't wait to smear me off the bottom of his shoe.

"Yes? Can I help you?"

"Yes, I'm sorry to bother you. The lady in the store asked if I'd get you to go back to the desk. Something about your credit card."

He huffed and flushed red, then pushed his chair back with a screech. "What? Don't be ridiculous. Move out of my way, I'll deal with this."

He shoulder barged me aside. I resisted the urge to slap his balding head as he rushed past me into the store, and strode past everyone toward the boat. As I passed the building, Lennon waved from beside the fuel pump.

I turned to face the bushes beside the store. "Sabrina. Now."

She appeared and stepped through the brush loaded down with her bag and our weapons. I took some of the load as the boat's engine turned over and burst into life. Monica waved at us to hurry. I didn't need an invitation and followed Sabrina as she ran along the jetty. Lennon had climbed in and held out his arms to take everything off us. He staggered back onto the white leather seats as our armory hit him.

"Sorry dude," I said. Behind me, I heard shouting from the store and looked over my shoulder. Bald guy had rumbled us and was running across the walkway. I held onto the chrome rail to keep the boat close as Sabrina stepped onto the engine cover and then I clambered aboard myself. As soon as my feet hit the floor Monica pushed on two levers and the engine jolted us forward. The momentum sent me sprawling onto the back seat and into Sabrina's lap. I lay there smiling as Monica wrenched the wheel to one side and swung the boat away from the dock and powered it out into the water.

It was a beautiful boat but, unlike with the trucks we'd taken, I didn't feel the slightest hint of guilt over taking it from such an obnoxious person. With the flickering light from a tiki torch dancing on his head, he stood on the edge of the jetty like a lighthouse at sunset. I stumbled upright in time to see the wash caused by Monica's speedy exit splash against the side of the dock and soak him. I resisted the urge to wave.

My heart still pounded. It might have been from the adrenaline surge or the run across the walkway but, with the wind in my face, all I felt was exhilaration. Lennon and Monica were laughing together by the helm. Sabrina sat relaxed on the back seat with her hair streaming out behind her. She gazed at me and smiled.

I gathered our weapons and carried them down a narrow flight of steps into the cuddy. It was a tight space, but luxurious just the same. Walnut and white leather lined the top of the cabin to match the outside trim. The seats were covered in a smooth waterproof fabric. Two small hatches in the roof let in the fading sunlight, but I had to switch on the built in overhead lights before I could look around properly. The front of the cuddy had an open compartment filled with oxygen tanks and masks, and half a dozen scuba suits hung from hooks above it. Under a seat to one side was a life vest. Its fluorescent fabric glowed in the light. I pulled it out and slid my arms into it and then clipped the lock around my waist. It wouldn't do for me to fall overboard before we even reached our destination. My stomach tumbled as the first thought of what might lie ahead knocked on the door in my mind.

A decent sized monitor sat on a shelf just inside the entrance with a jumble of equipment, a keyboard and a wireless mouse beneath it. I pulled open a small drawer below the shelf. It held a few scraps of paper and a small box of business cards. I pulled a card. The statement 'Adriana Jones – Treasure Hunter' splashed across it in vivid colors. Resisting the urge to laugh, I closed the door and ventured back up the steps, grasping the sides of the small entrance for support as the boat bounced across the water.

Lennon raised his hands in a mock effort to shield his eyes and shouted over the sound of rushing wind and racing engines. "Holy crap Howard, you look like you lost a fluorescent paintball fight."

"Believe me," I shouted back, "you have no idea how much more at ease I am wearing this thing."

Monica eased off the throttle and the noise level dropped enough for us to talk without shouting. Sabrina leaned forward and rested her arms on her knees. She looked concerned. "Paul. You can swim, right?"

"Oh yes," I said, "I can swim. I just don't like too." Now seemed as good a time as any to get this out. "I fell into a pool when I was a kid. Almost drowned. In fact, my Dad had to do the old 'lay them on their side, and give them a good squeeze' trick to bring me back. It scared the shit out of me. I've been nervous around water since then, but don't worry. When push comes to shove, I'll be okay. You can count on me."

"All right, and you don't have to worry either," said Sabrina. "We'll keep an eye on you. Right guys?"

Everyone nodded. I nodded a silent thank you back to them. Lennon took a seat on the side of the boat and kept watch on the water behind us.

The scenery whizzed by us in the boat's lights. It wasn't a blur, but we moved at a good rate of knots in the narrow river. Monica did a great job of keeping the boat in the center, away from the banks. I couldn't see the bottom of the river so it was hard to tell just how deep the water was beneath us. Behind us flowed nothing but frothing white water, floating away like a huge whale fin. Nothing followed us, but there were other boats moored when we left so I figured we should still keep an eye out. The bald guy might have had a friend back there to help him out, or they could call the river police.

"How long until we reach the ocean?" I asked.

Monica turned to face me, the first time she'd looked away from the river since we took the boat. "I'm not sure, but it won't be too much longer. This is the only way out though. It would be nice if there's no one waiting for us at the exit. Once we reach the ocean, I'll slow down and we'll work out how to program this GPS."

She pointed to the console in front of her. Dials of various sizes lined up in neat rows. I leaned closer to check them out, but most of the labels were foreign to me. I did recognize the fuel gauges, and they both reassuringly indicated full tanks. Two more dials indicated that boats had taps and drives, although I had no idea what they were. Above them was a panel set into the fiberglass, which glowed with a map of our position. I followed the snaking river to see where we'd come out into the ocean, but the end of the river was off the screen.

"You know those coordinates?" I asked.

She nodded. "Yep. I saw them so many times trying to work out what they were that they're burned into my brain."

"I tried too," I said, "but I gave up because I didn't believe that they would actually take us out into the ocean."

"Believe it," she said. "You might as well throw your card away."

"I would, but what's this?" I pulled the card from my pocket and showed her the back of it. Underneath the coordinates was another line of writing.

KYCB1873 was printed in precise black lettering.

"Got me," said Monica. "Safe deposit box? I tried everything but that and came up empty."

I laughed. "Yeah. You, me and Sabrina had the same idea. She checked it out. It's not a safe deposit box."

"Maybe it's the registration number for Beck's ship? Regardless, I have that number burned into my brain too."

She pointed to the screen. The small winding line that represented the river on the GPS screen grew wider a distance from now and, after that, there was nothing but blue. "There's the ocean. You ready?"

I cinched the buckle on the life vest with renewed determination. It tightened against my churning stomach and I hoped my voice wouldn't betray my nerves.

"As ready as I'm going to be."

CHAPTER FORTY-FOUR

Beck took a few deep breaths before he answered his counterpart. The Consortium didn't run without cost and the people paying the cost were the most arrogant idiots he'd come across. He sat in his office, feet on the desk, wearing a poker face. The monotone voice continued and grated in the earpiece like a storm warning. He had to interrupt. "You should reign in your dogs, Mr. Miller, they're getting restless. You know what happens to restless dogs. We put them out of their misery."

The voice at the other end of the line dropped the calm and continued as if it was a heartbeat away from cardiac arrest. "But he just told me you fool. He's coming for you and he knows where you are."

Beck imagined his caller's phone covered in sweaty fingerprints and spittle. "Watch your tongue Miller. You might be high and mighty in your courtroom, with your shiny bench and your little hammer, but don't forget I can find out where you live. We appreciate your money, we really do, but you should stick to pushing pencils and nailing bad guys. Let the real men do the dirty work. You don't want me climbing through your bedroom window at night, do you? It wouldn't be pleasant. I could swing you from your chandeliers with one of your robes.

Or even one of your stupid wigs. It's been a while since I visited London. I miss it."

"Don't you dare threaten me. You might find where I live but I could have you..."

"Have me what, you dickless pencil pusher? Do as you're told. Go and put your frock on and let me get on with our mission because you're pissing me off. I'll be seeing you." Beck disconnected the call and calmly replaced the handset. He left the control room and sauntered through the corridors until, almost on autopilot, he arrived at the main room. The hub of the wheel.

Jones was standing in front of one of the screens when Beck entered the room. The clock on the wall read 4:28:15. Less than five hours. The green dots on the screens were stationary. All the drones were in position. They were ready for the final command.

"Looking good?" asked Beck.

"Yes, Sir," said Jones. "Perfect."

So, the cavalry was coming. Let them. They had no idea where he was and, even if they did, they had no way to get to him. By the time they worked everything out, the Middle East would be rubble.

———————

The beam of light off the front of the boat bounced and jerked and lit up what looked like a huge nest of roiling and coiled snakes in the water. Beyond the waves lay nothing but darkness. Slow moving lights that appeared almost stationary broke up the distant horizon.

"Shipping lanes," said Monica.

"Huh?" I said. "It's so dark out there."

"Yeah, we have our lights and the moonlight out here, but that's it. Those lights far in the distance, they're tankers and transporters. They're how stuff gets from A to B. Shipping. They have designated lanes and routes they stick to. I'm guessing Kyle is beyond them, using them as a kind of smoke screen to hide behind."

"They seem miles away."

"They are," she laughed. "Don't worry. This boat is full of fuel and it's fast. I managed to get the GPS programmed. It says we should get to him in plenty of time. We need to start thinking about what we'll do when we get there."

The thought had occurred to me. The easy part was getting into position to do something, but once we got there, then what? We didn't have cannons or grappling hooks like pirates, or sophisticated weaponry like the Navy. We were a ragtag bunch of people with no one to trust and no idea of how to do what we needed to do to stop the bad guys. Like we'd discussed, Beck might be in a rowing boat with a laptop, or he might be on a cruiser with helicopters and infrared sighting. Until we got there we had no idea what we might be up against.

Monica was right about the distance though. The boat ate up the miles and plowed through the increasing current like a sharp knife. The lights that were pinpricks were now actual lights in the near distance. Lennon and Sabrina sat in silence and seemed to be conserving energy. Mine peaked and spiked, and my stomach tossed around like a tumble dryer load. The overhead lights in the cuddy lit up the rest room in front of me with a welcoming glow.

The boat bounced higher as the wake from the large boats crashed into us. Monica adjusted something on the cockpit and the nose of the boat lowered, but it still buffeted the water with loud cracks. I held on to the side rail for support. My stomach was talking to me. "I need to answer a call of nature."

"Well, you're not at school anymore," said Monica. "You don't need permission. Unless you need someone to come and hold your hand?"

I grimaced. "Yeah. Okay, well I just thought…"

She gave me a smile and looked forward once more. "I'm just playing, Paul."

I swallowed my pride, made my way to the small door and pulled it open. It was obvious whoever had designed this boat knew that they'd never need to relieve themselves in it. The bathroom looked to be around three feet wide and five feet tall with a toilet designed for an elf placed in it. I shucked off the life vest and tossed it into the cuddy.

"Are you…"

Sabrina's voice drifted to me from the back of the boat, but didn't have the power to beat the noise of the engine. I stepped back onto the main deck and walked up to her. She looked amazing and was still reclined across the back seat. I leaned forward and shouted as the boat shook me around. "I'm sorry?"

"I said are you okay? You look pale."

"Yes, I'm okay," I said.

"Good. You know, I didn't get to use my drone," she said with a pout.

"Use it for what?"

"I was looking forward to trying it out at the marina to scout for a boat. This happened way too easily."

"It did," I said, "but let's not curse good fortune. It's about time we had some luck. Who knows, we're nowhere near done yet. You might still get the opportunity."

I leaned forward to kiss her and could feel Lennon's eyes burning a hole in my back. The boat rocked and I missed my target and planted a smeared kiss across her nose.

"Why don't you try that again," she laughed.

I leaned in again, and her warm breath washed across my face. She closed her eyes in anticipation as a large wave crashed against the side of the boat. I heard Monica make a 'Whoa' kind of noise. In the corner of my eye I saw Lennon jerk and grab the sides of his seat. Sabrina left her seat in an impressive feat of levitation as I flew over her and across the back of the boat. I cracked my head against the chrome rail and it rang enough to play a tune. Then I rolled like an Olympian diver over the engine compartment and splashed into the freezing sea.

The wash from the boats propellers tossed me around like a piece of laundry, and I lost all sense of direction. My first instinct was to take a deep breath before the violent water dragged me under forever, but the icy shock had frozen me. I rolled and tumbled. The voice in my head screamed instructions to stay calm that my brain ignored. All I could think of in my disoriented state were sharks and piranhas or getting flattened by a cruise ship. So, I panicked.

Years ago, a holiday with family went horribly wrong when I slipped and fell into the deep end of a swimming pool. As soon as I hit the water, cramps seized my calves and I sank to the bottom. No matter how much I thrashed and clawed at the water, I laid on the bottom of the pool as the legs of other swimmers kicked gracefully in the distance. Dad said I was only gone for a few seconds, but I remember every one of them. The way my vision filled in from the edges as if it was tissue-absorbing ink. The way my head pounded and my limbs grew heavier. Then the panic turned to serenity as if my mind accepted its fate and found peace. A huge commotion in the water above me snapped me out of the fugue and I drew in my first breath of water. The next thing I knew, I awoke lying on the side of the pool, coughing and vomiting out my stomach contents. Later that day, Dad punched the lifeguard in the face. He'd missed the entire event because he was flirting with one of the hotel waitresses.

The rolling settled as the boat's wash spread itself out across the ocean and, by either fluke or fate, my flailing arms dragged me up into moonlight. As my head broke through I had enough time to heave in a breath of precious air before I began to sink again. I forgot every one of the videos I saw on treading water and thrashed about to grab its surface. The water was jet black and stung my eyes so I closed them. Images of Kacie plastered themselves against the back of them and urged me to fight.

I fought.

The first thing that came to mind was eggbeater. The gears in my brain engaged. Eggbeater. Try to relax, hold out your arms and kick your legs in the same motion as an eggbeater. That's how you tread water. Through the panic it was easier said than done. My chest began to complain at the lack of oxygen and that familiar feeling in my head returned. The closing in and the darkness, darker than the back of my closed eyes. I resigned myself to the water and relaxed.

In slow motion, my body began to drift upwards. I drew in my knees and kicked through the heavy water, and I rose quicker. My heartbeat thumped in my ears, fast and frantic, and then cold air hit me again and the moonlight reappeared. Water lapped against my face as I spun my head to look for the boat. I heard it before I saw it, and turned my head once more.

It was heading right for me.

CHAPTER FORTY-FIVE

Sabrina's scream got everyone's attention.

"Stop the boat, Paul fell overboard!"

The boat banked as Monica eased the throttle back and spun the wheel. Sabrina slid across the back seat and crashed into the cushioned side with a groan.

Lennon stood and raced to the back of the boat, held onto the side rails and leaned out into the night. He scanned the dark water. Mirror flashes of light bounced back off the choppy waves and made it harder still to fix on any one point. "Are there any more lights on this thing? I can barely see ten feet ahead."

"That's it," said Monica. "How far back were we when he fell?"

"God knows. I'm not even sure we're on the right line," said Sabrina. "Just troll back as slow as possible. If we hit him with the boat..."

"We won't hit him with the boat," said Lennon. "You look along your side and I'll look over mine. We'll find him."

The engine purred as the boat sliced through the water leaving little wake, but the sound ruined any chance they had of hearing a cry for help. Small branches and debris floated past that hadn't been visible when it was racing and both Lennon and Sabrina called out false alarms. Lights from the tankers twinkled in the distance. One of them headed in their direction. Sabrina lifted a finger to point as a head broke the water's surface to the side of her.

"There! Stop the boat!"

The engine wound down, until it sputtered and Monica swung the boat across to follow Sabrina's pointed finger. It moved forward under its own momentum as Lennon joined Sabrina. Howard's head bobbed up through the water and Sabrina shouted out as he disappeared beneath the surface again. They scanned the ripples as the water settled. He reappeared right in front of them.

"Monica! Turn away now, we're going to hit him," shouted Lennon. He almost fell overboard as the boat swerved, and he leaned over to grab Howard's arm. His fingers brushed across fabric, and then the boat floated out of range. Howard sank again. Sabrina leaped out of her seat and ran toward the front of the boat and vanished into the cuddy. She returned with the life vest and threw it out into the ocean. Howard resurfaced again. They could hear his gasp and see the panic in his eyes. The vest landed to one side of him. He fumbled and latched on to it at the second attempt and clung to it like a prize.

Sabrina guided Monica to float alongside him. Lennon leaned out again. "Howard. You have to trust me, all right? Hold onto one arm of the vest and raise the other up as high as you can. I'll grab it and drag you to the boat."

Howard slid an arm through one side of the vest and strained to hold the loose flap as high as he could. The water lapped at his face and the vest trembled in mid-air with the effort. As the boat drifted toward him Lennon reached out, scooped his arm through the armhole and grabbed the side rail. His chest muscles screamed as the slack tightened. He drug Howard alongside then pulled his arm closer until he could lift the vest and the man partially clear of the water.

"There are steps back here," said Sabrina. She pointed to the back of the boat at the chrome rails that dipped into the sea. "Monica, kill the engines."

The spinning propellers slowed to a stop.

"Yeah, I don't want to be diced up like a steak," said Howard between breaths.

"You got the strength to swim back there and get aboard?" said Lennon.

Howard nodded. He paddled around the side of the boat, got a foot on the stairs and clambered onto the engine compartment. Lennon and Sabrina took an arm each and dragged him the rest of the way onto the back seat.

"We need to get him into the cuddy and get those wet clothes off him before he freezes," said Lennon. The corners of his mouth curled into a tiny smile. "Sabrina, why don't you take care of that? Monica, let's get going again."

Sabrina pointed across the ocean. "Yes, Monica, get us out of here before that thing reaches us."

The tanker that was a small light in the distance was now a large vessel heading right for them. Its tall nose blocked out part of the night sky and was bound to obscure the small boat from view.

Monica choked the engine and hit the ignition. Nothing happened. She looked over her shoulder, frowned and tried again. Still nothing.

They were dead in the water.

"You choked the engine, didn't you?"

Lennon stared at the tanker but his voice was directed at Monica. "You choked it, right?"

"Shit," she said, "yes, I did. I shouldn't have done that. The engine is already warm."

"That's right," said Lennon, "so you've flooded the engine. I'm no expert on boats. Do we have to wait as long on a boat as we would in a car?"

The tanker rolled toward them like an icebreaker, relentless and constant. It would take miles of ocean to come to a halt and it was now bearing down on them. They could see the waves split apart as the nose of the huge vessel cut through them with ease. The people on board would never even realize they'd hit something and continue to sail on through the wreckage.

"I don't know," said Monica. "I've never come across this situation before."

Sabrina stood and walked to the helm. "Treat it like a car. Open the throttle completely and start the engine."

Lennon looked at her with a frown. "And that will start it?"

"No," she said, "but it will flush out the excess gas. Then you can start the engine."

A massive blast of sound shocked everyone as the tanker sounded its horn.

"They've seen us," said Monica. "We'll be okay. They'll swerve, right?"

Sabrina barged her out of the way, opened the throttle and cranked the engine. "They don't have room or time to swerve. They're assuming we won't be dumb enough to just sit here."

The rear of the boat spluttered and churned and the sharp scent of gasoline filled the air. Another turn of the engine and the smell grew thicker.

The horn blared again. The tanker seemed close enough to touch even though it was still hundreds of yards away. Its silhouette blocked out the sky and its shadow from the moon loomed over the boat.

"Is it working? Start the engine," yelled Lennon over the din.

"I'm trying," said Sabrina. She turned the engine over again. It turned over, but failed to catch. The boat was now rocking back and forth from the wake pushed forward from the tanker and its horn sounded again, deafeningly close.

Sabrina closed her eyes and said a silent prayer, then turned the engine over once more. It chugged and rolled and, at last, burst into life.

"Go, go, go," yelled Monica.

"I don't know how to drive a boat," shouted Sabrina. She gestured at the multiple dials and levers. "I just got it started. Now, get over here and deal with this!"

Sabrina slid back as Monica stepped behind the wheel and rammed the twin levers forward to power the engine. At the same time, she spun the wheel to put the back of the boat parallel with the tanker.

Their combined screams couldn't drown out the roar of the engine as the boat's nose lifted and the propellers churned water. They lurched forward. Lennon and Sabrina fell backwards. Howard moaned from the rear seat. The huge tanker steamed by them with one more blast of its horn and sent a mini tsunami into the back of the boat.

CHAPTER FORTY-SIX

I've never been surfing before but, as long as I survived the next few minutes, at least I could say I'd experienced it.

I lay across the back seat, shivering and soaked to the skin. The taste of bile still stuck to the inside of my mouth, and my bones ached as if I'd climbed a mountain. My colleagues lay scattered around the floor like litter, while the nose of the boat pointed upwards to the sky. The ocean had vanished. A tremendous rush of water roared behind the boat and pushed it forward at an unreasonable speed. Everyone around me screamed, but all I heard was the overpowering rumble of the wave we were riding. There was no way we could stay afloat. If this wave had altered its course by as little as an inch, the people searching for us would find nothing but flotsam. I closed my eyes and braced myself for another icy splash.

We seemed to fly forever, but when I grew tired of waiting for the inevitable I opened my eyes. Bit by bit the nose of the boat dipped as the wave behind us receded. The stars re-appeared a twinkle at a time and then, at last, the ocean leveled out again and the moonlight rippled across steady waves. The engine still screamed like a banshee. Monica picked herself up, pulled back the throttle to a reasonable level, and turned to face us. "I can't believe we didn't flip. I'm getting tired of asking this, but is everyone okay?"

"Shit," said Lennon. "I don't think I've experienced that kind of rush in all my years of training." He stumbled on drunken legs to the helm and squeezed Monica's shoulder.

Sabrina walked back to me on her knees and cradled my head. "Are you okay?" she asked.

The tenderness in her voice pushed through the chill that enveloped me, and I forced my mouth into a grim smile. My teeth chattered as I spoke. "Yeah, but I'm so cold. Would you help me inside the cuddy?"

She stood and looped her arms beneath mine, helped me off the seat, and together we stumbled below deck. She flicked on the lights and opened cupboard after cupboard, until a stack of fleece blankets tumbled out of one of the floor lockers. A few minutes later, my clothes hung in strategic drying positions and I was swaddled in fleece like a newborn baby. She threw one over my head and rubbed it vigorously to dry my dripping hair and laughed as my head bobbed and shook all over the place. It was a nice sound and the warmth from the friction felt amazing.

"Sit tight," she said afterwards. "I'll get an update on where we are and I'll be right back."

"Not going anywhere," I said. "I'll be right here." I lay back against the vinyl and closed my eyes. It was an effort to talk.

She mussed my tangled hair and walked out onto the deck. Snippets of the chatter outside drifted toward me in the darkness but I only made out the odd word. As they faded, I gathered the good news was the boat was still in one piece and the controls had survived our close call. I caught nothing else.

My world was tossing and turning again. I was under water. The liquid was pushing against my closed mouth and worming into my nose, trying to fill my lungs. I knew that if I relented for a second it would overwhelm me. I'd be doomed to float, lifeless and almost weightless,

around the ocean where I'd never be found. A murky film coated my
eyes, but through it I saw a light drifting toward me. The light spoke.

"…help you up. I'll help you…"

My lungs were ready to explode, the pressure in my chest immense
and paralyzing. Everything shook again as my head pounded and my
temples bulged. Then the light grew larger, until it got too close, so
dazzling that I had to squint my eyes to focus.

"Come on, Paul. Wake up. I'll help you up. I'll help you get
dressed."

The pounding stopped. The shaking didn't. Sabrina pushed against
my shoulder, again and again, until I rolled over and looked at her. I
awoke wide-eyed from the nightmare.

"It's okay," she said. "You're safe." She pushed back my hair and
kissed my forehead. "Come on, I'll help you get dressed. We're a few
miles away now. I thought you'd like to be awake when we arrived."

It was a struggle, but between us we got me into my stiff clothes.
They felt as if they'd been washed in starch and everything chafed in
all the wrong places. Still, they held warmth.

"Wow, I crashed. I must have needed that sleep," I said. "Thanks
for letting me."

"The only thing any of us could do was rest," she said. "Monica's
been a star out there. Since that tanker she's managed to avoid everything else. She reckons we're about five minutes away from being
within visual range of the co-ordinates. We made a plan to get us close
and then I'll finally use our drone to check out the area. It's dark, but
anything out there should have lights on, even if only for its safety."

I followed her out onto the deck. Monica and Lennon gave me
friendly shots to the arm. Seems there's nothing like a close call with
death and saving the world to bring a few people together. We huddled
around the helm and watched the GPS screen, which showed little
since we were miles into the Atlantic. All the lights on the boat were
turned off, so only the moon ahead lighted the way. I looked around
and saw nothing but nighttime flecked with starlight. At every compass
point around us, the far distance held nothing but a solid black
darkness.

A small blip appeared on the screen and Monica drew back the throttles and let the boat drift. The engine puttered away behind us. "I don't dare turn it off," she said. "Call me paranoid. One close shave is one too many. I'm not being helpless again."

"Fair enough," said Lennon. He pointed over the front of the boat. "So that's where the co-ordinates say he should be?"

As if she hadn't scanned the screen a thousand times, Monica checked the readout on the GPS. "Yes. It should be right there. Right in front of us, maybe a couple hundred yards away."

He disappeared below deck and returned with the rifle. The barrel rested on the windshield and swung from side to side as he looked through the scope. After a few sweeps he set it on the seat. "Well," he said, "if he's out there he's not in a boat. Looks to me like we're in the middle of nowhere. And we're all alone."

———————

It took Sabrina a while to get the drone and the controller to connect to the boat's Wi-Fi, but she got it to link together. The machine rested on the engine cover at the rear of the boat. Her laptop sat in what had become Lennon's seat and she and I sat on the rear bench as he and Monica hunched over the screen.

She flicked her thumbs over the controller and the drone's propellers whirred into action and the device floated into the air. It buzzed and swayed like an angry wasp drunk on late season apples.

"I see it," giggled Monica. She pointed at the screen like a kid in a toy store. "That is so cool. I want one. Can I get one?"

"You can have this one if it works," said Sabrina. "Here goes nothing. Eyes open people."

The drone lifted away from the boat and floated across us, over the nose and away into the distance. As it moved out of sight, Sabrina moved and sat in front of the laptop.

"Okay. I have no idea what we're looking for, so shout out if anything unusual appears."

The screen looked as if it was showing television interference as the waves flew underneath the camera. Each blink of reflected light flashed for a millisecond before darkness covered the screen again. Sabrina flicked her thumb across the controller and the image spun and moved in another direction. Still nothing. She made another adjustment. Still nothing.

For the first time, I had doubts about the numbers. What if they weren't co-ordinates? Had we gone through all this to end up floating in the middle of the ocean while wars started thousands of miles away? Hell, what if they were his lottery syndicate numbers? What if they were clothing sizes for his wardrobe? They could have been anything, but we'd all been convinced they would give us his location.

It was obvious from the mood of the group that everyone felt the same way. They glared at the screen transfixed, like they were expecting a last-minute touchdown in a Super Bowl. Shoulders were hunched, brows furrowed, and the tension crackled.

Something flitted across the screen.

"Whoa," I said, and pointed at the laptop. "What was that?"

The waves grew smaller as Sabrina lifted the drone higher to give us a wider view. They rippled and rolled into one another, but nothing moved. Then the shape flitted again. Something sliced through the water, dark and sleek, barely visible. This time Sabrina followed it with the camera.

I tilted my head as if it would give me a better image. "Is that a shark fin?"

We stared at the screen, as if we were willing it to talk, as another shape followed the first.

"Shit," said Lennon. "There it is again. That's a fucking shark. No doubt about it."

"That has to be another," I said. "The first one's still moving away."

Another fin split the water.

"That's three," said Sabrina. "Hang on a moment. Let's widen the view even more. Keep those things in focus."

More ocean appeared as she manipulated the camera and the three fins were joined by a forth. Then a fifth. The convoy moved forward, making the slightest of turns but maintaining the same heading. They seemed to be swimming in a wide circle.

"What the hell is this," said Lennon, "a shark pool party?"

"Something's not right," said Monica. "I swam with sharks on vacation once, it was great. But sharks don't swim in perfect circles, they weave while they're searching for prey. That looks too rigid, too programmed. They're like robots."

That sounded so familiar. Then it clicked. I looked at Sabrina. She looked back at me. We both looked at Monica, all of us with a wide-eyed enlightenment, while Lennon looked baffled and frowned.

The three of us spoke together.

"Ghost Swimmer."

We looked back at the screen in time to see, one by one, all five fins dip beneath the surface and vanish.

"Okay," said Lennon, "what the hell is a ghost swimmer. What am I missing?"

Sabrina reached into her bag of tricks and pulled out Monica's file. She held up a hand to ward off the impending onslaught as Monica took a sharp intake of breath and opened her mouth to vent.

"I know," she said, "and I'm sorry. Again. You can have your stuff back when we're done. I told you, necessary evil."

"Whatever," said Monica. "At least let me explain my research. Pass that over here."

Sabrina passed the manila folder. Monica withdrew a few pictures and passed them to Lennon.

"Ghost Swimmer is a project conducted by the US Navy as part of Project NEMO. They designed an underwater surveillance drone built to resemble a large tuna. You couldn't tell on the screen, but that thing's five feet long and weighs a ton. In motion, it swims like a shark and can dive to three hundred feet. It only needs to surface to communicate and so can stay underwater for ages. They designed it for checking boats in port, but I suspect it's doing something more unorthodox here since we're out in the middle of nowhere."

"So it's got nothing to do with DARPA?" said Sabrina.

"No. Kyle dug out that information but I reckon he did that more as a red herring. Nothing like a bunch of acronyms to get your attention. Do you have any idea what seeing the DARPA logo does to anyone that works in research? Talk about an aphrodisiac. I think it was just a huge smoke screen though. He already had what he needed, he just wanted to be sure that, if I found that stuff, I didn't catch on before he could move forward with it."

"Damn," said Lennon. "Sucks to be married to military types." He realized his lifestyle was no different, coughed, and added with a shrug, "Of course, they're not all the same."

I stepped into the group. "Okay, so now what? We can't follow them since they're underwater."

"No," said Monica, "but we can get close. If they are drones, then they're following a pre-programmed route. I'll get us to where we lost them. Next time, we'll see if we can track them when they dive again. Anyone any good with scuba gear? There's a pile of the stuff hanging back there."

"We'll need more light," I said as my stomach churned yet again at the thought of diving. "Let me check in the cuddy for any torches we can use."

I moved to the front of the deck and ducked under the small entrance. The tossing of the boat had not been kind to the cuddy. The laptop was still stuck to the side shelf with Velcro, but the bathroom door had swung open and the contents of the cabinets and the scuba suits were strewn around the cabin floor. Items moved underfoot as I weaved through the assault course until I stepped on something that shot my leg forward. If the laptop shelf was any further away, I'd have been speaking in a squeaky voice for a while, but I grabbed onto the edge and kept myself upright.

As my foot stepped on whatever had skidded, the laptop screen lit up. A bright yellow and orange logo appeared on screen, a life vest that had 'Adriana Jones – Treasure Hunter' stenciled across the top and bottom of it. I remembered the name, although I didn't need to, her tanned image smiled from the middle of the vest too. The blond woman we'd walked by at the marina. Despite her partners' display of testosterone this was her boat.

I rummaged through the mess and picked up a wireless mouse from under my foot, placed it on the shelf and clicked a button. The logo disappeared and the screen filled with a dazzle of color. It appeared to be an x-ray type view of everything under the boat. A myriad of shapes floated around and undulated, swaying with the current. Everything was disjointed and random, other than a solid curve of white that peeked into the left of the screen. It looked like the side of a huge bicycle tire. Something big was right beneath us. I poked my head through the entrance.

"Er, guys, come and take a look at this."

Monica was the first below deck, since she'd been camped out at the helm. She looked at the screen and then stepped aside as Lennon and Sabrina squeezed into the tight space.

"Okay," she said, "that looks promising. Watch that image while I move the boat and see what happens."

She moved back to the helm, adjusted the throttle enough to move the boat, and maneuvered us to one side. I watched the screen transfixed as if it was about to show a space shuttle launch. The shapes floated and danced, and the bike tire image grew until it filled the screen. My common sense suggested that if I rotated the mouse wheel backwards, the screen might zoom out. My common sense was right and a wider view of what lay beneath us appeared. The curve of the image continued to grow as it drifted across the screen and went from a slight curve to the side of a wheel. Then spokes appeared. The spokes met at a central hub as more of the image appeared, and then more spokes branched off on its other side.

It was a huge wheel. I couldn't tell from the screen how deep the image was below us, but in relation to everything else around it, it was massive. Whatever it was, it had no business sitting in the middle of the Atlantic Ocean. Someone had put it there. It was nothing Mother Nature would throw together, and it sat at the exact location of our co-ordinates.

We'd found our bad guy.

CHAPTER FORTY-SEVEN

"Sir," said the operator, "we have unusual movement above us."

Beck strolled to the front of the control room and stared at the screen. A small blip hovered above the facility's image. "What is that, a fishing boat? They're a bit off course aren't they?"

"Sir, we've been pinged. Whatever the vessel is, they're aware we're here. There aren't many fishing boats with sonar capable of anything other than short-range searches. If that is a fishing boat then it's kitted out for serious work."

That got Becks attention. "How long's it been sitting there?"

"Just moved into position, Sir."

"Okay," said Beck. "I wonder how we missed them getting close. Keep an eye on it and get information from the drones. If anything else shows up, let me know."

"Yes, sir. Sir, are we expecting visitors?" said the operator.

Beck turned away to hide his wry smile. "None I'm aware of. That's a strange statement. How many unexpected visitors have you welcomed here?"

"Well... none."

"Correct. We don't get visitors, which is why I said let me know."

"Will do, Sir." The operator focused on the screen as Beck walked away to his office.

There was no feasible way they'd found this location, but Miller, the idiot judge in London, had warned him. What had he said? He's coming for you and he knows where you are. Yeah, right. An under-water facility almost two hundred miles out into the Atlantic Ocean. It was about as James Bond as you could get.

His part of the operation took up a few rooms on the west side. Four hatches gave access into the place, one in each quadrant, plus the underground dock for the submersibles. Even if they'd lucked out and had found him they still had to get to this depth. And then what? The access hatches were airtight and needed secure keypad entry to open. And each section of the ring stood isolated from the others with locked doors opened by specific key cards.

Beck laughed to himself. The notion they'd found him was ridicu-lous but there was one person who might have discovered the location. If he'd been careless.

The wife.

His work was stored digitally. Nothing existed on paper. He had made notes but they were always shredded. Still, he'd promised himself he would not underestimate her. His wife was a clever girl. Rugged and resourceful too, but no amount of rugged or resourceful could dive deep into the ocean and open a locked door without the access code. She'd drown trying. Along with Miller's henchman.

He smiled. There had to be a way to get a visual of the entrance hatches. Watching his wife's bloated body floating away to the surface would be a divorce for the records.

CHAPTER FORTY-EIGHT

"What the hell is that?"

Lennon leaned forward and peered at the screen. "It's not moving. How could something that big exist underwater and not float around?"

"Plenty of ways," said Monica, "but probably ballast. Weight distribution. Submarines work the same way. Technology is always moving forward. Believe me, you aren't aware of half of what's out there. Things exist that the public can't know about. It would freak them out."

"Yeah," I said, "let's leave that alone. I'm freaked out enough with what's going on right now. So, are we assuming that's Beck?"

"I'd say we are," said Monica. "He's definitely out here somewhere and, since there's nothing on the surface, I'd say this fits the bill."

"Okay," I said, "so what's our next move?"

Sabrina pointed to the screen. "We have to get down there. I'm sure this sonar can measure depth but I'll be damned if I know how to do it."

The following silence confirmed no one else did either.

"So," she continued, "I say we take advantage of these scuba suits. They may or may not get us deep enough but there's only one way to

find out. One problem though. I see small waterproof pouches for electronics in them but no compartments large enough to carry any of our
bigger firepower. We'll be stuck to transporting a pistol each. Nothing
more."

"It is what it is," said Lennon. "If we've assumed correctly, and
from what we know of Beck, he probably has an arsenal of his own.
We'll just have to be careful until we can borrow some of his."

I'd done a lot of borrowing this week. One more day couldn't hurt.
"How long do we have left?" I asked.

Monica was about to answer when small shapes appeared on the
screen. First one, then others floated in from the left, and followed a
familiar slight curve.

"Look," I said. "The Ghost Swimmers are back."

Five small blips drifted sideways across the screen. We ran out onto
the deck as they swam behind the boat inches away from hitting us.
Their fins scythed through the water and created little waves of wash
that rippled and vanished. After a few feet they dived again into the
black water and out of sight.

I went back into the cuddy and glared at the laptop screen. There
they were, sticking to their route. Their images grew smaller,
presumably as they sank deeper. They shrank until they were tiny
dots that swam right across one side of the circular image, through
the central hub and then grew larger as they rose again on the opposite side.

"I have an idea," I said. "This might sound crazy, but hear me out
and see what you think. I doubt it'll get us in the door, but it might get
us somewhere close."

In my younger days, I owned a motorcycle. Sometimes, more in
summer, I found it a challenge to slip into the protective leathers I wore
while riding. I don't know how the bondage community does it, but
those things take some serious effort to get in to.

It seems scuba suits are no different. By the time the four of us had
each found a suit to fit and had squeezed ourselves into them, the
Ghost Swimmers had passed us by twice more. As I zipped the pistol
into the waterproof pouch, I was already sweating inside my second

skin. To the side of us, a metal fin split the water's surface for the third time. The other four followed, right on schedule.

My plan hinged on a huge stroke of luck. We'd seen the drones sink below the surface and pass over whatever lay beneath us, but we couldn't tell how close to the structure they swam. The oxygen tanks in the boat were full and the fluorescents on our headbands cast out solid beams of light. Monica told us that a full tank of air should last around forty-five minutes. However, the deeper we dived, the more oxygen the tanks would expel. The increasing water pressure compressed the air in the hoses and would force us to use more. We settled on a time limit of thirty minutes. If we couldn't reach the structure in thirty minutes, we'd swim to the surface and rethink things. On the screen the drones seemed to pass across the structure in no time at all, so I was quietly confident. And completely terrified. We had no idea what was waiting for us. And even if the drones got us deep enough we still had to gain entry into the structure.

Lennon stood on the rear of the boat and waited for the first drone to swim alongside us. He was wind milling his arms like a high diver. I think he was trying to impress Monica. As it drew level with the boat he dived overboard in a perfect arc and cut through the water. The metal shark didn't miss a beat and swam right next to him as he surfaced. He reached out, curled his hand around the fin, and allowed himself to be dragged along.

Monica went next. The second drone followed its leader's exact course, and she leaped off the engine cover with a squeal of delight when it grew close enough. It carried her off into the darkness.

Sabrina turned to face me. "You okay with doing this?"

"It was my plan," I said. I adjusted the headband that held the light on my forehead just to give my shaking hands something to do.

"Yeah, and you did a good job coming up with it. But when your turn comes to jump are you going to follow through? Do you want to go next and I'll just push you overboard to be sure?"

I don't know if she saw my frown through the scuba mask. "Er, thanks? I appreciate your looking out for me but I'll be okay. Thanks again just the same." I pointed past her. "Here's your ride. Hop on!"

She gave me a playful punch that would leave a bruise. "See you down there," she shouted and threw herself over the side of the boat. She latched onto the fin as she surfaced.

Ghost Swimmer number four circled around. I pushed the mouth-piece between my lips and sucked in a good gulp of oxygen. The pure air made my head swim but cleared in time for me to judge my entry into the water. I stepped onto the rear of the boat. As my beam of light glinted off its metal casing, I closed my eyes and jumped into the ocean.

I seemed to sink forever and then floated to the surface. The scuba suit made an amazing difference. There was no freezing cold blast as I entered the water like earlier, and the weightlessness made me feel strong and liberated. With a faint whirring noise the metal shark swam by me, its tail swishing from side to side to power it forward. I grabbed the fin and the machine pulled me along with it. Sabrina glanced back to check on me and gave me a thumbs up. The lights from Lennon and Monica shone ahead of her and lit up the water's surface with tiny searchlights. As I lifted my hand to return the thumbs up, Lennon vanished beneath the surface. His light turned the water green, dimmed and flickered, and then faded to nothing. Then Monica went under. Sabrina followed and, as my stomach lurched once more, my metal ride dragged me beneath the surface and into the darkness.

The drone's strength increased once we submerged. Its power hummed through my body as it dragged me along the ocean's ceiling. Once we dived beneath it, there was no surface tension to cut through and it moved through the depths and pulled me along with no effort.

The light on my headband showed little at first and my eyes needed to adjust to their new surroundings. It took a moment but images started to clarify before me. My three colleagues led the descent. Lights swiveled and searched as they tried to take in their surround-ings. I could vaguely make out their silhouettes through the murky water as their personal rides pulled them deeper. Beneath me lay pure darkness. There were no runway lights or beacons to welcome what-ever vessels might transport people to the place. The ocean didn't do signposts and streetlights.

Oxygen flowed through the mouthpiece as I concentrated on Monica's advice. Through my shaky nerves I remembered to breathe out slowly as I entered the water. Now I reminded myself to breathe in for a few seconds. I had to get past the carbon dioxide I'd just exhaled, hold my breath, and breathe back out again. They don't mention this stuff on the Discovery Channel.

As Ghost Swimmer number four continued to pull me deeper, small fish swam by me. This was their world and I was trespassing. I had a moment of panic when I thought of real sharks but even my luck had to be better than that. The beam of my light shone through the swirling bubbles that Sabrina and her ride churned up, and small bits of debris floated past my mask. She looked at me again and held up a thumb. I relaxed enough to do the same. The blood rushed through my ears. It was the only sound I heard over my breathing. The rubber mouthpiece chafed against my lips but I clamped my teeth tighter. If I lost it, I'd be dead in moments.

As I dove deeper, I'd expected pressure to be exerted on me to make my head compress or my lungs scream in distress, but I moved through the water at peace. It was as if I was riding a fairground attraction, but without the clanking gears and the pull of chains. We continued to sink. When I'd watched the screen back on the boat, the drones had reached their maximum depth in a few minutes before they moved across and then surfaced again. I had no way to know, but I felt as if I'd been underwater for at least ten minutes.

Something beneath me caught my eye. Something red shimmered before being covered again by the gloom. Our lights were still being pulled in that slight curve and the view ahead was still bubbles and debris. Then I saw it again. A brief flash, but this time in multiple locations. I strained my eyes and waited until it flashed once more. Four red lights were blinking in the black depths of the ocean.

The others had noticed them too. Their lights moved erratically as heads turned and tilted to get the best angle to see what lay below us. The red flashes blinked again, forming a perfect square. They made me think of the four points of a compass or the bases on a field. I focused to find what would equate as the pitcher's mound but the depths defeated me. My ride tilted, banked like a turning plane and aimed straight for one of the flashes. As I got deeper still, the combined radiance from our lights picked out the shadow of an image. I made out the curve we'd seen on the laptop screen.

The red flashed again and everything was clear.

The flashes were beacons mounted on top of poles which, in turn, were mounted to the outside of a huge gray structure. When they flashed, a red glow washed over the structure and highlighted a hatch built into the curved side. Stair rungs led up to the hatch, although no one would have cause to use them in the ocean. Maybe they were part of the construction phase. The lights flashed again and this time I picked out brackets around the entrance. The whole thing just hung there, suspended in millions of gallons of water, and stretched back into the distance. The opposite side was too far away to see until its light flashed. I couldn't even guess at its size in the shifting water but it had to be a good half-mile across. The image we'd seen on the boat was very accurate; it was a massive, floating wheel.

The drones circled around the structure like vultures, and then swooped toward it. The first one was a few feet away when its nose raised and it began to climb. Lennon pushed himself off it, pulled his arms to his side and arrowed himself down toward the hatch. The Ghost Swimmer rocked against the force, then corrected itself and began a smooth ascent. Lennon bounced against the side of the ring, grabbed onto one of the stair grips and held out his other hand ready for Monica.

Monica was a quick learner. As her drone grew closer she launched herself toward Lennon, her flippers kicking against resistance until she too crashed into the wall and grabbed his hand.

Sabrina went next. Her drone rose and left as she drifted away from it on her back and swam like a mermaid to the others. She landed gracefully on the steps and held out her hand for me. My drone showed no signs of stopping. Fear rose again in my throat as I grew closer, but its tail made a tiny adjustment and altered its course. As it rose, I let go of the fin and kicked my legs. I reached out my arm and had begun my descent when the fifth drone caught up with me. The movement flashed in the corner of my eye and I glanced through the side of my face piece as its fin whipped right by me.

It caught the hose that ran from my helmet to the oxygen tank and dragged me backwards. I snatched out for the tail of my transport but it swam away, oblivious to my peril. My forward motion tightened the hose. The fin snagged, stalled and then powered forward to sever my supply, and the fifth drone swam away in an eruption of bubbles.

As the hose waved around like a severed limb, I took in another breath. Everything seemed to be okay as my lungs filled with air. I released it and took another, but this time no air flowed. My chest caught and my lungs protested. I tried again. Still nothing. The others waved at me to push on and join them but my brain told me to breathe. I tried again as the sides of my vision darkened.

I was suffocating.

CHAPTER FORTY-NINE

So this was how my life was going to end. After the events of the last few days it seemed ridiculous to go out to a metal fish. Pressure built up behind my eyes, but I still saw Sabrina launch herself off the side of the building and barrel toward me. She still resembled a mermaid, as she forced herself forward with the flippers on her feet. My last sight could have been a lot worse.

I thought of the things I hadn't done. I'd never jumped from a plane, never surfed, and never fished with my daughter. And Kacie; would she ever know what happened? Getting killed on land meant that, eventually, my body would most likely be found. But here, at who knew what depth, and over two hundred miles out in the Atlantic Ocean? I'd be consumed by marine life before anyone realized I was gone.

As my vision failed my others senses heightened. The hose still streamed bubbles out behind me and buffeted into my back. With great effort, I turned my head enough to see the severed end wafting around in the water. My arm snaked out and grabbed it and pushed the end between my lips. The pressure of the air forced my head backwards, but not before I gulped precious oxygen along with a few drops of ocean. The urge to cough almost overwhelmed me, but before my lungs could expel the mixture, Sabrina was at my side. She wrenched the hose from my hand and forced her mouthpiece between my lips. The pain as the rubber gnashed the skin into my teeth felt amazing and I sucked greedily on it. The black edges of my vision melted away and left spots instead. My head pounded and my eyes rested against a dull ache, but I was breathing.

Sabrina waved her hand in front of my face to get my attention. She needed her mouthpiece back. I relaxed my grip and handed it over. She took a few breaths, then passed it back as she took my hand, and pulled me toward the building. The others reached out as we got closer and guided me to the stairs. I curled my fingers around a rung and nodded my thanks. Monica made an open/close sign with her hand and she and Lennon floated off over the top.

My body had recovered quicker than I expected. My heartbeat had stopped triple timing, the shaking had subsided and the pain behind my eyes had reduced to a dull throb.

I assumed Monica and Lennon had gone to find another way into the building. Sabrina had me breathe from her mouthpiece again and then took it back and floated across to the hatch. She beckoned for me to join her. I pushed off the stairs and rose to meet her, where she pointed to the side of the structure. I shook my head and raised my shoulders in a non-understanding shrug. She pointed again, harder this time, so I swam closer to the section she indicated. Up close, I could make out a hairline crack that formed a perfect circle in the side. It looked like a gas cap cover. She clawed at its edges with the thick tips of her gloves but nothing moved. The fabric wouldn't allow her any purchase. I chose the more masculine cave man method and hammered against it with the side of a clenched fist. Bubbles fluttered from the side of the crack and then, like a jack-in-a-box, it popped open.

Sabrina looked at me wide eyed and shook her head. I smiled, shrugged and took another breath of oxygen. An illuminated keypad sat at the back of the opening, big alphanumeric keys, two rows of letters across the top and the numbers zero through nine across the bottom. If this was a government research facility the password wasn't going to be someone's dog's name or favorite football team. I gazed at Sabrina. She gazed back nonplussed. We had no idea.

Lennon and Monica reappeared over the top of the structure and swam toward us, both shaking their heads. No entrances elsewhere. We had the hatch, but without the combination we were still at the end of the road.

The others bustled against us as they drifted closer. Monica punched her fist in the air and smiled as if she'd won the lottery, then pointed at the panel. She tapped the side of her head and moved up to it.

The first key she pressed flashed a green 'K' into the murky water. Then a 'Y'. I was such an idiot.

The code on the back of the business card.

I took another breath from Sabrina's mouthpiece as Monica finished entering the combination. As the last digit flashed, she pushed herself away and waited. Nothing happened.

She leaned in to enter the code again. Maybe she was thinking her bulky gloves had hit a wrong key, when the hatch popped open. Lennon grabbed a handle and pulled. The door swung back on thick hydraulic hinges. He ducked his head through the opening and swam inside, fearless and eager to get the job done. After another breath Sabrina pushed me forward and I followed him into a small room. My light lit up the far wall about ten feet away. Another door faced me. The others squeezed into the space behind us and Sabrina pulled the door. It closed smoothly, assisted by the hydraulics.

We looked around the room and at each other and waited to see what would happen next. The floor vibrated as something beneath us activated and the water began to flow out. Vents had opened in the four corners. I held my breath for the last time, as the level washed down my face mask. Once it reached my neck I heaved in massive gulps of the fresh air that pumped through ceiling vents as if the supply might run out again. As the water trickled away I slid the face mask up and off my head.

"Well that was different. Why hasn't the other door opened?"

It turned out to be a good thing. Rubber clothing and flippers littered the floor as everyone shucked off their tanks and stripped back to regular clothing. It was a damn sight easier to remove than to put on. I retrieved the pistol from its waterproof pocket and tucked it into my waistband.

"The air pressure is being balanced," said Lennon. "I don't have a clue how deep we are and decompression is normally for ascending divers. They must stick to a natural air intake ratio, otherwise they pay for it later."

"Yeah, I've had the bends," said Monica. "Only once though. It taught me a quick lesson."

"Okay," I said, "for the divers among us that just don't because they hate water, what are the bends?"

"Painful is what they are," said Monica. "While you're diving you're breathing pressurized air. You get the bends when you rise too quickly though, not when you descend. Who knows, perhaps there's more of this structure way below us that we can't see. Anyway, the pressure difference causes air bubbles to move around inside your body. Eight times out of ten, they cause joint pain. And it hurts like hell. This chamber is decompressing. It doesn't need to in our case, but it does give us time to get ready for when that door opens. That's what matters to me."

Our group resembled Robin Hood's band of merry men, but we were ready. I grabbed my pistol as the next door clicked and popped open.

"Come on," I said, "let's finish this."

CHAPTER FIFTY

Image captures from the Ghost Swimmers showed a decent sized boat above them, but they were too dark to make out the identity of four silhouettes. They were enough for Beck to switch his mindset. He was ready for confrontation.

"Sir, there's unexpected activity at the west hatch," said the operator. "It just opened and resealed. The room is draining as we speak."

A small warning light flashed on the console before him to confirm the report. Beck stood so suddenly the stool behind him skidded across the carpet on its casters. He marched to the screen and looked at the display.

The facility was split into four sections; north, south, east and west. Airtight security doors partitioned each quadrant to allow them to be annexed in the event of flooding or attack. The west side housed the science division; lots of white coats and thick glasses pottering around and tapping at keyboards. The east wing, which held the control room, was the base for Consortium operations. The other side had no idea what happened here. The storage and power areas separated the north and south sections.

A diagnostic scrolled below the diagram, which showed the time of entry and the code used to open the hatch. The entry code was his.

"Well, well, well. You sneaky little bitch."

"I'm sorry, Sir?" said the operator.

Beck wouldn't allow a single moment of weakness to show. He'd been found. He considered his access code to be more secure than his bank account details. Only one person could have found it.

He considered the work it must have taken for her to get here. This was too secret a location for her to stumble across, so she must have worked out where he was and then found the means to get here. And that was after she'd untied herself and escaped a trained killer. In another life, she'd have made the perfect wife. In this one she had now become a potential threat.

There were no written logs of his location or codes, so how had she found him? And what did she hope to achieve? She knew nothing of the plan or of The Consortium. Had he been careless, and she'd over-heard a conversation or found a classified document somewhere? It seemed impossible and yet the hatch had opened. With his code. It had to be her.

And she wasn't alone.

"They're still on the opposite side of the complex," he said. "Dis-patch that quadrant's security detail."

Each wing had a two-man team to keep order. Although their job description said 'security detail', not much security was required in an undersea research facility full of scientists. They were more like token law keepers; people trained marginally better than the scientists and computer operators to keep order should anyone get any ideas of grandeur or go stir crazy in the concrete confines. Beck didn't know the team in the west wing, but against a soon to be ex-wife and her accomplices they should be able to neutralize the threat. His command team wouldn't even hear about it.

"They've responded, Sir. They're on their way."

"Good. Monitor the situation," said Beck.

He strode over to his office, took a seat and lifted the bottle of Glenfiddich from his desk drawer. The neck of the bottle clanged against the side of the glass as he poured a shot. The first sign of nerves had crept in. He checked his watch. Less than an hour to launch.

Fifty-five minutes to be precise. Precision counted and he and Jones needed to turn their keys at the right time. Everything was in place and waiting. He tipped his head back and downed the shot.

It was the wife. How much of a threat could she be?

The other door in the airlock resembled the side of a tank, but it swung open with ease. A smaller entrance hall with a corridor was revealed on the other side. The far end of the corridor stopped at a tee junction.

We crept out of the airlock and tiptoed across the hall and up to the entrance of the first corridor. A stretch of wall about five feet across stood on either side of it. Sabrina and I stood against the wall on the left, Lennon and Monica took the right.

"So," I said, "what's the plan? We're basically standing in the rim of a wheel. Do we walk in circles until we find a bad guy?"

"That sounds like a plan," said Lennon, "except that we need to find the computer or terminal or whatever to plug that flash drive in to. And there's our problem. The damned thing might be a huge mainframe or a single laptop. I can say one thing for sure, and that's that bad guys don't leave their weaponry unguarded. Whatever and wherever it is, it won't be easy to get to."

"So logic dictates it'll be in the center of this thing," I said. "You wouldn't leave your super weapon on one side of a wheel, when you could arm the entire rim with protection and plant it smack bang in the center of the hub."

Sabrina looked at me as if I'd discovered how to find world peace. "That makes perfect sense. Let's get to the center."

"You have the flash drive, right Monica?" said Lennon.

She felt through the outside of her pocket and nodded.

"Want me to take that?"

In the second she took to react, Monica's internal conflict fought in her eyes. They flitted to one side and back while she weighed up her trust. Then logic took over. Lennon was the best trained of the group. It made sense for him to protect our only defense.

She placed the drive into Lennon's outstretched palm. He slid it into his front pocket as Sabrina edged to the corner.

"Come on," she said. "I'll lead."

As her head peered around the corner voices sounded, young and chatty, like two kids passing time. She shrunk back beside me and we listened. The voices grew closer and stopped. They'd reached the end of the corridor and must have noticed the airlock door was open. Then a radio squelched and a quieter conversation took place.

Soft footsteps padded toward us as they approached. Lennon caught my eye, held up two fingers and mouthed 'Two voices?'

I nodded a yes, and he stepped up to the edge of the wall and raised his pistol. The rest of us copied him and waited.

The steps grew closer until a faint shadow cast across the floor. Security in a place like this couldn't get much action so I hoped they wouldn't be too much of a test. Sure enough, the first guard poked his unguarded head through the entrance after the barrel of his small pistol and turned to face Lennon. A burst of nausea rippled through my stomach as Lennon smashed his elbow into the guy's nose. Cartilage shattered with a crunch and he dropped to the ground. Lennon raised his boot to finish the job but didn't need to. There was no movement. It was a solid connection. Lights out. In a flurry of movement, he rounded the corner and burst forward. I followed.

A lone guard stood transfixed, mouth agape in shock and surprise. Before he could swing his gun around, Lennon bore down on him and slammed his pistol into soft tissue. Lips split and teeth cracked as he followed the blow with a solid punch that knocked the guy to the ground. The pistol clattered away along the corridor and he curled up in a ball and whimpered. I was glad Lennon had the drive.

His breathing was quicker than usual, but still composed and measured. "Enough killing for one day, right?"

"Agreed. I have an idea," said Monica, and gestured over her shoulder with a thumb. "Put them in the airlock. This door won't open from the inside, only when an outside door opens first. There'll be an override somewhere though, so we'll either get this done and free them... or it won't matter."

Lennon coerced the second guy to stand, and we shoved him inside the airlock. The girls grabbed the pistols and dragged the first guy in behind him by his ankles. The second guard stood against the wall shaking as the shock of his situation sank in.

"Okay," I said to him. "Strip."

The guard's eyes widened. He must have imagined the worst possible scenario.

"Dude, look around you. Two guys. Two girls. You're safe now, as long as you cooperate. I just want your uniform so we blend in with your colleagues."

"That's a good idea," said Lennon and gestured to the terrified man with his pistol. "Now strip, before I do it for you."

The guy stepped out of his clothing as Sabrina and Monica stripped the other.

"The keycard," I said and gestured for him to toss it over. He slipped the lanyard over his head, bunched it up and threw it underhanded. I caught it and turned it over in my hands. "Where will this get me?"

"Around this quadrant and into the adjacent ones," he said. "No further."

"And how many quadrants are there?" I said and then stopped. "Forget that question, they're quadrants. That means there's four." Damn it, I'd been doing so well. "Okay, so where's Beck?"

"Beck?" he said. "Never heard of him. Look man, I just make sure the weirdoes don't go stir crazy in here and fight each other. That's it. I don't know anyone named Beck, I swear."

The stress and fear in his voice convinced me he told the truth. Across the room, Lennon was struggling to suit up in the other guy's clothes. They were a snug fit and his face flushed. He sucked in his already taut stomach and zipped up the pants.

"One size less and I'd be speaking in a squeaky voice," he said. He grabbed the other keycard and smoothed out his new uniform. "Okay. Are we good?"

We nodded.

"Let's lock these guys up and get us a bad guy."

The entrance corridor led out to the massive circular ring we'd seen from the boat. A wider corridor curved away left and right from our entrance.

"Okay, which way?" I asked.

"I don't think it matters if your theory works," said Sabrina. "We need to walk one way or the other and find a branch that will take us into the center. That's where the action is."

"Agreed," I said and turned to the right. A sales seminar I attended years ago claimed that certain cultures believed right to be a way of strength. Omens that came from the right were lucky, ones from the left... not so much. If I couldn't decide between directions I always turned right.

The rest of the group followed.

I ran my right hand along a solid concrete wall, curved and smooth, with vents cut into it at intervals. Cool air pumped through them. To the left of the hall was another wall, but on this wall, now and then, paneled doors with narrow windows broke up the run. They reminded me of the doors to school classrooms. Most of the windows showed small rooms loaded with equipment and flashing lights. Intelligent looking men in glasses and white coats milled around or gathered in groups to talk. This section was some sort of science center. I had to wonder if the regular looking people in the rooms knew of the mayhem their facility was about to cause.

My watch showed we had less than an hour to launch, if we'd guessed the timeline correctly. No big explosions had sounded since we'd been here; no alarms or sirens were ringing, so I assumed we still had time. A couple of white coats exited a room and walked toward us. Lennon and I assumed our confident guard poses, and the coats nodded and walked right by us. The uniforms worked, which didn't surprise me. In my experience of selling drugs to the medical profession, most scientists were too preoccupied to notice you, or considered you so far beneath them they didn't give you the time of day. These guys didn't seem to be any different.

We followed the slight curve and met no one else as the first branch to the left appeared. I brushed my fingers against the pistol in my pocket for reassurance. The girls did something similar, while Lennon just looked ahead with a steeled focus and led the way up to the corner. He appeared implacable and driven while my stomach tumbled and churned. The joys of military training.

"Okay," he said, "I'll take the lead. If anyone comes toward us be alert and watch them, but wait until danger presents itself before you shoot. I can't imagine many of these guys pose much of a threat, and we agreed on no more killing. If a threat presents itself, try to fire in bursts of two, a double tap. Aim for the chest. Remember, we don't have much ammo. Don't waste it."

The icy coldness of the pep talk chilled me, but it made perfect sense. I had to remind myself why we were here. I felt for the pistol again, wrapped my fingers around the grip, and followed Lennon around the corner.

The corridor stretched away in a straight line to the center for a while, then curved away out of sight. We made our way to the bend uninterrupted and, as we rounded the turn, found out why. The concrete walls ended in a bulkhead. No windows. No door. Just a solid gray wall of nothing. It was probably a structural support and definitely a dead end. I put my ear against the cold wall to see if I could hear anything on the other side but there was nothing but the hiss of the air vents.

The girls glanced at each other and frowned. Lennon didn't miss a beat. "Okay, wrong corridor. Back we go and onto the next one. We keep moving right. Sooner or later we'll find our bad guy."

We followed him back to the outer ring and were a couple feet away from the entrance when the radio on my uniform beeped.

"Try them again," said Beck. "You're sure you're paging the right team?"

The operator hit a button. "West wing security team, respond."

Silence.

Louder. "West wing security team, please respond."

Beck turned away from the desk and moved into his office, muttering under his breath as he walked. "If you want a job done properly, do it your fucking self."

Until now, the facility had never been breached. Despite the regulations and procedures that ran the operation, unauthorized access seemed impossible. There were no drills or rules to follow for that. The security teams were not adequately trained and, given its location, it was deemed pointless to equip an armory.

He checked his pistol, more out of habit than necessity. There was no point carrying a weapon not primed for use. The shiny brass winked back at him and he tucked the gun into the rear of his waistband, left his office and walked out into the corridor. He turned right and strode past the kitchen and food storage area and past the main branch that led to the center room.

The bulkhead door that separated the east quadrant from the north quadrant was a huge slab of steel with a small window set in its center at eye level. There was no handle. Beck swiped his card across a control panel set in the wall. Gears shifted and whirred and the door clicked and swung open on automated hinges. It was designed this way to avoid accidental closing, or worse, not closing at all. Human nature meant that doors were left ajar. In most places, an acceptable failing. Deep beneath The Atlantic, in a billion-dollar facility, failings could be deadly.

A sensor hummed as Beck walked across the threshold and then, after a small pause, the door began its slow swing to close again. He was feet away from it when it completed the arc and closed airtight with a faint click.

The north quadrant held everything needed to keep things moving in the facility, every hour of the day, for three hundred and sixty-five days a year. Backup hardware, software filing systems, lab equipment, and suits and replacement parts for the submersibles. Tools to repair every item in the place. Bulk food storage, which delivered into each section as needed. And water. Despite the billions of gallons that pushed and squeezed against the outside of the facility, clean water was the most important resource in the place. A filtration system provided shower and bathroom water, but it hadn't tested clean enough to drink. Seven days with no water will kill any man.

A door opened a few feet away and Beck reached a hand behind him and rested his fingers against the gun's grip. A middle-aged man appeared with a clipboard, looked up and nodded a greeting, then disappeared into the next room. Beck breathed out and relaxed his arm. The man had almost died doing inventory.

Beck continued his careful walk and checked through each window as he moved. The north quadrant's security team sat in a small office watching TV. He ignored them, kept walking and repeated his mantra.

If you want a job done properly, do it yourself.

"West wing security team, please respond."

The second request came through with a lot more urgency than the first. I suspected the owner of the scratchy voice had someone in authority standing nearby making demands. When the voice first blared from the shoulder radio, we paused in a single motion like a well-trained dance troupe. As my hand moved to the jacket's collar, Lennon glared and raised a hand.

"We might have the element of surprise right now. Don't ruin that by answering."

"Yeah, good point." I thrust my hand into a pocket to emphasize how much I wasn't answering that call.

I waited for another call but the radio remained silent. We continued up to the outer corridor and turned left at the corner with confidence and attitude, as if we knew our way around the place. The corridor was empty, so we relaxed a little and moved forward again. Due to the curve of the wall, we could see no more than fifteen feet ahead. I kept expecting someone to come marching around the corner. Still, the uniforms seemed to work. We passed more rooms like the others, research rooms or self-contained labs with the men and women in the white coats hard at work. One after another of the doors with the small windows went by but we found no more branches into the center. We ran, at last, into a large solid looking door that barred the way.

"Next quadrant?" I suggested.

Lennon nodded. "Swipe the card and let's find out if that guard told the truth."

I waved the card against the panel on the wall and, after a faint click, the door swung out toward me. It moved much slower than I expected and left plenty of time to get out of the way. I could tell by its thickness and construction it must have weighed a ton. Once that thing closed, nothing and no one was getting through. Lennon moved first and the rest of us followed in a single file line. As we each passed under the door something hummed overhead. I craned my neck and saw a tiny glass circle recessed into the top of the doorframe. Monica moved beside me.

"Camera?" I said.

"Probably a sensor. The door's automated. Imagine it closing on you if it didn't realize you were there. It'd crush you to death. Make quite a mess."

"Yeah, when I go I don't want to go with death by door. Something much quicker please."

She smiled and moved past me.

The next quadrant was identical to the other. Nothing changed in the decor and the same filtered air pumped through ceiling vents, but the rooms were different. There were no white coats or flashing lights. No labs or computers. Just room after room of supplies. Not much work got done in this wing.

We passed rooms full of everything needed to keep a place like this running. Since we'd moved in only one direction when we left the airlock, I didn't know how big each quadrant was. When I spotted a huge stack of water bottles through one of the little windows, I signaled for the team to stop. The events earlier in the ocean had left my mouth and throat sore, and the bottles looked as good as medicine. Somehow, my voice hadn't got raspy yet, but it was just a matter of time. I felt like I was taking in sand every time I swallowed. The room was empty, so we entered, grabbed a bottle each and looked around.

It resembled a supermarket, with gray steel racks lined up in rows and loaded with canned goods. One side held medical supplies; dressings, masks and sterile tape. I assumed any drugs were kept isolated or refrigerated. Everything looked normal until we saw the back wall.

Brown boxes, each labeled with a bar code, were stacked to one side from floor to ceiling. To the side of the boxes was a panel of flashing lights and a huge louvered vent.

Curiosity got the better of me. I moved deeper into the room to check them out. The rest of the team followed me.

CHAPTER FIFTY-ONE

He was halfway around the north quadrant and there was still no sign of intruders. Beck liked to think that the security team would at least have checked out the breach, but, since it was in the next wing, they'd probably assumed the next team would deal with it. Civilian security wasn't trained well enough in his experience, hence the desire to take care of things himself.

His attention was split. His peripheral vision watched the corridor ahead as it was revealed bit by bit by the curve. His main focus was through the small windows that looked into each room. Everything seemed normal and no figures moved in any of them. Someone had taken water from one of the packs in storage and left the opened pack sitting there. It looked as if an autopsy was carried out on the package. The plastic skin hung raggedly down the sides of the body, while some of the innards were missing.

Each window revealed nothing unusual and Beck reached the containment door between the north and west wings without incident. He swiped his keycard across the panel, waited for the click and for the door to swing back, then drew his pistol and moved forward.

People bustled and mixed in the rooms ahead but everything seemed to be in order. No one looked concerned and work went on as normal. If someone uninvited had entered one of the rooms, there would be noise or confusion, but window after window passed until the airlock corridor lay just ahead. Beck moved across to the closer wall and edged forward, pistol raised. He swung around the corner to face the airlock and aimed to shoot but the passageway was empty. The airlock door was closed. Nothing seemed out of place.

He moved toward the door in small, hesitant steps and approached the entrance. The wall dropped back on either side, the perfect place for someone to be waiting. He crouched and then dived forward past the entrance and fell into a roll, came upright on the other side of the wall and swiveled around. Nothing but empty walls faced him.

The technology in this place was way too advanced to give a false reading. Someone had opened that access door. He moved back toward the main corridor and was past the entrance when something caught his eye. A foot off the floor, on the left wall, a small line of blood droplets had spattered up the surface. The floor was clean, and the blood was too dark to be arterial. Something had connected with soft tissue at a fast pace to make it spray like that. A hard punch or a kick. Beck pressed the button on his radio.

"Override the airlock door in the west quadrant."

A few seconds after the reply, the door clicked open with a hiss and swung back. The security team lay inside against the sidewall, bloodied and embarrassed in their underwear.

"What the fuck happened to you two?" asked Beck.

"Who the hell are you?" asked the guy whose mouth was still in one piece.

"I'm the bloke that runs this place," said Beck. He raised the pistol. "Now, one more time. What happened here?"

"A group of people came through the airlock," said the guard. He stared at the floor between his feet. "Four of them. Two men, two women. They jumped us and took our uniforms. It happened so quickly, we never stood a chance."

The other guard nodded an agreement as blood and saliva still dripped from his shattered mouth.

"And where did they go from here?"

"No idea," said the guard. "They made us strip and then locked us in here. I don't know where they are, but they're in the facility somewhere and they're dressed like us."

Every nerve and sensor in Beck's body fired. His senses climbed a notch and his instincts for survival kicked in. "Both of you, get to the infirmary. I'll deal with this."

He turned and sprinted back down the corridor, turned the corner and ran. Room after room passed in a blur until he slammed into the bulkhead that sectioned off the east quadrant from the north.

He swiped his card and, as the door swung slowly open, raced through it and headed to the branch that led to the hub.

The panel of lights that had distracted me was an array of sensors that, according to the labels beneath them, managed temperature, air and humidity control. It made sense. We were who knew how many feet under the ocean. The outside temperature wouldn't fluctuate much, but with the computer equipment and human bodies inside the building, the heat would rise in no time without the correct measures in place to control it. Humidity would be an obvious problem under water. With the amount of electronics in the section we'd just left, it was one that couldn't be allowed to happen.

What the panel didn't do was give me any clue as to the whereabouts of the equipment that we were looking for, the heavy-duty stuff. The reason we were here. We still had no choice but to follow our collective gut and try to get to the middle of the structure.

I drained my water bottle and placed it to one side and turned to face the door. A dark blur flew past the window. Monica was beside me and saw the same thing. She pointed, open-mouthed as her voice caught in her throat. "I think that... that was... that was him. That was Beck. I'm sure of it."

Lennon leaped forward, grabbed the door handle and yanked it open and we streamed out of the room as a unit. The shape was visible for a second and then disappeared around the curve. We followed at full sprint. Our feet made no sound on the solid floor but I heard the familiar click and hum of an opening door. We arrived at the bulkhead between this quadrant and the next in time to find it swinging shut.

Beck was nowhere to be seen. Lennon dived through the opening, followed by Monica, then Sabrina. It looked to be a foot wide as I dived toward it. The sensor in the frame above was covered, so the door continued to close on its arc. My shoulders jammed, and I twisted sideways to squeeze my body through the small gap. The interruption in momentum dropped me to the floor. The door was still closing as I scrambled to cross the threshold, while I tried to catch my breath. My legs straddled the line between this quadrant and the next so I withdrew them with a jerk as the door closed. It snagged the sole of my shoe, tore it off my foot and crushed it like paper against the solid frame.

I got to my feet and doubled my pace to catch the others. Lennon still led the way. We passed a room that looked like a kitchen. I saw the backs of two men as I flew past the window and looked forward again in time to see an arm shoot out of a side corridor and take Lennon out at the throat. His bottom half still ran at full speed, but his upper torso stopped on the spot. His legs cartwheeled into the air, throwing his body backwards and crashing to the ground. I winced as his head hit the concrete with a sickening thud and he lay motionless.

Beck stepped out from around the corner with a pistol raised. He panned it across the three of us and smiled. "Well, would you look what the cat dragged in. Looks like we're left with the three musketeers."

We stood still. I breathed in ragged bursts of filtered air as Monica and Sabrina looked at Beck as if they wanted to kill him. I'm sure Monica did.

"What?" he continued with a shrug of his shoulders. "No brave soldiers going to leap into action and take out the bad guy?" He looked at Monica and winked. "Sorry about earlier babe, needs must and all that. I have to say, I'm very impressed. You found me. There are black ops units from all over the world that have tried and failed."

Monica didn't flinch. "You made it easy, you moron. You wrote the coordinates on a note pad. Just how well trained are you?"

Beck's cool demeanor flickered for an instant and a glimpse of psychopath showed. Then it vanished and the smug grin reappeared. "Didn't seem to do you a lot of good though did it?" He glanced at his watch. "Twenty minutes to spare. So near and yet so far. Seems a shame to kill you, what with all the effort you made, but I can't have any loose ends. Who wants to go first? Any volunteers?"

A door opened behind us. I turned my head as the two guys from the kitchen moved in to cut us off, but Beck walked around us and into the corridor to join them. We'd be neatly lined up and he wouldn't hit his men if his rounds went right through us. As Beck stepped over him, Lennon's eyes flicked open. He'd been playing possum to give himself an edge. He swung his legs around and whipped Beck's feet out from under him. As he tumbled toward me, Monica gave him a good thump to the face to help him on his way. He hit the ground and his pistol clattered across the floor and out of reach. As he fell, Sabrina and I launched backwards. One of the kitchen guys stood right behind me. I slammed my head under his chin and propelled myself forward off my toes. The sound of his splintering teeth turned my stomach, but, as he collapsed, I rained down blow after blow until he lay out cold. Sabrina slammed the edge of her hand karate style into her guy's throat and crushed his windpipe. He gagged and gasped for air as she landed a cross and hook combination to nose and temple that sent him sprawling next to his colleague.

Beck scrambled to his feet and ran head down and disappeared through the kitchen door.

Monica scooped up his gun and we went after him.

The window was one of those thick rectangular things with little squares of wire reinforcement running through it. Through the squares I saw row after row of shelving. The place had more flour than any bakery I'd ever seen and in the back of my mind I considered them sandbags. They'd absorb any bullets that might head our way. Unfortunately, they also stacked together like a solid wall so I couldn't see past them.

I tiptoed on unbalanced feet and glanced down to make sure Beck wasn't hiding below the window and then pushed on the latch. My knuckles throbbed from the impact of the punch earlier and I already knew they'd swell later. The door opened a fraction and Lennon ducked in front of me, crouched and pushed it open with his shoulder. He was good, so I made sure I stayed right behind him. He pivoted from side to side, pistol raised and steady, and then focused ahead. We separated like a trained unit. Monica went left to take the aisle on that side. Sabrina went right to the far side, and I pulled myself away from Lennon to the take the aisle next her. Lennon went dead ahead from the door.

The room was split into two sections down the center, with four aisles on either side. I couldn't see anything other than the far wall. Eight solid rows of storage. Beck might be around any of these corners. I'd already witnessed his violence when he took out Lennon. Had that been me, I'd still be lying on the ground concussed. That's if we weren't dead already. I slipped off my other shoe and both socks so I could walk easier. My bare feet didn't make a sound as I padded forward. The floor killed any noise.

It didn't kill the sound of a scuffle to my left. Lennon's voice got as far as making a guttural sound before rapid pummeling echoed off the ceiling. I heard a thump as a body hit the floor and then a metallic scrape as Lennon's pistol skidded beneath the shelving in front of me. My heartbeat sped up, adrenaline kicked in and I rushed to the intersection and spun around the corner. Lennon's feet peeped out from the next aisle. His toes pointed at the ceiling.

Monica and Sabrina appeared to either side and kept watch while I examined him. A strong pulse still beat in his neck but he was out cold. Blood ran in a tiny stream from his broken nose. I turned him on his side and looked up at the ladies. They were ready to keep moving, although I knew Monica wanted to check on Lennon, but now we weren't able to cover all the aisles. I went back, picked up Lennon's pistol, and we moved forward again. My chest hammered as if it housed a drum kit, my shoulders tensed around my ears and I held my breath. I inched forward, step by step, tried to breathe, and hoped I was walking in unison with the colleagues on either side of me. Monica had taken Lennon's aisle, which meant we had to take a chance on the far one. My nose itched from the dust in the air and I stopped to pinch it. A sneeze now would give away my position. I was halfway down the aisle when it happened again. A noise to my left, muffled and struggling. Then a thump followed by a crumpling sound. No metal hit the floor this time, and I raced to the far wall and rounded the corner. Sabrina appeared at the same time and we took the turn together. It was Monica's turn to lay out cold, her legs folded beneath her like a rag doll. Worse still, her head lolled against Beck's knees. He aimed her gun right at us.

"This is weird. I think I actually feel guilty for beating the wife like that," he said, "but you should have stayed out of the way. Drop the guns."

I considered my options. I know Sabrina was doing the same. We were two against one. Even if he shot one of us, the other could take him out and still try to stop whatever was about to happen. We had about ten minutes left if what Beck had said was true.

As if he read our minds, he angled the pistol down and jammed the barrel into the top of Monica's head. "I said put the guns down. Last chance, unless you want her death on your conscience."

I already felt surprise that I'd sacrifice myself, but I wouldn't be responsible for someone else's death. He might kill us all anyway, but I had to believe we'd have another chance to disarm him. I knelt and placed the gun on the ground with a shaking hand. Sabrina did the same.

"Okay," he said. "Sensible move." He paused and smiled. "Now, it's a bit cramped in here, don't you think? Why don't we retire to the kitchen?"

CHAPTER FIFTY-TWO

The entrance to the kitchen was one of those stable doors where the door is cut in two across the middle and either half can swing in both directions. Sabrina pushed against the louvers and swung the top half open and barged the bottom with her hip. I considered swinging the top half back into Beck's face, but he kept a reasonable distance. He and Lennon had similar training. Beck was like Lennon's evil twin.

We lined up with our backs against a granite counter top. Beck walked to within six feet of us, stopped and hoisted himself up onto the counter on the opposite side. To his left was a row of refrigerators and a preparation area plastered with spices and storage containers. To the right a stainless steel rack hung from the ceiling and held a collection of heavy-duty pots and pans that dangled like shiny branches.

"Why don't you just get on with it," said Sabrina. "Don't you have world domination to attend to?"

I had to admire Sabrina's nerve. Mine crackled and jumped, and I was fighting the bile rising in my stomach. Beck laughed. It was a stereotype, but he cackled like a lunatic.

"I still have ten minutes. Can't be a minute too soon. To be honest, I was getting nervous. This little fracas has helped calm me a bit, so thanks for that. So was the wife telling the truth? You found me because I left a note somewhere? That seems very slapdash of me."

I had no intention of inflating his ego. Sabrina remained tight-lipped too and nudged my side.

"No conversation?" he continued. "Maybe I should just put you out of my misery then." He slid off the counter and sauntered across to us, waving the gun around like a toy. Sabrina nudged me again, but I couldn't work out what she was trying to signal. She stepped away from the counter and turned to face Beck.

"Okay, I'll play your game." She glanced over Beck's shoulder as she spoke and I followed her eyes. I looked around the room distract-edly and caught a shadow moving through the door's louvers.

"Monica said you left an imprint on a notepad at your house. We didn't believe you could be out here in the middle of nowhere, but then we thought you might be in a boat."

Her plan was working. Beck turned to face her as the bottom half of the door edged open.

"It's not quite a boat is it?" he laughed. "Hard to imagine another war will start from a place that hardly anyone knows even exists. Even the nerds on the other side of the building have no idea what we're doing."

Monica squeezed through the doorway. She looked bleary-eyed, but she moved with the grace of a ballerina and crept into the kitchen.

"Why would you do this?" asked Sabrina. "Money? How will you spend it when there's no world left? Are you that stupid?"

Beck's eyes narrowed and the psychopath reappeared. "Stupid, huh? I'll show you stupid." He raised the pistol. A crack echoed through the kitchen. Sabrina jumped, Monica paused, and I fell to the ground. Then the pain came.

I clutched at my leg and let out a howl. The bullet punched through the muscle in my thigh, exited out the back and went through the cabinet door behind me. Blood seeped through my fingers and fire spread away from the unwanted hole in me.

I opened my clenched eyes to see Beck smiling. "She thinks I'm stupid," he said. "Someone who says that to a man holding a gun is really stupid, don't you…"

That was as far as he got. Another sound echoed through the kitchen, a loud metallic clang against a solid surface. Shock registered in Beck's eyes and then his body folded and dropped to the floor in front of us. Monica stood over him with a cast iron skillet in her hand and a wicked grin on her face.

"Well," she said, "I could have nailed the bastard like that in my kitchen and saved us a lot of work and pain." She glanced across at me. "Sorry about your leg, by the way. If I'd known he would do that, I'd have smacked him sooner."

The ladies helped me to my feet and wrapped a large dishcloth around my leg. Blood soaked through the white material in no time and it oozed as I winced and pressed my fingers against it. Sabrina took another cloth and tied it tighter above the first.

"It was a through and through," said Monica. "No major damage, but we need to stop you leaking. I took care of Lennon's nose too. It'll be sore when he wakes up, but at least it'll point in the right direction. I think he's quite good looking, I'd hate for our adventure to spoil his looks."

I cringed at the image of Lennon's nose being jolted back into place as, right on cue, he stumbled through the door and frowned at me. He looked from me to Beck and then back again as if he was trying to piece together the events he'd missed. "You got shot?"

"Yeah," I said with a nod. "Through and through." I sounded like a pro, and felt like we were about to compare war wounds. My nerves had settled, and I was ready for my first man-to-man discussion about gunshots.

"Cool. Welcome to the club. Now, how much time do we have?"

Okay. End of discussion and back to business.

"Minutes," said Sabrina. "Come on. Can you walk?"

I put weight on the leg and it screamed a protest that went all the way to the pit of my stomach. "Yeah, I'll be all right," I said through clenched teeth. "Let's go. Beck slammed into Lennon from a corridor not too far from here. Let's check it out. If he ran back there, then we have to be close to what we're looking for."

We tied Beck to the fridge door handles with miles of shrink-wrap and made our way out of the kitchen and into the corridor. The only sound was the pumping air, relentless and welcome. My leg complained at every step but in a few minutes, if we didn't find what we needed, I'd have bigger problems than that.

We reached the branch in the corridor without incident and ventured along it. It was the same as the others until we rounded the curve and faced a solid door. Like with the bulkheads, there were no windows, just the panel to one side. Unlike the others, this door had a handle. Lennon stepped forward and swiped his card. The little red light above the panel remained lit as its green brother sat idle and dim. I hobbled forward and tried my card. Again, the lights mocked us.

"Wait a second," said Sabrina. "Beck had a card on a lanyard around his neck. I remember it swinging when he stood over Paul. It makes sense that the boss would carry a skeleton key card. I'll be right back."

She turned and sprinted up the corridor and out of sight and returned less than a minute later with the card. My heart swelled as she ran toward us. If this was my time to go, at least I could punch out knowing I'd experienced Sabrina. In my mind she was a diamond; hard and sharp, but beautiful too, and the symbol for passion and love. She was probably my perfect woman. If we could just stop World War Three from happening and get out of here without getting shot again, who knew what the future might hold.

She didn't mention Beck, but handed Lennon the card while she frowned at me. "Paul, your eyes have glazed over. Are you okay? Do you feel shock setting in?"

I was about to explain my thoughts when Lennon shouted. The green light had illuminated and the door clicked and opened.

Beeping sounds bled through the opening. Lennon pulled the door wider and stepped around it. A voice spoke from inside the room. A British accent. "And who the fuck are you?"

It was followed by a gunshot.

Blood sprayed up the wall like flicked paint and Lennon staggered back and collapsed in the doorway. A red pool welled out from beneath him and ran into the curve of the wall. I slid down the opposite side, clutched my knees through the pain and trembled.

Despite Sabrina's misunderstanding of my situation, shock had caught up with me. The blood loss from the leg wound didn't help either. While I sat useless and shaking against the wall, Sabrina and Monica moved in a blur of action. Lennon's body lying over the door threshold must have triggered the sensor in the frame above and prevented it from closing. Monica dragged him behind the safety of the door just enough to rifle his trouser pockets and take the flash drive. The door remained open as shots rang out and pinged off the concrete while she searched.

"Come in here again and I'll take your fucking head off," shouted the voice.

I couldn't see a way to get inside without being taken out as soon as we appeared in the doorway. Sabrina had other ideas. She crouched in front of me and lifted my head with a finger.

"Paul, pull it together. This is the final push. They've guarded this room, so it has to be where we use the drive. I think I have a way to get us in, but it will take all of us to make it work. Can you get it together? Can you do that for me?"

Kacie's face pushed forward in my mind. My little girl, depending on me to save her world. There were no cameras recording these moments. I wouldn't appear on television like the movie we'd talked about on the phone. Maybe no one would ever know who stopped the next war. But it didn't matter. We had to do it. I nodded, and she wiped the hair from my forehead and kissed it.

"That's my boy. Hold down the fort and keep an eye on Lennon." She pressed a gun into my sweating palm and ran off up the corridor and out of sight.

More shots rang out as Monica searched Lennon's body again, this time for a pulse. Tears streamed down her face as she pressed his neck and leaned into his face to check for breathing. There was a lot of blood. Her hands were slicked with red that shined in the fluorescent light.

"Is he alive?"

"I don't know," she sobbed. "I can't get close enough to check."

"We have the key card. Drag him clear and let's tend to him. Let the door close. We can open it again when we need to."

I pushed off the concrete and staggered over to her. We each grabbed an arm and pulled until Lennon was behind the door. It swung closed and clicked shut just as the voice shouted again.

"Try again, bitches." The laughter ended as the door resealed with a dull thud.

Lennon's shoulder was a mass of clotting blood. It looked as if he had his through and through to match mine, but I didn't know if the bullet had nicked anything important on its passage through his body. His eyelids fluttered and moved but his breathing was steady. I braced my weight on my good leg and helped Monica pull him upright against the wall to slow the bleeding.

She could see my concern. "It's not pumping out of him, so there's no arterial damage. Where did Sabrina go?"

"No idea. She said she had a plan to get us in the room so I reckon we sit tight and wait."

She waved Beck's keycard. "We can still get in and just storm the place."

"No. Just because we heard one voice doesn't mean there's only one person in there."

We sat with our backs to the wall on either side of Lennon. He murmured occasionally as if he was stuck in a bad dream. I supposed he was. The frustration of sitting powerless built as the minutes ticked away. It wasn't like we were waiting for a game to kick off. A major war was about to start and we were propped against a wall like three drunks.

Monica stood and clutched the keycard. "Enough. We can't wait any longer. Are you coming?"

I picked up Lennon's pistol in my other hand, stood as best I could, and shuffled over to her. With a gun in each hand I nodded. "Go for it. This is for you, Kacie."

She lifted the card and was inches away from the panel when Sabrina's voice boomed behind us. "Stop! Wait a minute."

She slid to a halt beside us, pistol in one hand and medical supplies in the other. I opened the box, took out dressings and got to work patching up Lennon.

"Here," she said and handed me a surgical face mask. "Put this over your nose and mouth."

"I don't think Lennon's too concerned about my germs right now."

"It's for your benefit. Stop asking questions and put it on. You'll see why in a moment."

I slid the mask over my nose and mouth and covered Lennon's face too. The girls did the same.

"So what was your plan?" I asked.

"Just wait a minute. I was counting on you closing the door. Trust me, it'll open without our help in a moment and we'll have all the advantage we need."

We stood in a line outside the door and waited. Lennon rested against the wall. His eyes had opened as I tended to his shoulder, and he seemed to be okay other than the hole in his shoulder and two huge bumps on his head. He complained of dizziness so I propped him in the corner behind where the door would open. He'd be out of sight. I told him to stay there. He was in no shape to argue.

The seconds continued to count down, and I glanced across at Sabrina. She glared back. "Patience. Any second now."

"What did you do?"

She let out a resigned sigh. "Remember the control panel with the lights in that storage room?"

"Yes. Humidity, air control and temperature."

"Correct. Remember the air intake to the side of it?"

I frowned and tried to piece her puzzle together. "Yeah. So?"

"The panel allows the user to direct air flow into individual rooms at different rates."

I still frowned. "Okay…"

"Now, remember the sacks of flour in the kitchen?"

The penny finally dropped, and she spoke as if a light bulb just illuminated above my head.

"There you go, welcome aboard sailor. Imagine air pumped into the room filled with fifty pounds of self-raising flour. How long would you be able to breathe?"

Right on cue, the door clicked open and a plume of white dust billowed out around the edges. A gasping cough barked behind it. The door swung open inch by inch and more of the powder drifted into the corridor. I raised my two pistols, the girls raised theirs, and we ducked low and advanced.

The room looked like an airport in a snowstorm. Flour swirled and created small drifts as the air continued to pump it around the room. Any filters must have overloaded, but Sabrina had directed a hurricane through the air system and rendered them useless anyway. Small lights glowed and blinked in the fog and the clock on the back wall still counted down. We had just over two minutes to find the correct workstation and plug in the flash drive. It wouldn't be easy; the room was full of desks and consoles. All of them looked as if the cleaning maid had quit years ago.

I dropped to the floor as the supersonic whine of a bullet flew past my ear and ricocheted off the wall behind me. The wound in my leg reminded me of its presence and sent pain shooting through me. I clenched my teeth to hold back the scream that built in my throat as a comforting hand landed on my back. Sabrina was next to me and motioned for me to stay put. I shook my head, got to my knees and moved forward.

The voice coughed and gagged and screamed abuse from somewhere to my left. Sabrina followed me as I shuffled in that direction, leaving snow plough furrows on the dusted floor. Monica crept around to the right and disappeared behind a row of desks.

A muzzle flash blinked in the distance, an orange star lit against a white sky. Sabrina rose and fired off a volley of shots. I lifted both pistol's gangster style and did the same. Metal clinked and glass shattered but the abuse still came followed by another round of gunfire.

Sabrina spoke, her voice muffled behind the mask. "We shoot once more, two rounds each. This guy's military. He's taken good cover, but we shoot then he shoots. This time, we shoot then shoot again. Concentrate on the muzzle flash. He'll come from behind cover to return fire, and we might get lucky. We don't have time for anything else."

I nodded once and blinked dust out of my eyes, then lifted in time with her, squeezed the trigger twice and waited. Sure enough, a shadow moved in the haze. We fired again. Bullets whistled and thudded and then a pink spray flared in the motes of flour and dragged them backwards and out of sight. Metal clattered and the mist swirled as a body fell through it.

Sabrina was up in an instant. "Cover me. Assume he wasn't alone."

I knelt upright and scanned the room as she bolted over to the guy's position. Nothing moved. If there were other people in here they would have responded by now, so I hurried over to join her.

The guy lay on his back, dust already forming on his hair and eyebrows. He was turning into a ghost quicker than he should. One eye stared at the ceiling. The other was missing, replaced by a gaping hole. Lucky shot. The pizza from earlier lurked at the back of my throat, and I swallowed it for the second time.

A chain draped off his neck and coiled on the floor on top of a silver key. It looked important, so I lifted his head, slipped it off, and put it in my pocket. As my stomach heaved again I caught movement from across the room. The ghost of Monica waved its arms through the smog. "Guys, I think I've found it. Come on!"

We shuffled across to her. The clock on the wall behind her glowed, the red neon numbers bright, and then fading outwards into a pink mist. It said 00:01:44.

I hoped she'd found it.

CHAPTER FIFTY-THREE

Monica blew and wafted clouds of flour off the console. Even through the dust it looked like something from a Star Trek movie set. It should have been obvious to us as soon as we walked into the room. The curve of the wall held multiple screens and, once Monica cleared them, they showed maps of different regions covered in green dots that seemed to hover. The clock was dead center. Beneath it sat two workstations, both with laptops. Both laptops had keypads built into them, protected by clear plastic covers. I handed Sabrina the dead guy's key.

"Those dots have to be drones," she said. "Good God, there are thousands of them."

Monica ran her fingers down the side of the machine in front of her. "There's a USB port right here. Do I plug the flash drive in and see what happens?"

The clock read 00:01:15.

I wiped my eyes again. They were drying and white powder caked my eyelashes. "Do it, we're almost out of time."

She leaned over the computer. As she fumbled to find the slot, a gunshot cracked behind us. We dropped to the ground. I peeked over a console as Beck marched into the room. Somehow he'd cut his ties.

Even through the flour, I could see thick welts across his arms. I ducked and hid.

"You arrogant bastards. How dare you come into my fucking office and balls up years of planning. I'll take out every single…"

His voice cut off and his breath whistled as if he'd walked into a wall. I peered over the top of the console again. He'd disappeared. Then he stood and kicked at something below him. Fueled by adrenaline, I ignored my aching leg and vaulted the console.

Most of the flour had drifted through the open door at this end of the room. Lennon lay on the ground curled into a fetal position as Beck swung kick after kick into his vulnerable body. He didn't see me as I flew off the console and used my weight and momentum to smash my fist into the side of his head. Pain shot through my wrist and up my arm as small bones splintered, but Beck staggered back and dropped to one knee. I followed him as my damaged leg buckled.

He shook his head. "Fucking hell mate, that was a good one. All right, now let me show you how a real man does it."

He stood and tried to disguise the shake in his knees. I stood and favored my good leg. I'd stunned him but he moved on me anyway and swung a blurred fist at my head. I ducked backwards as it flew by me like a hammer and leaned in to punch his exposed ribs. My hand screamed as I connected, and I pulled back. Beck smiled. "Did that one hurt, sweetheart? Looks like you've done some damage."

Sabrina screamed across the room. "Paul! Fifty seconds!"

I looked into Beck's manic eyes. I had to finish him while he was still rocked otherwise he'd kill me. As I stepped forward again Lennon stood up behind him and slammed the edge of his hand across the back of his neck. I needed the distraction. Beck's eyes squeezed closed at the blow. I knew I couldn't punch, my hand was useless, so I flattened out my palm and slammed it to the underside of his nose as hard as I could. Bone and gristle crunched and snapped and I felt it force upwards into his head. Blood gushed over my hand. His eyes shot open as fragments tore through his brain and then he toppled backwards like a felled tree and landed in a plume of powder on the floor. I doubled over as my stomach convulsed once more and the pizza spattered beside him.

"We need another key!" Monica was frantic.

My mind was a blur but Lennon was already on his knees rifling Beck's pockets. I joined him and searched. No keychain or necklace. Nothing but paper in the inside pockets. Lennon used his good arm to roll the body over. Beck's limp arm splattered into my pizza deposit.

The pants pockets were empty too.

Monica shouted again. "Twenty seconds. Come on!"

I had a random thought. Beck was English. They have this tradition of carrying everything in their front pockets. Probably a pickpocket thing. I swallowed my pride, rolled him back over and dug around. My hand flashed across a wallet and then my nail snagged something metal. I dug harder into the fabric and under the wallet and forced my nail into a small round hole and dragged out the second key.

The powder was finally settling as I launched the key in Monica's direction. It glinted in the light as it arced across the room. Monica caught it in a clenched fist and flipped open the plastic cover that protected the keypad.

The clock read 00:00:09.

Both girls pushed their keys into the pads and then looked at each other. "Now, or on zero?" asked Monica.

As she spoke, the dots on the screen went from green to black. The countdown reached one. Then zero.

"Now," said Sabrina.

They turned the keys.

Nothing happened.

The dots hovered in position and looked even more ominous now they were black. Colored green, they looked like a video game. Black meant death. Sabrina was right; there were thousands of them, every one armed and ready to unleash a wave of destruction.

Lennon and I leaned into each other, casualties of war. The girls gazed up at the monitors, their mouths agape as reality hit home. We'd failed. Millions of people were about to be killed or injured, and just as many displaced. My daughter would grow up in a world that wouldn't know peace, a world I wouldn't want to bring a child into.

Then, in an instant, the black switched back to green. The static screens blurred into life as the dots moved, slowly and controlled. The whole wall looked like the target of a thousand laser sights. My eyes flicked from one screen to the next and found the same pattern on each one.

It took a moment to sink in, but as the drones went back to their programmed routes we realized we'd done it. Monica and Sabrina grabbed each other and jumped up and down together, shouting and whooping. Lennon backed away and indicated his shoulder as I turned to him. I used my decent hand to fist bump him instead.

I held Sabrina and kissed her. "Now we have to get back to land so we can tell the authorities about this place. This can't happen again."

"Agreed," she said. She slid the key into her pocket. "You keep the other, Monica. Whatever happens, no one is using this room again without these. Get rid of it miles away from here. Do a Gollum and throw it in a volcano or something."

She laughed and nodded, then Sabrina threw my arm over her shoulder, and we made our way out of the room. As we reached the door, mumbling voices carried around the corner. I winced as I paused with my weight on the injured leg and shuffled to the other. "Shit. You think maybe these aren't the only screens being monitored? Thinking about it, why would they have one guy guarding something so important?"

"Look where we are," said Lennon. "This guy must have had the surprise of his life. He expected no one but his boss through that door. The less people know what's going on, the less chance there is of something leaking. We were lucky, we have a girl scout." He gestured to Monica, who blushed and raised her pistol.

"Come on," she said. "Let's hope it's a bunch of white coats."

It wasn't a bunch of white coats, but it wasn't security either, more like a group of fit programmers. They were disorganized and looked terrified, huddled together like a pack of nervous kittens. As we rounded the corner, the lead guy caught sight of Monica's pistol and paused. His weapon pointed to the ground and shook in his hand. She screamed at the top of her voice, fired a round over them and charged.

Four pairs of eyes shot wide open in surprise and a chorus of male screams erupted, then the group turned and sprinted back around the corner. Monica followed, still screaming. After the shock wore off, we caught up with her and found her standing beside a closed door. She looked back at us and smiled as we reached her.

"What the fuck was that?" said Lennon. "That was the craziest thing I've ever seen, and I've seen some crazy shit!"

"Worked though didn't it?" she said. "I'll keep you on your toes, don't you worry. They were clearly not military types though, and they should know how we can get out of here." She glanced through the window again. "They're huddled behind the desks at the far end of the room babbling to one another. It seems we took out the big bully, and the rest of the kids have folded. Paul, swipe the keycard and let's speak to them."

I did as I was told and swiped the keycard.

CHAPTER FIFTY-FOUR

No coercion was required, no interrogation or nails pulled with pliers. The four techs told us about an underground terminal where we could find a fleet of small submarines. I'd seen them on National Geographic. Submersibles. One or two-man vessels designed for underwater exploration. In our case they'd be getaway vehicles.

We left the room and Lennon shot out the door panel to make sure we wouldn't be followed. Monica took great pleasure in shooting up most of the equipment too so no one could contact the outside world. She was worrying me again, but it looked like she was Lennon's problem now.

Beck's keycard got us through the next bulkhead and we found the entrance that took us 'below deck'. I felt as if I'd walked into the wrong side of an aquarium. Most of the structure was thick glass and looked out under the ocean. It was an incredible sight and ironic that a place ready to commit such evil acts could be home to such beauty.

We clanged and hobbled down a flight of metal steps and on to a concourse that stretched off toward a pair of huge doors that looked as if they'd let us out of here. As promised, a row of vessels bobbed up and down at the side of a pier like a floating taxi rank. I placed my hand at the small of Sabrina's back as we reached the front of the line and swept out my other arm in a grand gesture. "Your carriage awaits, ma'am."

She smiled and kissed me, then lifted the glass dome that formed the roof of the small sub. Two reclined seats lay side by side, with a cockpit that looked a little more complicated than the one from the boat. "Looks cozy in there," she said. "Want to take her for a spin?"

She slid a hand over my rear as the others snickered behind us. "You, or the sub?" I asked.

"Well, we did just save the world. We should celebrate."

"And I did just get shot, so there are parts of me that could use some TLC, so…"

"Hate to interrupt the lovefest," said Monica, "but has anyone here ever piloted one of these?"

Sabrina stepped back, lifted the dome on the second vessel and pointed out the controls. The girls helped Lennon into the far seat of the sub. He reclined and gave a mock salute with his good arm. The color had bleached from his face. He'd lost a lot of blood and I hoped Monica would at least get him to the surface alive. She was jumping around like she'd drunk a dozen Red Bulls, and I feared for his physical wellbeing. He smiled at me as if he knew he would get lucky. I suspected he was right.

As Monica clambered into the other seat, Sabrina walked back to me. "Wait here a sec, okay? I need to check something."

She jogged off along the pier to the far end and gazed up at the huge exit doors. When she stood in front of them, their actual size became apparent. They towered over her and it made me wonder what else was moored in here that would need that kind of clearance. Whatever it was, it wasn't here now, and I was grateful for that.

A minute later she was back by my side. "You can't see it from here, but there's a small dome above the doors. I think it's a sensor. When we get close enough, the sensor should open the doors and we can leave. Monica, when we get outside don't worry about direction, just aim up and follow me. Let's get to the surface as soon as possible, since we don't know what the battery life is on these things.

Once we get up top we can get back on the boat and signal someone."

Monica stuck a thumb in the air and Sabrina helped me into a sub and closed the hatch. The seat was surprisingly comfortable, so I laid back and rested my throbbing leg. She leaned forward and started the engines. A small hum vibrated through the machine as it drifted toward the doors. They opened as we approached and let us into a smaller room with solid walls. The water level remained the same, and we glided through the entrance and waited for the other sub to join us. As Monica pulled up alongside, the huge doors closed again and the room filled with water. Then the doors in front of us opened, and we sailed out and into the ocean.

The ride to the surface was much easier and a lot more peaceful than the dive down. It would have been nice if we'd had time to explore our surroundings. Sabrina had seen the battery gage on the sub's dashboard and they had a full charge, but we needed to alert someone about what we'd found. Lennon and I had also lost a lot of blood and we needed patching up by a professional.

"You think we should report this anonymously?" said Sabrina.

"Why would we do that?" I asked. "We're as good as heroes. I was hoping Kacie would get to see me on TV."

"We've left bodies along the way and broken about a dozen laws. The authorities can get a bit twitchy about that kind of stuff. I also doubt Lennon wants to be on TV either, what with him being part of the whole thing to begin with."

"Good point. Let's get back to land first, and I'll make a call. Then I can leave a pack somewhere with all the details in it. The powers that be can take it from there."

The two subs made a steady climb toward the surface, but not so fast as to cause the bends I'd been warned about. Before long, the dark water lightened to a pale green as the moonlight shone through the surface and we broke through it with a splash. The small vessel bounced about as the other sub joined us a few feet away. I could see through the port window that Monica was laughing. There was no sign of Lennon but I could see her talking to him. I signaled we were headed to the boat, and she gestured that we should leave them alone for a while. It looked as if Lennon was about to get lucky under the moonlight after all.

Sabrina gazed down at me and twirled her hair again. I recognized that look. Clearly I hadn't lost too much blood, as the General began to stir in anticipation.

"We could follow their lead right here, but I need to get you back on the boat. It's time to celebrate and I have just the way to do it, but not here. We're going to need more room."

My leg throbbed and ached but there are some things that make working through pain acceptable. As Sabrina steered us toward the boat, I lay back in my seat and stared at the moon. There was a time, a few hours ago, when I thought I'd never see it again. When we got back to dry land, I'd make that call and put together a package explaining everything, and then I'd call Kacie. I'd promised her a vacation and I intended to keep that promise. It was time to become a good father again.

I needed to call work too, but something inside nagged at me to leave it for a while and take some time to get to know this amazing woman seated next to me. We deserved some normal time together.

Sabrina turned and smiled. "You've gone quiet. Everything okay?"

"Everything's great," I said. I couldn't help but wonder if she'd like a vacation too. I'd go anywhere with her. Anywhere, on or off land... except Kentucky.

I'm not doing that again.

ACKNOWLEDGMENTS

I once read that the art of writing is a solitary endeavor. I suppose that is a true statement, but the art (and it is an art) of getting that writing out to you, the reader, is anything but.

So many amazing people have helped get my story published that I'm bound to forget someone, so first of all, to that person…you know who you are. Sorry, and thank you!

My heartfelt thanks and gratitude go to…

…the unfortunate people that suffered through my first manuscript (and this may be where I've forgotten someone) – Barry Ashley, Liz Brewer, Madison Culler, Kenneth Morris, Gary Platt, and my siblings Lynn and Steve Williams. Thank you for your honesty in pointing out my many mistakes.

…Lynn Tincher, for going a hundred steps further and turning my finished draft into a proper story.

…Tony Acree and my fellow Hydra authors, for friendship, faith in my work, and constant encouragement. Check them all out here, they're lovely… http://www.hydrapublications.com/

…Stephen Zimmer and everyone at Imaginarium, for showing me that it can be done, and how to do it. If you read or write, do yourself a

favor and visit Imaginarium – it gets bigger and better each year…
http://www.entertheimaginarium.com/

…all of the wonderful people that have offered friendship and cheered me toward the finish line, like my good friends at the Kentuckiana Authors FB Group and the very talented Welcome Cole.

…my family and friends, and the people that help to put the Sparkle in my writing.

…Cathy, for endless patience and the scary ability to control two very needy cats.

…and to YOU! Thanks for reading.

Much love to you all.

Mick Williams.

ABOUT THE AUTHOR

Mick Williams wrote his first short story (which linked a local celebrity to a spate of killings) in High School. His teacher noted 'he has quite an imagination'…she never mentioned whether it was good or bad. Since then he has written a romantic comedy and three adventure/thrillers.

After a decade in Kentucky, USA, he has recently relocated back to his hometown of Stoke-on-Trent, England, and shares a house with his wife and two demanding and needy cats, Crash and Thud.

In between working and writing, he is an avid reader and enjoys watching football. Both kinds.